Kotuku

Kotuku

by Deborah Savage

Houghton Mifflin Company
Boston 2002

www.houghtonmifflinbooks.com

Book design by Lisa Diercks
The text of this book is set in Monotype Walbaum.

Library of Congress Cataloging-in-Publication Data
    Savage, Deborah.
    Kotuku / by Deborah Savage.
        p. cm.
    Summary: Still having difficulty facing the death of her best friend, Wim
must deal with a difficult great-aunt and Maori visitors from New Zealand
who uncover a dark family secret.
    ISBN 0-618-04756-5
    [1. Identity—Fiction. 2. Grief—Fiction. 3. Great aunts—Fiction.] I. Title.
    PZ7.S2588 Ko 2002
    [Fic]—dc21   2001039027

Printed in the United States of America
QUM 10 9 8 7 6 5 4 3 2 1

To my wonderful editor at Houghton Mifflin Company,

Amy Flynn,

whose support, generosity, and hard work

have helped me through the best and worst of times

Kotuku

One ꩜

Wim woke that morning to find the man with the tattooed face watching her. His head was inches from hers on the other pillow.

He'd never come so close before.

She didn't move. Dawn filtered through the lace curtains. They stirred slightly in the breeze. She felt the touch of air as a breath against her skin. She was waiting, as she always waited, watching the intricate pattern of spirals and lines shimmer across his dark skin, letting herself be caught by his black eyes. The curtains billowed; lacy shadows drifted across the bed, across her outstretched arm, over his cheek.

The house was silent. Wim was alone, but unafraid. She breathed in the sweet, musky scent of low tide. A sense of promise rose in her like a green wave shot through with light, lifting her, carrying her toward . . . she did not know what. There was always this premonition of something almost reached, almost realized; *he* brought it. He always brought it.

She stirred slightly and the man with the tattooed face dissolved. There remained merely the shadows from the lace curtains, more defined now in the rising sun. Wim lay in bed a moment longer, letting the familiar sadness subside, and only then did she remember: *Jilly.* Jilly. Today. June 13. It had been a year. She had been dreading this day, and now it had arrived and she had not even remembered.

She threw her legs over the side of the bed, scraping her toes against the sandy floor in her haste to find her boots and pull on her barn clothes. Jilly was gone, a year ago today. Today, as then, a whole summer stretched out before Wim. She yanked on her jeans, held her tee shirt to her nose, sniffed, and flung it in the corner. She paused, drew a deep breath. This summer she had the Kid, and that would make all the difference. She pulled on a clean shirt, shaking her thick hair out of her face, and focused her thoughts on the horse. The Karate Kid. Master of the killer kick. She'd found him in April. He hadn't been the Kid then, back on that gray, drizzly day when she'd driven the Dune Forest Stables truck down an unfamiliar sand road to pick up some used saddles Evelyn had heard were for sale. He'd been no more than an emaciated shadow, barely discernible in the fog against the weathered gray boards of a shed.

Wim would not have noticed the horse even then, if the man with the tattooed face had not shown her.

She paused again, one boot on, one off. Strange. That April day had been the last time he'd appeared, until today. Two months. A long time between visits. She frowned and laced up her boots. She'd caught him watching her from among the stunted pine trees along the sand road, the pattern on his face etched like the pine needles against the fog. She had turned to meet his gaze and so had seen the cramped enclosure half hidden behind the shed. The horse was standing at the far corner, head drooped so low its muzzle was brushing the mud. She recalled that moment, how utterly still the world had been.

The roar of her father's van approaching from down the street broke into the remembered silence. A mockingbird erupted into song from the tree outside her window, and down in the yard, Bart the terrier yapped. Wim grabbed her pack and dashed down the stairs. She was late getting to the barn to let the horses out into the paddocks. Sam Thorpe's van backfired to a stop, the door slammed, and beyond the quiet West End neighborhood Wim could hear the faint sound of traffic on Commercial Street in the center of town. Every summer, the Provincetown streets seemed to jam bumper-to-bumper with cars and campers earlier than the year before.

She ate a yogurt quickly, wiping her mouth with the back of her hand as her father came into the kitchen. He dropped a handful of mail on the table, commenting, "Late start, huh?" Then he added, without looking up, "Oh, that's right . . . on vacation now?" He riffled absently through the mail, picked up a bill, opened it, and frowned.

Wim mumbled, "Yeah." Sam's questions were often rhetorical. She knew he was too preoccupied for conversation.

Her father dropped the bill, went to the sink, and splashed water on his face. "It's too damn hot too damn early," he complained as he scrubbed his face dry. "Evelyn must be happy. Lots of early tourists this year. Business picking up already?"

She said "yeah" again, noncommital. Sam was really only

interested in his own business. Besides, "business" and "Dune Forest Stables" seemed to contradict each other. Tammy, Evelyn's partner, did struggle to bring the two terms into sync, but Evelyn resented the summer season as much as Wim did, barely tolerating the plodding trail rides through the dunes, the endless cycle of riding lessons, the weekend riding camps, and the buggy tours down Commercial Street that brought in the necessary revenue. Dune Forest Stables, as far as Evelyn was concerned, existed solely as a haven for the horses she'd saved from mistreatment or neglect. Evelyn took them in, Wim brought them back to life, and Tammy tried valiantly to turn them into something approximating a business asset.

"We need to leave right at four," Sam was saying. "Try to get back here by half past three—you ought to be able to take a half-day off, for what those two pay you—"

"I don't care what they pay me," Wim shot back, her automatic response to Sam's habitual disapproval of her job. She sifted through the mail. Bills, as always, creating a perpetually bewildered frown on Sam's face. Junk mail. Fliers. The monthly newsletter from the Provincetown Historical Society.

"I know. I know." Sam sighed, paused. "Look—just try to get back here on time. I'm really counting on you. Aunt Kia's never been easy to handle in the best of circumstances, and at the airport after a long flight . . . well, you know. She's just a lot more confused these days—"

"I know, Dad. I said I'd go. I'll be here."

"And don't forget to take those boxes in the study out to the cottage. They're all packed—just put them in the back room. I've cleared a space out there."

"I know. I will," Wim murmured.

It had all been discussed several times. She was going with Sam to Logan Airport to meet this senile old woman who would be living with them until a room was available at the Rose Point Nursing Home in Truro. But Sam Thorpe was a worrier. Life was never settled. Her mother usually dismissed his anxieties, treating her husband at times as though he were one of her hospital patients, but around Sam, Wim often felt like a horse hooked to cross-ties, confined and jittery. She tried to ignore it now, picking up an unopened envelope from the pile of mail. "Samuel Williamson Thorpe," she read aloud, holding it up to the light curiously.

Her father glanced at her. *First time he's looked at me since he came in,* Wim thought. She held out the envelope. "That's what's written on it. Here. Who knows you by that name?"

Sam shrugged and started out the door. "Can't deal with the mail now. I've got a new guy opening the store this morning, and . . . " His voice trailed off as he went out.

She watched from the door as her father drove away. The van's muffler popped and rumbled in the quiet street. Morning light glinted off metallic letters on the van's side: CAPE MARINE HARDWARE AND SUPPLIES. Harsh, salty winters had weathered the paint so the letters were peeling and wearing away. *Like Dad,* Wim thought. She pushed the door open to go outside and realized she still held the letter addressed to Samuel Williamson Thorpe. She studied it, squinting in the sunlight. The handwriting seemed old-fashioned, elegant, as if to match the ancestry the name was born of—the long line of wealthy merchant ship captains of whom her father was inordinately proud. *The only thing he's really proud of,* she mused, absently stuffing the letter into the back pocket of her jeans. A cool morning breeze was coming in off the water and she rubbed her arms as she walked around to the back of the house.

"Angelo! Bart!" she called. "SueSue!" Three dogs emerged from hollows under the foundation of a gray-shingled cottage that sat between the house and the harbor beach. Bart scrabbled from beneath the overgrown rose bushes that obscured the back of the cottage, and Sue wagged foolishly out of a tangle of trumpet vines near the doorway. Wim greeted them all, but her eyes were on old Angelo as he struggled to his unsteady feet and shook himself. She murmured to him lovingly and he leaned against her. "Who could abandon you? Whoever could abandon you?" she whispered, rubbing his knobbed head.

As she filled the water bucket and fed them, she wondered unexpectedly if Great Aunt Kia would be like Angelo. Stiff, sleepy, senile. Bart gnawed on her boot and she playfully nudged him away. "They should all be euthanized," her mother, Carol, had commented more than once after Wim had given up trying to find homes for these least desirable of all the abandoned pets she found wandering the Provincetown streets every year after the summer season was over. Who wanted ancient Angelo, or the terror that was Bart, or stupid Sue? "You spend your whole paycheck on those useless animals," her father often complained.

Her reply was always the same. "It's my money," she'd say. "That's what I want to spend it on."

"Wouldn't it make more sense to save it for college?" Sam would mutter. But he always seemed more baffled than annoyed, and Wim never tried to answer.

How could she explain something she herself did not understand? She had no ambitions beyond staying here, where she'd been born, on this narrow, curved spit of sand poking out into the Atlantic Ocean. She had no desire to do anything beyond working at Dune Forest Stables and taking care of the animals. Pensive, she gazed over the rose hedge to the harbor beach. Dune grass rustled softly in the breeze. The sun had faded behind a lowering sky and waves were beginning to whiten the rocks out on the breakwater. She lifted her face, tasting the change in the weather. Tasting, too, the sudden memory of Jilly that rose, unbidden, to tighten her throat. She turned abruptly to go, calling the dogs into the truck, and drove to the barn.

The horses had been turned out. Two girls who traded work for their horses' board were mucking out stalls. Evelyn was sprawled on the sofa in the tiny barn office, booted feet propped up on the desk, radio blaring the Hyannis oldies station. She raised her eyebrows when Wim arrived, and Wim muttered sheepishly, "Sorry."

Evelyn waved her hand expansively. "First day of vacation. You could've taken the whole day off. Anyway, I know your aunt's coming—"

"Great-aunt," Wim corrected quickly. She leaned across Evelyn and pulled the calendar out from under her feet. "No trail rides today?" she asked, studying it.

"No, thank God," Evelyn answered with fervent relief. They looked at the calendar together, the older woman's head bent close to her own, and discussed the upcoming week. It had been Tammy's idea to officially make Wim the barn manager last year. Evelyn had looked at her partner with a bemused snort. "What d'you mean *make* her barn manager? Cripes, Tam, she's been managing that barn since she was eleven."

Tammy had replied, with the stubborn patience that had saved Evelyn from financial ruin countless times, "It's a *business* thing, Ev. Commercial riding stables have barn managers. Besides—" She'd given Wim a conspiratorial smile. "It would be a good excuse to pay her more. You know. A raise."

Evelyn didn't need an excuse, only to be reminded. And they were both, Wim knew, trying their best to make her feel better, to take her mind off what had happened. But it had happened to all of them, and their trying only reminded her of what they couldn't talk about.

"Since you're taking off early today anyway," Evelyn said now, "why don't you indulge yourself completely and work with your honey out there—" She inclined her head in the direction of the back paddock. "He needs it. We're going to have to sedate him again to trim those damn hooves."

"Oh, don't," Wim begged. "Not yet. Give me another week, Ev. His hooves aren't that bad yet."

The Kid. Undisputed pariah of all the Dune Forest misfits. Untouchable. Beautiful. She went out to the small corral behind the barn where he had been kept since they'd rescued him. As always, she caught her breath at the sight of him. The horse watched her from the far side of the corral. Powerfully built, compact, his dappled gray coat shimmering like water in the broken sunlight. His mane and tail, still matted with burrs, nonetheless were white as the sand. Wim leaned on the fence, chin propped on her arms. He was lovely. And lethal.

She could watch him all day. Not speaking, not doing anything. Just watching.

And the horse watched back. Gradually, over the last two months, in the hours after school and on weekends, Wim had begun to sense what drove him, what fueled his tremendous rage. She would move up and down the corral fence, the horse would move up and down the fence on the far side; they had come to know the space between them. Wim had no plans for him, no expectations; she was content simply to be with him.

Evelyn had understood. "It's enough, girl," she'd said. "Don't ask him a thing more. He doesn't want to be asked anything."

Evelyn was the only person who accepted that Wim did not want to be a horse trainer. Or a competitive rider. Or a dog breeder, a veterinarian, a farmer, a zoologist. She didn't want to *be* anything. For the past six years, since she'd been eleven years old, Wim had come to the barn, taken care of the horses, looked after stray dogs and cats until she found homes for them, and *watched*. Just watched.

Today both she and the Kid were restless. The horse paced along the trail he'd worn by the back fence, and Wim gazed past him into the thickets of scrub pine. The sounds from the yard irritated her—cars driving up, doors slamming, the calls of children, even Evelyn's strident voice as she yelled for Tammy from the barn. The usual commotion felt unusually jarring. She made a low sound in her throat meant to soothe the Kid, but it was as much to soothe herself. Twice she went back into the barn to check the time on the office clock. Finally Evelyn, between bites of a tuna sandwich, grunted, "Why'nt you just take off, Wimmie. You're making me nervous." She chewed reflectively a moment, then added, "So who exactly is this old coot Sam's picking up at Logan? Seems like she's a pretty big deal to him."

"She's Dad's aunt." Wim shrugged. "I guess she's more like his mother, actually. She raised him and Uncle Alex down in Florida from when they were little boys, after their own mother died. I don't know her. I've never met her." She paused. "Ginny and Bea know her, though. Because they were all living in Florida before I was born. They don't like her. They say she was bossy."

Evelyn snorted and tossed the remains of her sandwich to the waiting Bart. "Well, there's a couple of pots calling the kettle black. I wouldn't form any impressions based on what those sisters of yours like or don't like." She heaved herself off the sofa. "Well, if things get too crowded, you're welcome to set up residence here. There's Jilly's room—"

Their eyes flew to each other. Wim's in horror, Evelyn's in consternation. It was always an accident, the name coming up between them. "No—no." Wim spoke softly, the way she would to a frightened horse. "No, it's okay. Mom and Dad hired a home health aide. She'll be there every day. It won't be a problem." She paused, then repeated vaguely, "I don't know her."

The restlessness pursued her as she did a quick check of the stalls, made sure the outside horses had water, gave instructions to the girls who would do the evening chores. But then, after all, she didn't drive straight home but went instead the long way around on the beach road to the salt marshes. The wind was from the southwest, with the deceptively soft freshness that preceded rain. She hadn't intended to get out, but only to gaze across the marshes and tidal creeks from the truck, out of habit to see what was there. She folded her arms across the open window and took a long breath of the salty air.

This low green world created a solitude within her as richly textured as the marsh grasses rolling silver under the wind. In the sweep of an osprey's flight or the brief flare of a fox slipping through the undergrowth of the beech woods she found a pure, untamed joy. Gazing now over the marsh, Wim gauged the tide by instinct. Full, but on the ebb. She would have known this even if the shore birds had not been flocking in, waiting for the rich mud exposed by the receding water. The grassy marsh stretched as far as Wim could see, bounded by dunes and beech forest and laced by a labyrinth of clear, narrow tidal creeks. From the truck she could see wafting shadows of grass on the water's surface.

It was the man with the tattooed face who showed her the white bird. He appeared now in his most diaphanous form, staring up at her through the pale gold water. But even as his lined face dissolved and became a swirl of weed against the sandy bottom, Wim had turned her head. And transfixed, saw the great white bird far out in the marsh. She knew immediately that she was not looking at one of the delicate little snowy egrets that often fished during the summer in the tidal estuaries. This bird was much larger, equal in size to the great blue herons that had gathered along a mud flat midway out in the marsh.

Wim shaded her eyes. The late afternoon sun illuminated the plumage of the bird so it appeared to be lit from within by molten gold. Moving carefully, she slipped from the truck and crept down the bank to the edge of the creek, her feet sinking into the tangle of weed wrack. She made her way cautiously along the water, focused on the flame of white out in the marsh. It was as if the great bird burned with some essential message that she had only to get near enough to receive, and although she was moving slowly, her heart was beating hard. By the decayed remains of a fishing boat half submerged in the mud she stopped, crouching in its shadow and squinting against the glare. *Great egret,* she decided. It had to be. A great egret was unusual this far north, but not unheard of.

But the bird moved then, stalking closer along the shadowed edge of grass. The angle of the sun made it possible to see the color of its long legs—not the shiny black of a great egret, but an unmistakable bright yellow. Wim caught her breath. Hardly daring to believe, she slipped behind the boat, pulled off her boots and jeans and tossed them up on the bank.

The water here was shallow and sun-warmed. In places, the creek was no wider than her own body, and as she drifted along in the soft current, the water was so clear beneath her it was almost invisible. She swam like an otter, hardly moving her limbs, silent, molding herself to the water's movement, raising her head occasionally above the grasses to keep the bird in sight. She'd been coming here since childhood, losing herself in the secret world of the marsh, and she knew all the intricate meanderings of the channels. Shoals of translucent fish darted ahead of her shadow; flounders burst from their camouflage in clouds of sand beneath her. Her dark hair, normally thick and unruly, streamed around her like a graceful water weed. Here, where she could expand perfectly into solitude, she felt soft but safe, like a hermit crab emerging from a tight shell in a sheltered pool.

Wim paused more frequently now, looking across the tops of the grasses to keep her bearing. The great blue herons were spread out over a vast expanse of marsh, some stalking half hidden through the grass, some frozen in alert patience on the creek banks. But the magnificent white bird seemed at once more distant than the others and more reachable. Wim was a practiced watcher; she knew how to move a breath at a time, knew how to quiet herself until even her thoughts were unobtrusive. She drifted her silent way into the heart of the marsh. The afternoon sun was again under cloud and the wind, without resistance on this open, watery plain, streamed in waves through the rustling grasses and masked whatever inadvertent sound she made.

At a bend in the creek where a spit of sand jutted into the water, she paused and assessed her position. She could not see over the grass on the sand spit, but she knew the white bird was hunting just beyond it. She pulled herself up and inched on her stomach through the coarse grass, parted it with her hands, and froze, hardly breathing.

There it was, rarest of the rare, thousands of miles north of its southern coastal range, standing with one yellow leg cocked not more than six feet from where she lay. Neck curved gracefully, powerful beak poised, the great white heron could have been a sculpture of flawless marble. Shadows of the wind-torn grasses danced over feathers carved with such delicate precision it seemed the slightest breath of air would stir them to flight. Yet the bird itself was absolutely still. In her awe, Wim slid through the last screen of grass and lay in full sight of the bird, but the heron did not move. And in that stillness, suddenly, she knew why the man with the tattooed face had brought her to this, on this day.

Jilly had always stood just this way, poised in this space of stillness, before beginning to dance. Whether performing on stage or in her room with only Wim for an audience, Jilly would stand motionless for a moment, tall, her white skin luminous, her blond hair pulled back from her graceful neck, one long slender leg drawn up. And like this bird, there had been in that stillness a sense of some elemental force longing to release, of some spirit needing to break ties with the earth.

A misting rain had begun to gust in from the sea, so she didn't realize at first that her face was wet with her own tears. Wim was so close to the great white heron she could see the water beading like pearls on the bird's feathers and trickling down the curved, motionless neck. She lost all sense of time. She would watch forever, aching for the bird to move, to release her from the vision of Jilly. And she would watch forever because she would gladly live forever, caught and held by this vision. But the tears were blurring her eyes now, coming more insistently until she was struggling to keep from making a sound. She clenched her teeth. She had not spoken Jilly's name since the day she had walked away from the hospital room for the last time. More than a year. And she would not. She would not.

She must have made a sound. Without warning, the great white heron lifted its wings and rose straight up, neck tucked in, yellow legs trailing. For a moment the bird seemed to hang suspended directly above her; she might have reached out a hand and touched its foot. Then the wind gusted, the huge wings flapped slowly once, twice, and the bird beat powerfully out across the marsh and disappeared into the mist.

It took Wim a long time to make her way back. The receding tidal water had in many places become too shallow for swimming, and she had to struggle knee-deep through the sandy muck. The wind turned her wet tee shirt into a cold weight, and by the time she reached the place she had left the rest of her clothing, she was shivering so violently she could not pull on her jeans. She yanked at them ineffectively, shook them in frustration. Her tee shirt sagged around her knees. She grabbed her boots and, dragging the jeans, clambered up the bank, exhausted. Bart yapped at her from the truck. She looked back. The rain had closed in over the marsh, obscuring all but the vaguest suggestion of creeks and pale dunes beyond. No white bird in the distance. But closer, a sudden flash of white . . .

She lunged for it. Caught for a moment in the grass, then flipped by the wind and scudded across the surface of the creek, was the letter to her father addressed in the old-fashioned writing, fallen from the pocket of her jeans. Helpless, she watched it eddy gently for a moment on the sea-bound current, watched it swirl more swiftly and disappear. Wim stood a moment longer, inexplicably shaken by the feeling that she had lost something of immeasurable importance. Bart yapped again. *Probably just junk mail,* she told herself, and got in the truck.

Only when she pulled up to the house did she realize that she was late and that her father had probably long since left for the airport. She ran inside. The clock in the kitchen showed a quarter after four. She heard a car pull up outside, heard a car door slam, and thought with relief: *He's late too. He got held up at the store.* She went down the hall toward the door calling eagerly, "Dad? Dad?"

She was barefoot. Her skin, streaked gray with sandy mud, was scratched from the rough marsh grass. Her clammy tee shirt clung to her legs. She pushed the damp hair from her face and opened the screen door to the figure coming toward her. "Dad?" But even as she spoke, she knew it was not her father.

It was a man. He stopped on the walk when he saw her. "I'm looking for Samuel Williamson Thorpe," he said.

Their eyes met. Two pairs of eyes, each black as a moonless sea. Skin like her own, brown-gold as kelp. Wim stared.

It was the man with the tattooed face. Without the tattoo.

Two ඓ

They might have stared at each other no more than a moment or as long as an hour or a lifetime. She didn't know. She saw every detail, though, with a strangely heightened clarity. The man was not tall, but he was thickset and powerfully built, giving the impression of great size. Close-cropped black hair accentuated the broad plane of his forehead and his prominent cheekbones. His mouth and nose also were full and strongly defined. His presence hit her with a physical shock. She felt she had looked into his eyes all her life. And mirrored in his eyes was the same recognition she knew must be in her own. But the man did not appear to be startled.

When the mockingbird burst into song from the cottage roof behind the house, the sound somehow freed Wim. She dropped her eyes and stepped back. The man said apologetically, "Oh, look, I'm sorry to bother you—" His voice had the same brown warmth as his skin. He frowned a little and checked a slip of paper he was holding. "But can you just tell me . . . I have got the correct address, haven't I? Samuel Williamson Thorpe?"

She glanced up and his gaze, unwavering and somehow generous, served oddly to steady her. "He's my father," she managed to reply. "But he's not home right now."

The man gave a half-smile and a shake of his head. "Serves me right, eh. When I wrote, I assured him I'd phone first—" He folded the paper and put it in his pocket. "He did get my letter, then? Do you know? David Te Makara—from New Zealand?"

Samuel Williamson Thorpe. She saw the envelope drifting on the tide. "I'm not sure," she faltered.

"Oh well, look," the man said. "I don't want to be a bother. Your father doesn't know me—I explained everything in my letter, but—" He shrugged, dug in his jeans pocket, and brought out a business card, holding it out to her in his large hand. It was almost impossible to take it without brushing her fingers against his. She snatched it from him, disconcerted, and read it more to compose herself than from curiosity. *David Te Makara. Department of History. Auckland University, Auckland, New Zealand.* Underneath, in smaller lettering, was *Lecturer in Colonial and Pre-Colonial Maori History.*

"Oh, okay," Wim blurted, relieved. "My father's the secretary of the Provincetown Historical Society. You must have got his name from them. He's always talking to people about his family history and—" She knew that she was babbling. A compelling silence, somehow present whether either of them spoke or not, was rising between them like a flood tide. It rushed, warm as blood, through her whole body. Desperately, Wim looked at the ground and shifted on her bare feet.

When she looked up again she was startled to notice for the first time that a girl was standing behind the man. She was observing Wim from beneath stern dark brows but otherwise gave no sign of acknowledgment. Her unyielding gaze might have contained a challenge if it had not been so purposefully disinterested. Her features were similar to the man's, broad and well defined, but her short hair was artfully chopped into spikes and her ears and nose were pierced in several places by small silver rings. She was dressed, with shrewd carelessness, in faded black. David Te Makara, following Wim's stare, put his arm around the girl's squared shoulders.

"My niece. Tangi Robertson," he said.

The girl corrected abruptly, "Tangi *Te Aniwa*," and deftly moved away from the man's embrace. A faint darkening on his face was the only sign that he had noticed her rudeness. The wind brought another spit of rain and the man pulled his denim jacket closed. "My apologies," he said to Wim, his manner suddenly distant. "I won't trouble you any further. Will you please tell your father I stopped by? And if he wants to phone me at the hotel, I'll be there a few more days. I'll just leave a number where he can reach me— "

He was holding his hand out to her. Wim was all at once acutely aware of her appearance, the wet shirt clinging to her body, her hair dripping in a tangle over her shoulders. It was all she could do not to reach out her hand to him. But she knew if she tried to touch him, he would dissolve. He always disappeared when she reached out to him . . .

"He wants the card," the girl spoke unexpectedly and with indifference. "He wants to write the number on the card."

"Oh," said Wim. Feeling foolish, she handed the business card back to the man. He scrawled a number on it and gave it to her, smiling at her with such frank fullness her whole being was suffused with warmth. "Thank you," he said. Then, after the slightest hesitation, he added, "I don't know your name."

"Charlotte Williamson Thorpe," she blurted.

"Ah." His eyes flicked suddenly from her to the girl and he let out his breath with unexpected force, as if he had been holding it.

She said, flustered at herself, "But I never use that name. It's Wim, really. You know—the way William was written in the old days . . . Wm. It was my father's idea . . ." Her voice stumbled against the silence again, a palpable, dynamic presence between them. The man still seemed distracted, but he said with perfect courtesy, "Well, g'day then, Wim. Thank you." He gave her a quick, incongruous grin, added softly, "Perhaps we'll meet again," and left, the girl marching beside him.

Wim went into the house and, feeling dazed, wandered into the room her father called his study but which had now been converted to a bedroom for Great-Aunt Kia. Ginny's childhood bed had been moved in and positioned against one wall, and Sam's desk had been relegated to the corner, but otherwise the room was as it had always been. She'd never found it inviting, a mixture of unintentional neglect and the clutter of her father's perpetual research on his family history. A heavy mirror that took up one entire wall had once graced in ostentatious splendor the captain's cabin of a ship—not the cabin of Captain Charles Williamson Thorpe, the most illustrious of the Thorpe ancestors, but that of some cousin of lesser reknown whose modest mail and goods packet had plied the waters between Cape Cod and Boston for many years.

Wim faced herself in the mirror. Something tremendous had just happened; she could feel it. She'd been touched at a depth in herself she'd never known before, but as she searched the image in the glass, she could see nothing more than what she had always seen. She pressed her hand against her chest. Her heart was racing; that was all.

Gradually she forced herself to calm. She lugged one of the cardboard boxes to the hallway. Sam had packed it carelessly, although she knew the things in it were of value to him. Material for the historical novel he had been intending to write for as long as Wim could remember but which had never progressed beyond pages and pages of notes. Magazine articles; publications from various historical societies; old letters, ledgers, and logs from six generations of Cape Cod merchant ships captained or owned by Thorpes. She shoved the heavy box toward the door and went back for another.

This one contained family photo albums. Curious, glad for the distraction, she knelt in the hallway and opened the album on top to pictures and memorabilia from her sisters' high school years. Innumerable shots of Ginny and Bea, always together, obvious sisters, undoubtedly Thorpes. In several photos, Ginny was wearing a sweatshirt with PROVINCETOWN HIGH CLASS OF '89 in blue letters across the front. Ginny had been eighteen that year, and Bea seventeen—the same age Wim was now. Ten years ago. Wim had been seven when these photos were taken, hardly old enough to have any sense of these older girls' connection with herself. There were volumes of photo albums like this, illustrating each milestone in her sisters' lives, recording the life of a family Wim did not know. Bea and Ginny had always been as close as twins, exhibiting the typical Thorpe ruddy skin, their faces heavily freckled under straight red hair that streaked blond in the Cape Cod sun, looking into the camera with the blue eyes they shared with both parents.

Wim leafed in a desultory way through another album. Bea and Ginny, ten and eleven years old respectively . . . and all at once, a third child, and the two sisters peering at this tawny-skinned, dark-haired baby as if a changeling had been dropped in their midst. "Whew! Just look at her!" Uncle Alex had teased Sam on his visit ten years ago from Florida. "Now that's what I'd call a throwback! She's Aunt Kia all over again, isn't she, Sam? How'd you manage that?"

She'd only remembered the incident because Bea had giggled, "Throwback! Isn't that what you do with fish you don't want? Hey, Wimmie, can I call you Little Fish?" And Ginny had joined in, and they'd called her Little Fish until they grew bored with it.

Wim paused, remembering, studying the pictures of herself as a young child. Her curiosity deepened despite herself and she dug around in the box until she found an album with a much earlier date. These were the Florida years, long before Wim had been born. She'd never looked much through these pictures. They gave her a strangely sad, unsettled feeling, like the aftermath of a dream she couldn't quite remember. To her, these might have been pictures of a fictional family from a book whose characters she was nevertheless very familiar with. They had been the Florida Thorpes then: her father, Sam, and his brother, Alex, all the cousins, and the presiding matriarch of the clan, Katherine Irene Thorpe.

She turned the pages slowly at first, not sure what she was looking for. But there was a growing urgency in her; she sought for something among all the images of two little red-haired girls and their equally fair cousins, the images of a younger, much happier-looking Sam and an oddly maternal Carol, the scenes of barbecues and bicycles and beaches. Then she stopped. Peered closer. There, in the background: a blurred figure half turned away from the camera. And on another page, an out-of-focus woman's form. She turned another page, caught her breath in astonishment.

She might have been looking at an older version of herself. The hand-printed caption read "Kia, on Gunrunner, 1945." The woman sitting so composed on a tall black horse was neither of regal height nor dressed in full equestrian fashion. The saddle was utilitarian and well used. But the overall effect was of poised command. The mature, darkly arresting eyes were looking straight at the camera from a face framed by unruly black hair. Beyond the self-possession obvious in the woman's bearing was an unidentifiable quality that expected respect, even deference. Straight dark brows, wide somber mouth. Wim resisted going back in the room to look in the mirror. There was no question of the resemblance. She stared at the old photo for several minutes. 1945. Her father's aunt was eighty-four now; when this picture was taken, she'd been thirty.

She flipped through more pages, but the album kept falling back to the picture of the woman on a horse, and Wim, with sudden unease, closed it and shoved it deep into the box. She scrambled to her feet, hesitated a moment, then went slowly back into the room. The low afternoon light coming in the window turned the mirror glass dark. She had to stand very close to see. She tilted her head so the light fell along her cheekbones, washed over her broad, high forehead. She held out her arms, ran one hand over the tanned forearm, turned her arm to expose the paler skin. Under her fingers rose the electrical prickle of goosebumps. Disconcerted, as if the eyes watching her from the mirror were not her own, she drew in her breath and stepped back hurriedly.

It was true: she looked extraordinarily like her great-aunt, Katherine Irene Thorpe. But Kia herself looked like the two strangers who had just showed up on the doorstep.

All at once she was exhausted, and she sat in the oak swivel chair at Sam's desk. On the wall above the desk, unexamined for years by anyone except her father, hung a framed genealogical chart, hand-lettered, with ornate embellishments. Dust covered the glass. Wim reached up to wipe it clear. The family tree began with Captain Charles Williamson Thorpe, born in 1777, and ended with Virginia Thorpe and Beatrice Thorpe — Sam had commissioned the chart before Wim was born. "But we named you after Charles Williamson," her father had assured her once, apologetically, as if that fact alone would compensate for being left off the family tree. "A most admirable and distinguished man."

This was before anyone realized that, despite the heritage of success reaching unbroken back through the generations to Captain Thorpe himself, Wim had no desire to distinguish herself at all. She had no aspirations or ambitions to explore beyond the horizon; she was content to be who she was where she had always been. She ran her eyes down the faded chart, reading names that had graced headstones in Cape Cod graveyards for 250 years. All those Thorpes, with those proud and repetitive names—Charles Williamson and Williamson Alexander, Thomas Alexander and Samuel Williamson—each in their day seeking and commanding great respect. Mutinously, she swiveled the chair away. This family legacy of magnificent dreams—did any of it really matter? Wim kicked the chair back from the desk. It was absurd to look to the past for anything; looking back only broke hearts—something she, by the accident of her birth, was living proof of. She, Wim, was a dream *breaker*. No matter how tactfully the story had always been presented to her, she knew the truth of it: She knew how Sam had finally risked selling his Florida hardware business and moved his family to Cape Cod to restore the neglected Thorpe ancestral home and work on the historical novels he had always dreamed of writing. She knew how her mother had been accepted into medical school in Boston and had planned to pursue her lifelong aspiration of becoming a doctor. But to the surprise of both, Wim had come along. "A welcome oversight," Sam had once jokingly reassured her. And because of it, he had considered it more prudent to once again open a business, which grew successfully to include stores all over the Cape, and his writing study lay unused except to store his research material. And Carol, with a new baby, had turned down her medical school acceptance and continued, as before, to work as a nurse.

The phone rang and Wim jumped up guiltily. "Hi, Dad,"

she answered and mumbled through apologies. "No, Mom isn't home yet. It's only half past six."

"She said she'd try to get home before seven," Sam interrupted. "Anyway, just tell her Ginny's here at the airport with me. She took off early from work and met me at Logan."

She felt, irrationally, the old jealousy. "That's better anyway, Dad," she said as cheerfully as she could. "Your aunt doesn't know me, after all. It's better that Ginny's there."

But later, carrying the boxes out to the cottage, the unreasonable feelings hit her again. The cottage had always been her sisters' territory, undisputed for years until, as a small child, Wim had tried to join their partnership. Here in the cottage, Ginny and Bea had shared secrets and built playhouses and later had reserved it as a sanctuary for themselves and their friends. How could their five-year-old sister have been a welcome witness to the whispered dramas of teenagers? So Wim had been tricked away, coerced away, sometimes forcibly evicted, until the cottage took on the ambiance of an exclusive, secret club. Even after she'd met Jilly . . .

She paused in the main room of the cottage, holding the last box she'd brought from the house. By the time she'd turned eleven, and Ginny and Bea had been away at college for years, the old restrictions had still applied. "Don't let Wim go in there with her friend," they had each implored. "They'll just mess things up. All my stuff's in there, Mom!" And, "Dad, she just shoved all my stuff in a pile! It's a mess! I can't find anything. Can't her friend do her dancing somewhere else?"

The cottage would always belong, by birthright, to them. Whether they were absent or not, her sisters' presence claimed the space. So the barn had become Wim's world. Jilly had taken her there, introduced her to Evelyn and Tammy. Tammy was Jilly's aunt, and Jilly had stayed with her and Evelyn during the summer vacations until she was fourteen, when she'd moved into their home permanently to escape the chaos of her own.

The man with the tattooed face had brought Jilly into Wim's life, just as he brought everything that was important to her. He would appear; she would catch the slight movement in her periphery vision and turn her head. And whatever she saw by looking in a different direction, she *met*. Completely, with all her being. One day, it had been Jilly.

She kicked open the door to the back room of the cottage, dropped the box, and left, slamming the door behind her.

Later, after the flurry of Sam's arrival, after his old aunt was settled in her room and after the endlessly involved discussion around the kitchen table between her father and mother and Ginny, Wim escaped to her room. But she could not sleep. The wind gusted intermittently through the oak tree outside her window. The rain had stopped. It was a cool June night. The smell of the ocean carried with it something intangible, disturbing her because she felt on the point of identifying it and could not. So she lay awake and thought about the great white heron, her mind's eye tracing every detail of the graceful form. She was compelled by the restless excitement that had haunted her all day to *get closer*, to understand the purpose of its almost eerie perfection. And as the white bird carried her on slow wingbeats deeper into thought, she was startled suddenly to find the man from New Zealand confronting her. Unwillingly, she remembered his eyes as he'd looked at her, his brown hand giving her the business card, his smile. She jumped out of bed, pulled on her jeans and boots, and went down the stairs.

But she was not able to slip quietly away. Ginny was sitting in the dark on the front steps, smoking. She glanced up, puzzled, when Wim came out and asked, "You going out? It's past midnight."

"Just to the barn."

Without preamble, with the self-confident, assertive manner that had made Ginny a success already in the business world, her sister said, "You weren't bothered that I met Dad at the airport, were you? You know what a worrywart he is. He'd convinced himself that he would need help with Aunt Kia, and that was that. And since you were late getting back from the barn—" Ginny gave a short laugh and dragged at her cigarette, blowing the smoke playfully at Wim. "Don't look so guilty! You're not responsible for Dad's neurotic worrying. I told him you'd grow out of those horses when you were good and ready."

"It wasn't the horses!" Wim muttered, stung.

Ginny laughed again and patted the step; Wim perched reluctantly beside her. "Oh, it doesn't matter about the horses," Ginny continued. "It's just Dad. You know. He worries about you." She made a face at Wim. "He thinks it's time you started thinking about a real job, something that will help toward college."

"I have a real job. And I'm not going to college."

Ginny rolled her eyes and waved her hand impatiently. "I know, I know. Whatever. Dad just means a job the way other kids have in the summers. Remember that summer before my senior year, when I worked at the Chowder Shack? Something like that. Where you could make a decent wage. Maybe even make a few friends."

Wim always knew, when talking with either sister, that she was being forced to walk along an unsteady plank that could flip and toss her at any moment. Ginny's was a well-ordered, reasonable world; she took care that everything she said made sense. But Wim could find no balance there. She squirmed on the step.

"It's just that he doesn't want to have to worry about you, too, now he's got Aunt Kia here," Ginny was continuing. "Not that it's your fault. Dad makes his own worries, after all. I don't know why he insists on Rose Point for Aunt Kia. It's got to be one of the most expensive nursing homes on the Cape." She blew smoke expansively and shook her head. "I hope that new wing opens soon. Aunt Kia was always strange, but boy, she's really senile now."

The old woman had not struck Wim as senile or "wandering in her mind," as Sam evasively put it. Katherine Irene Thorpe had arrived at the house tired, overwhelmed, and irritable. She had declined dinner, saying she only wanted to be alone and to go to bed. Her eyes had caught Wim's then; there had been unexpected humor in them, and the instantaneous acknowledgment of something shared. "You are Charlotte," Kia had said. She had studied Wim a moment, then added, as if confering a favor, "You may show me my room." But she had not expected Wim to carry her bag—she shouldered it herself.

Ginny was blithely continuing her commentary between thoughtful drags on her cigarette. "And anyway, I told Dad he shouldn't keep fussing at you. You're going into twelfth grade.

There's still time for you to decide what you want to do with your life. Not everyone is like me or Bea." She bumped Wim affectionately with her shoulder and laughed. "Thank God, huh! Besides, we didn't have something traumatic happen to us the way you did."

Wim jumped up. "I have to go," she said hurriedly. She walked to the truck, not pausing even when Ginny protested, "But I've got to leave for Boston tomorrow morning, Wimmie. We haven't had a chance to visit."

She fumbled in the dark with the keys, and it took her a moment to realize she was angry. Why was Ginny demanding an intimacy now that she'd never allowed to develop before, when they were all children at home? Wim started the truck, pulled onto the street, hesitated, then called out the window, "I'll try to get back before you leave," but she knew she wouldn't.

She wished she'd brought Angelo with her. He would have curled his bony body next to her on the seat, and if she stayed the night at the barn, he would burrow into the cushions of the office sofa with her. She could touch him. Not like the Kid. She parked the truck in the dusty yard and went silently around the barn to the corral. The horse was dozing in his usual place against the back fence, but he nickered softly when he saw her. She smiled. The greeting was a recent development.

"Beautiful animal," Evelyn had said softly, when she'd looked at the horse for the first time last April with Joe Blair, the Animal Control officer for Wellfleet.

"Awful mean, though," Joe had commented, shaking his head. "Don't know, Ev . . . might be this one's too much even for you."

Later, hearing of this, Tammy had rolled her eyes. "Could he possibly have said anything that would have made you want the horse *more?*" she'd said sarcastically. "But what are we supposed to *do* with him, Ev? He's useless. Can't ride him. Can't touch him. Can't even put him in with the other horses."

"He sure has a rage in him," Evelyn had agreed quietly. "Give him to Wim."

Wim leaned on the fence now and murmured to the Kid. The horse flicked his ears, switched his tail, shifted uneasily on his feet, but he listened. She talked to him about the places she loved. "There's space on the dunes," she crooned. "So much space. You could run forever. There's nothing to stop you. You don't have to go anywhere . . . you can just run and run, 'cause it's all open, and the wind is always blowing, and the sea . . . the sea is there, and the sand, and space—" When she paused, the horse craned his neck and pointed his ears in her direction. She continued softly, "Yes, it's true. And I will take you there. Yes I will. I promise. No halter. No saddle. Nothing holding you. You can run and run and run . . ."

As her voice murmured on, the horse came toward her across the corral in the summer darkness, a shimmering shadow drifting over silver sand.

She didn't move; he came until he stood close enough for her to see the continuous flutter of his nostrils as he took her in. Not close enough to touch, but enough for each to hear the other's soft breathing, for them to absorb each other's space into their own.

She didn't notice him move. But almost imperceptibly, in the breathing silence, she felt the brush of velvety muzzle warm against her skin. She closed her eyes. A snuffle on her neck, exploring, then a deliberate, more forceful lipping against her cheek. Only then did she realize he was tasting the salt of her tears.

Three ⟡

B y mid-June, the barn calendar was fully booked with trail rides, lessons, and buggy trips. Wim sighed, pushing the sweaty hair from her face, and checked the calendar against any amendments Tammy or Evelyn might have scrawled on the notepad beside it. Today there were lessons scheduled all morning, an afternoon trail ride for eight on the longest loop, and three buggy trips in the early evening. The phone rang. She sighed again and started to answer just as Evelyn poked her head in the office door. Wim handed her the receiver. Evelyn grunted "yes" once or twice, hung up, commented, "Very persuasive, that bunch." She scribbled something on the calendar.

"Red pen for add-ons," Wim reminded her automatically.

Evelyn made a face, switched pens, and grumbled, "You're worse'n Tammy. Is that what I pay you for?" She tapped the pen on the calendar. "Fifteen Cub Scouts from Boston. Cripes. It's gonna take the whole damn barn. Well, Tam can take 'em. She's better with kids anyway."

"Fifteen? So you'll have to use Muenster?"

Evelyn snorted. "Don't you start. Half of what ails that pony is play-acting. You know he's a sissy. C'mon! They're *Cub* Scouts. He won't even know anyone's on his back."

Wim brought the pony in from the big corral to brush him down. The horses designated for the day's trail rides were kept brushed and waiting in their stalls. Muenster followed her willingly. She never had to cross-tie him. Patient, soft little creature, round and yellow as cheese. Rescued from a carnival act. The others picked on him, and he was forever nursing bruises. Wim ran the shedder over his blond coat and watched for any favoring of the legs. The pony leaned against her and sleepily blinked his eyes. She worked on him, caressing more than brushing, and stopped frequently to rub his face.

Tammy's tall, angular form appeared silhouetted in the doorway at the end of the barn. "Hey, there, Wimmie," she called.

"This is the one place it would be *nice* if I didn't get called Wimmie."

Tammy chuckled and came toward her, pausing to drink from the hose. "Well, you were doing your off-in-dreamland thing, and I figured it would get your attention." She assessed Wim with a critical eye. "You look about beat, kiddo. You do the whole barn this morning?"

"I didn't mind. I was here anyway." She shrugged. "I stayed over last night."

Tammy leaned her shoulder against a stall door and watched Wim a moment in silence. Then, "So, the situation with your aunt's not working out," she stated.

Wim shrugged. "Oh, it's not really that—" She paused.

"Well, yes—she's difficult. She wakes up pretty early, and she doesn't always know where she is, and she wants to go home, so she wanders off."

"I thought Sam hired a home health aide."

Wim shrugged again, busying herself with a knot in Muenster's forelock. "She doesn't come in until seven."

Tammy cocked her head. "Yeah, I get it. Wim to the rescue, right? How early is 'pretty early'? Five? Four? That's ridiculous, Wim. Your dad's got to snap out of denial and get her into a home."

Wim blushed. "He's just waiting until Rose Point is ready. Anyway, I like her," she muttered defensively. "She's not senile. No, really, Tam. There *is* something different about her, but it's more sort of . . . mysterious. Like there's more going on in her than it seems." She frowned and continued. "I guess I wish Dad had spent a little more time interviewing health aides. He took the first one the agency sent. She just pumps Aunt Kia full of drugs. She says it's to keep her quiet so she won't hurt herself." She tossed the shedding comb in the tack box with an abrupt movement, and the pony looked around at her in mild surprise. "But it's just to make her easier to deal with."

Tammy said decisively, "It's your father's problem, Wim. Don't take it on yourself. Yeah, I know you, kiddo. You get over here at six, and if you've already been up running around after your old auntie for hours by then—"

Evelyn called out from the office, "You getting that pony ready for the Queen of England? For God's sake, finish up and put him in his stall. Wim! You hear me? You staying for lunch?" She emerged and strolled down the length of the barn, inspecting with an acute eye each horse as she passed, as she always did. She bumped Tammy affectionately with her shoulder. "Hey, Tam. Where've you been all morning?"

"Bills," said Tammy, laconic.

Evelyn rolled her eyes. "So that's why you look so worried! How many times do I have to tell you not to worry? Things work themselves out."

"*Tammy* works things out," Wim corrected. "It's me she's worrying about, anyway. She's just fussing."

"It's her aunt," Tammy explained.

"*Great*-aunt."

"Great-aunt, then. Doesn't matter," Tammy said impatiently. "Sam's bitten off more than he can chew, as usual, and didn't give it enough thought, and I bet Mom's not sticking around to deal with it, so guess who looks after the old dear? Along with the umpteen other things she looks after?"

A smile softened Evelyn's sunburned face and she draped one arm over Wim's shoulders. "How long have we known this girl?" she asked Tammy. "Going on seven years? You think she's gonna change? Be grateful, Tam. When we're old and drooling and doddering like poor old Angelo, guess who we'll have to look after *us?*" She twisted her mouth sardonically. "And for us two, she's gonna need all the practice she can get."

Wim went home for lunch, as she had begun to do a few days after Kia's arrival. Sometimes it was just to keep the old woman company while the health aide fixed sandwiches. If she could spare more time, she would take Kia out for a drive in the truck. They would go to the road overlooking the marshes and eat their lunch while Wim surveyed the ever-changing tidal grasslands. "What are you looking for, Charlotte?" Kia had asked the first time they did this.

"A great white heron," Wim had replied.

Kia had stirred. "Rare is rare," she'd said with unexpected force. "Don't expect magic twice in the same place."

She'd never told the old woman about seeing the bird. Kia returned Wim's startled look impassively and soon after began to doze off. Wim had taken her home. But Kia's words stayed with her, linking the bird to the memory of David Te Makara. *"Don't expect magic twice in the same place."* She did, though. More than two weeks had passed, but she had not been able to keep herself from looking, each time she came home, to see if he was standing again at the front door.

But the days became too crammed with activity to ponder magic. As the tourist season grew busier, Wim was consumed with work at the barn. Kia woke her around four o'clock every morning. By noon, when she went home for lunch, she had to struggle to keep from being lulled to sleep in the quiet, drowsy house. One day, coming home later than usual, Wim found the health aide dozing in the living room, the television on. The woman jerked awake. "Must be the heat," she muttered sheepishly. Wim said nothing, turning to look for Kia.

She found the old woman sitting on the edge of her bed, plucking at sodden sheets. In the warm room, the odor of urine was overpowering. Anger rose in Wim, acrid as the smell. It was the third time she'd come home to find Kia soaked. She knelt by the bed. "I'm sorry, Aunt Kia," she whispered, stricken. "I should have gotten here sooner."

She started to remove the woman's wet clothing, but Kia

slapped her hands away. "I'm not helpless," she said, scowling. "Leave me alone. I can take care of this."

While Kia was in the bathroom, Wim stripped the bed to the rubber pad and lugged the sheets to the basement laundry. Her dirty barn clothes had been collecting for weeks on the floor; she stuffed as much as she could in the washing machine and switched it on. As she shut the lid, something white swirling in the soapy water caught her eye. She fished it out.

It was the business card David Te Makara had given her, forgotten in the pocket of the shirt she'd been wearing the day she saw the white heron.

Kia had quick eyes. "What is that?" she asked, when Wim came back to her room. Wim was holding the card between two fingers so it would dry, her hand at her side.

She jammed the wet card into the pocket of her jeans. "Nothing," she said. She felt Kia's eyes follow her as she straightened up the room, made the bed with clean sheets, picked up the discarded clothing in the bathroom.

"Why am I here? Why are you keeping me in this place?" Kia suddenly demanded.

"I'm not—" Wim began, and sighed. "Aunt Kia, don't you remember? Uncle Alex decided to move to Puerto Rico. He knew you wouldn't like it there, so Dad and he thought you'd—"

Kia tossed her head and glared so fiercely that Wim stopped. They stared at each other across the room. Despite her age, there were only the faintest streaks of gray in the old woman's thick hair, which she wore, like Wim, braided loosely down her back. She sat erect and alert on the bed, her presence commanding a far greater space than her body. "You're just parroting what everyone else tells me," she snapped. "Do you think I don't remember what *they* say? I thought you were different, Charlotte." She paused a moment, then leaned intently toward Wim. "Why? Tell me why I'm here."

Wim was standing by the window, the shade cord in her hand. Disconcerted, unsure how to answer, she jerked the cord too hard and the shade rolled up with a loud snap. Kia's gaze suddenly darted from Wim to something beyond her, outside the window. The nature of her silence changed, too, as though she were listening. The skin on Wim's neck pricked. "What?" she whispered.

Then, as suddenly as before, Kia's gaze dropped. Her shoulders sagged perceptibly and she slumped on the bed, defeated. She shook her head slowly back and forth. "What? What?" she repeated Wim's question querulously. "What does it matter, *what?* You can't see anything. You don't have any idea what I see." She sounded so forlorn that Wim's throat tightened. In a hoarse whisper, almost inaudible, the old woman added, "I thought you did."

Wim was overwhelmed by the urge to cry out, "Yes I do! I *do* see!" But she could not say anything.

Kia stood abruptly in a decisive, fluid movement. "I am going home," she announced, gathering her handbag and a sweater from the chair beside the bed.

"Oh, Aunt Kia—"

The health aide appeared in the doorway, looking contrite. "Lunch is ready, if you're hungry," she said, addressing Kia and avoiding Wim's eyes. "I made your favorite. Tuna salad with curry. Coming?"

"Coming? Coming?" Kia mimicked her nastily. "I'm not a child. Stop trying to bribe me. You only want me to eat so you can give me those drugs. Then I'll go to sleep and *you*—" She jabbed one finger fiercely at the startled woman, "you can get back to your soap operas."

The health aide took a deep breath. "You need to sleep, Katherine. That's all those drugs are for. Your blood pressure—"

Kia threw her head back and laughed. "Sleep?" she chuckled, genuinely amused and without a hint of bitterness. "For goodness' sake. What do I need to sleep for? I'm eighty-four years old, you fool. I'll be gone soon enough. What do you want to preserve me for?" She waved her hand dismissively. "I've slept quite enough, thank you."

Still clutching her handbag and sweater, Kia pushed past the health aide in the doorway and went down the hall to the kitchen. "I'll eat because I'm hungry," she tossed the words haughtily over her shoulder. "And if I take your nasty little pills, it'll be so Charlotte can get back to her horses. Poor Charlotte—" She swung around to face Wim. "Poor Charlotte feels responsible for me, and she won't leave unless she thinks I'm all right. Isn't that so?"

"Yes," said Wim, truthfully. "But I'm not 'poor Charlotte.' I don't have to get back to the barn until three, if I don't want to." She paused. There went her free time with the Kid. Keeping her tone deferential, she asked, "Instead of going home, Aunt Kia, would you walk with me down the beach?" She turned to the aide. "I can make sure she takes her meds when we get back. You could leave early, if you want."

The aide glanced at the clock, hesitated. "Well—"

Kia said impatiently, "Yes, leave early. I don't want you here. I want to be with Charlotte." She sat at the table and took a huge bite of the tuna sandwich, chewing noisily and with obvious pleasure. The aide looked helplessly at Wim. Kia remarked, "I have been waiting a long time for Charlotte to take me to the sea."

"The harbor isn't exactly the sea, Aunt Kia."

Kia gazed at Wim a moment, her eyes strangely bright. The health aide hurriedly gathered her things, muttered a thanks, and went out of the kitchen. Kia smirked.

Wim said, "You don't really have to be so mean to her."

"Do you want me to give in to her?" growled Kia. They heard the front door open and close as the aide left, and the old woman observed with a shrug, "I suppose she's doing what she was hired to do. Babysit a sick, nutty old woman."

"You're not nutty!"

Kia chortled. "Yes, I know. But nutty is all they see. That's the joke of it, isn't it? Your silly father, God love him, can't see more than a horse with blinders. Never could. His brother's just as bad." She shook her head with rueful humor and got up. "Well, they've finally found a way to get back at me for taking their mother's place. That's what this is, you know."

"Dad would never—" Wim began, protesting, but Kia waved her words aside.

"Take me to the sea, Charlotte," she said. "I lost something there. I need to find it. Don't you remember?"

"Um . . ." Wim faltered. Kia was watching her again, eyes glittering like dark pebbles at the water's edge. She could feel agitation building in the old woman, the way static built in the air before a storm. "I don't remember," Wim admitted at last in a low voice. "But I will take you to the sea soon, Aunt Kia. I promise."

Satisfied, the old woman followed her without further comment across the yard and onto the harbor beach. They walked in silence for some time, reaching an abandoned wharf before Wim stopped. Kia wandered in among the barnacle-encrusted pilings and stood half hidden in the shadows. After several minutes she looked back at Wim. "I want to go home," she said softly. "I must go home to the sea before I die, Charlotte."

Wim hesitated. Sam would never take the old woman back to Florida. "This *is* your home, Aunt Kia," she answered carefully. "Really. You grew up here. Remember? You lived in our house when you were a little girl. Dad told me. He told me how you moved with your family to Florida so your father could have a horse ranch, and how your brother raised *his* family there, too—my dad and Uncle Alex—and when their mother died, you moved in with them to help out." She took small steps away from the wharf, hoping it would force Kia to come out, and kept talking. "Dad told me that he'd always wanted to move to Provincetown, to fix up the old family house. No one had been living in it for years. The historical society looked after it. It's called Thorpe House, Aunt Kia. Our ancestor built it . . . the ship captain. You know—you're the one who told Dad all the stories, when he was a little boy. He said it was your stories that made him want to come to Cape Cod to see where his ancestors had lived."

Kia was weaving trancelike in and out among the pilings. The light filtering down through the planks of the ruined wharf patterned her skin with shadows. Wim stopped speaking. Kia stopped. Wim could hardly make out her form. She spoke so softly Wim was not sure she heard the words or just knew, somehow, that she was saying them. Kia said, "I must, I must go to the sea."

"I told you I'd try —"

"Charlotte!" The old woman's voice struck out at her like an eel from its hiding place. "You aren't taking me seriously! You aren't listening!" She came suddenly to the edge of the shadows beneath the wharf, stooped, picked something from the sand. She held what she had found on the open palm of her hand and extended her arm into the sunlight. Wim heard the sharp intake of Kia's breath. There was a bright green flash as what the old woman held was touched by the sun. Then Kia closed her hand into a fist and moaned, "No. No. This isn't it. It can't be. We haven't come to the sea." She seemed suddenly to lose all her strength, and Wim was at her side in a second.

"Aunt Kia," Wim urged gently. "Let's go back to the house. You're tired." She took her by the arm and Kia came without protest. Her fist relaxed and a piece of polished green sea glass dropped from her fingers to the sand. Wim bent to get it but Kia said, "Just leave it. Leave it. It's only glass, Charlotte. It isn't what I am looking for. Leave it." The hopelessness was back in her voice, and Wim's eyes burned with unexpected tears. It was like watching old Angelo struggle to get up on a cold morning only to collapse on stiff legs. She couldn't help him. She couldn't fix what was wrong. She could only watch.

When they reached the gate in the rose hedge that opened from the beach into the back yard, Kia stopped and gazed at the house for several seconds. A puzzled flicker of recognition crossed her face. She narrowed her eyes, concentrating. "How . . . how old was I? When did I live here, Charlotte?" she asked.

"Dad said your family moved away when you were ten."

Kia nodded, startled. "Yes. Yes. I *do* remember. Ten. It was just after Grampy died — " She was looking around as if noticing everything for the first time. All at once her body stiffened. She pointed. "That's the cottage! That's where *he* hid. So he could watch the house. Grampy told me. Yes. I remember now!" Her voice had grown more vigorous. "He was watching for Grampy. He wasn't sure, you see . . . but then he saw Grampy's necklace. That's how he knew. Because it was the same as his own."

Kia clutched Wim's arm in agitation. "You don't go in there, do you, Charlotte? You have to be careful. *He* could be there. He wanted to take Grampy away with him. He might take *you*, but you must stay here and help me — "

The old woman was speaking almost incoherently now and Wim, alarm overcoming her bafflement, put her arm firmly around her shoulders and steered her through the gate. At that moment, Carol called to them from the house. "It's after three, Wim. Kia should be resting. And someone phoned you from the barn." Her mother walked across the yard toward them and Wim felt, with inexplicable panic, an irrational sense of loss. Kia had been about to tell her something. Something essential. She was sure of it and was filled with an absolute urgency to know what it was. Bewildered, she tried to brush the feeling away. It was obvious that Kia was confused. For a moment, just before her mother reached them, Wim almost convinced herself that Kia *was* senile after all.

But all afternoon, through the chatter of children on pony rides, through evening chores, Wim could not shake the residue of that inexplicable feeling of loss. She tried not to dwell on what the old woman had said. None of it made sense. Yet she could not help returning to it again and again. A strange longing built in her, and with it an unease, until she was so preoccupied she stumbled over a water bucket and startled a horse by dropping his measure of grain. She leaned her head against the horse's neck and rubbed her hand over his back to calm them both. *I'm just worried about her,* she told herself. *That's all.* She finished her chores quickly now, wanting to get home in time to sit a little with Kia before the old woman went to bed, and she realized, with quiet surprise, that she had come to love Kia the way she loved Angelo and the Kid.

Wim took vague notice of an unfamiliar car pulled up next to the house when she arrived, but she was tired and the dogs needed to be fed and watered. By the time she went up the back steps into the kitchen, she had forgotten about it. So she was completely unprepared, and stopped in the doorway, stunned. David Te Makara was sitting at the kitchen table, his niece Tangi beside him, holding Sam and Carol Thorpe in the spell of his voice.

She could not escape. Her vision suddenly tunneled, and all she could see was a tableau, David at the center, her father leaning eagerly toward him, listening, and her mother poised in the act of serving him a glass of iced tea. The glowering presence of the girl only accentuated the energy that seemed to emanate from the man and shimmer around them all like heat dancing on the surface of the sea.

Wim's eyes flew to David's. She wanted desperately to fight him off but could summon no resistance. When he smiled, she felt it in the pit of her stomach. He drew her into the room as surely as if he had reached out and taken her hand, yet he had not moved and had not spoken to her. She sat suddenly in the nearest chair. It was the chair closest to David. The whole room felt on fire.

Carol, fussing in an uncharacteristic way around the stove, said, "This is our youngest daughter, Wim. Wim, this is Mr. Te Mar—"

"Te Makara," said David. Smooth. His smile gracious. "David."

Sam looked so pleased and smug, it was as if he had been awarded David Te Makara as a prize in a contest. "Please forgive Wim the pungent odor of horses. She has a summer job at a riding stable," he said. Wim looked at the floor.

"Oh, it's the scent of home," David said with his easy smile. "I grew up with horses. We all did, in the back blocks. Spent entire summers mucking around on horses. Half wild they were, too. Wild as us kids, eh." He enveloped Wim in such a warm look that it transformed her father's dismissive words into something private and special shared only between them. He looked at her intently with his dark eyes and added softly, enigmatically, "I've been away from horses too long, I think."

There was a momentary silence. Then Carol said, "Well, you two better decide—are we ordering out for pizza or Chinese?"

"Pizza," said the girl, straightening momentarily from her slump. David laughed and shrugged. "She's the boss."

Sam told Wim, "Why don't you go clean up—David and Tangi are staying for dinner." He settled back in his chair. "We've been talking for hours. David's doing some fascinating work . . . research for his book—I've forgotten the title already."

"It's only got a working title yet, I'm afraid." David shrugged with pleasant self-effacement. "This week I'm calling it *Lost People: The New Zealand Maori in Exile*. Next week, who knows?"

Sam laughed, giving David a delighted glance. *The way silly Sue looks,* Wim thought in dismay, and stubbornly kept her own manner disinterested. "Just fascinating," Sam repeated, shaking his head in admiration. "So you were telling me about the Maori—I had no idea they were hired in such numbers to crew on whalers and traders. And in the early part of the nineteenth century, of course, most of those American ships came from right here on Cape Cod. Tough work, especially crewing on the whalers. Makes you wonder why they did it. And why so many Maori never returned to New Zealand, choosing to live in exile."

Interrupting unexpectedly, Tangi spoke again. "It wasn't New Zealand to Maori; it was *Aotearoa*." She made the comment disdainfully, as if it was so obvious she considered even saying it beneath her. "It was stolen from them when the *Pakeha* named it New Zealand. Maori became exiled in their own land, eh. They lost their *turangawaewae*. Missionaries stole their identity. Traders sold them guns and turned tribe against tribe. *Pakeha* settlers stole the land from under their feet—" She was speaking as if by rote with feverish intensity, but when David gave his niece a brief, implacable look, she sat back disgruntled and stared into space.

"*Turangawaewae* is a difficult concept to translate to non-Maori," David explained courteously, addressing Sam as if the girl had not spoken at all. "It means, roughly, 'standing place.' It has to do with belonging to the land of our ancestors, from which we have the authority to speak. Maori live within a context of tradition and ancestry, although that was greatly disrupted by the influence of British and American colonialism."

Wim stood up abruptly, ignoring her father's startled frown. Professor David Te Makara was obviously in love with the sound of his own voice, and his niece Tangi was the most unpleasant person Wim had ever met. She was suddenly so exhausted she could not tolerate them any longer. "Mom, where's Aunt Kia? Isn't she awake yet?" she asked, without attempting to wait for a pause in the conversation. The girl's eyes flashed at her, and Wim felt a perverse pleasure in her own rudeness.

Carol said, "I thought she should sleep a little longer. You took her for an awfully long walk—"

"But it's six-thirty!" Wim protested. "She's been sleeping for *hours.*"

"She needs the sleep, Wim. She's still adjusting," Carol stated impatiently.

Wim looked with mute appeal at her father but caught him direct an apologetic smile at David, as if to make an excuse for a misbehaving child. Incensed, she cried, "Dad!" but Sam shrugged. "Your mother's the nurse," he reminded her. "Let's leave those decisions up to her." He turned again to David.

"My elderly aunt. I told you about her." He leaned back in his chair. Wim could not remember ever seeing him so relaxed. All the usual tiredness was gone from his face, his expression animated and enthusiastic. "Now, you were telling me about those old sailing schedules you looked through when you were on the Vineyard . . . no mention of your Henry Cooper in them, either? Have you contacted the museum in New Bedford? I'd be happy to introduce you to the head curator there."

David inclined his head in acknowledgment. "I'd certainly appreciate your help. All I know about Henry Cooper is that he's my great-great-great-grandfather and that he left New Zealand on an American whaling ship bound for Cape Cod in 1856 and never returned. He was twenty-four years old. He'd been raised by American missionaries. At some point he seemed to give up his *Pakeha* name. That's all I've been able to find out."

"*Pakeha?*" asked Sam.

The girl spoke rebelliously. "*Pakeha.*" She almost spat the word with contempt. "Means 'white.' Missionaries wouldn't *allow* Maori to have Maori names."

"It's the name we have to work with," said David, once again intercepting the girl's words. "The records were kept by missionaries." He shrugged, defusing the tension with his smile. "Reckon I just haven't come across the right records yet, is all. You know that research is just a posh name for boring detective work."

Sam nodded eagerly. "I do know. I've been researching material for my novel for years. Ship's logs, letters, even an old journal no one's been able to read—it's in some kind of code.

I've got boxes of stuff—been in my family for generations."
He looked swiftly at his wife, then he offered, "You're welcome
to look through whatever I have, if it's any use to you. I don't
think there'd be a conflict, since I'm writing a novel."

Wim squirmed as she stood in the doorway of the kitchen.
Stop talking about that stupid novel! she thought furiously. *You
know you're never going to write it!*

David's eyes seemed to flicker once with some internal light,
then darken. "Thank you. That's very generous of you," he
said to Sam.

David Te Makara's voice might have been soft, but Wim
had caught that momentary change in his eyes. Was it *triumph?* Had he somehow maneuvered her father into offering
the use of his papers? She frowned to herself, uncertain. Perhaps what she'd seen had been more like . . . *relief?*

Puzzled, disturbed, she announced, "I'm going to go wake
Aunt Kia." She left the kitchen quickly, before her mother
could say anything. Pausing in the hallway, she listened to
David's warm, compelling voice. It was difficult to pull herself
away. She heard Sam's laugh. She hadn't heard her father
laugh in months. She shivered suddenly. The sun was down.
Kia would need a sweater when she woke.

The door to the room was partially open. The smell of urine
hit her again, staler this time. With the shades down the room
was dark, but she could see enough. She went in, lay her hand
on the damp sheets. Cool. She went back to the kitchen.

"Dad," she said, pointedly avoiding looking at her mother,
"Dad, Aunt Kia's run off again. I think she's been gone awhile
this time."

"Oh, not *again*," Sam groaned, getting up from the table. David stood immediately as well. Sam shook his head and gestured for David to sit. "No, no—go ahead and order the pizza. Don't wait for me. I won't be long. She never gets too far."

But David Te Makara continued politely to stand, as if, Wim thought angrily, he did not want Sam to stand higher than him. David was no taller than her father, but his presence made him appear to physically overwhelm him. "Dad," said Wim quickly. "I'll look for her. I know where she goes. She hates riding in your van, anyway."

She almost ran to the truck and had already put it in gear when the door to the house burst open and Tangi strode down the walk toward her. "I'm coming with you," she announced. Without waiting for a reply, she yanked open the door on the passenger side and slid onto the seat next to Wim. "Right, then. Let's go," the girl said brightly.

Wim was so shocked she could only stare, her hand frozen on the gearshift. Tangi had transformed almost beyond recognition. The glower was gone, replaced by a frank cheerfulness that made her seem much younger. Her voice, devoid of her earlier contempt, had an almost chatty quality. She looked at Wim and grinned. "Didn't mean to put you off, eh," she remarked. "I'm just sick to death of being here." She settled more comfortably in the seat and when Wim still did not respond, she continued, "Look, I *had* to get out of the house, eh. You can't imagine how many places Uncle David's dragged me around to. Anyway, I've had absolutely *heaps* of experience with old ladies. My Nana, for one. And Auntie Pat, and Mrs. Hohepa, and old *Kui* Ana. You wouldn't know them, of course, but believe me—they're *old*." She accented the last word with a jerk on the handle that rolled the window down. It made a grinding sound.

"Careful. It's an old truck," muttered Wim.

The girl surveyed her a long moment in silence. "I'll be a good help," she said finally. "You'll see."

Her tone and manner had changed again, imperceptibly, like a subtle shift in the weather. Wim said nothing. She drove slowly down Commercial Street, through late evening bicyclists and strolling couples, and headed past the marshes without a glance at the darkening grasses. The sky was glowing tangerine over Herring Cove, but Wim was sweeping the road ahead, looking for the solitary, determined figure of Aunt Kia.

Four ෨෧

Without asking, Tangi switched on the radio and fiddled impatiently until she found a Boston rap station. "Choice,"
she grunted with satisfaction, and she leaned back, eyes closed,
absorbed.

Wim tightened her grip on the steering wheel and ignored
her. They were in the dunes now, driving slowly along an
empty road in the deepening twilight. Despite her age, Kia had
proven herself to be a fast walker with exceptional stamina.
The last time she'd run off, Wim had found her at the visitor's
center on Race Point Road, several miles from home. She
peered ahead, trying to penetrate the dusk. The rap music was
setting her teeth on edge. Finally she pulled over and stopped.
"Are you serious about helping?" she demanded abruptly,
switching off the radio. Startled, Tangi gave her a furtive
glance and, to Wim's surprise, looked down at her hands in discomfort.

"Sorry," she muttered. "Don't get choice stations like that

in Auckland." She paused, cocked her head, and added more brightly, "So, yeah. What's she looking for, your auntie?"

"Looking for?"

"Yeah. You know," Tangi prompted. "When the old ones go walkabout like that, it's because they're looking for something. My Auntie Pat—that was my Nana's oldest sister—she always went looking for her little brother. He died when he was five, my mum told me. It was Auntie Pat's job to look after him, and she was only eight when he died. So anyway, that was it. When she got to be over ninety and went a bit gaga, she forgot that he'd died, like . . . eighty years before, and off she'd go walkabout, trying to find him. Gave them all a right turn, eh, 'cause sometimes she'd hitch a lift and go *miles*."

It took Wim a moment to gather herself after this rambling barrage of words, but eventually she said warily, "Well, she did tell me about losing something at the sea. I don't really know where she means, but she wants to find whatever it was."

"That's it, then," the girl said, satisfied. "She's heading for the sea."

Wim smiled despite herself. "The Cape's a peninsula," she reminded Tangi. "The sea is everywhere." She leaned forward, hooked her arms over the steering wheel, and gazed pensively into the summer night. Crickets filled the salt-sweet air, an owl hooted from the beech forest. "She could be anywhere," she sighed. "I've found her on Race Point Road, and in the center of town, and once she got halfway to Truro." She considered calling her father but knew he'd tell her to come home, and she'd have to stay there with David Te Makara. On the other hand, if she reported Aunt Kia missing again to Pete down at the police station, she'd have to endure the desk clerk's wise-cracks about there being a leash law in town. Caught by inde-cision, she turned to the open window and let the sea breeze wash over her face. "Maybe everyone's right," she said, half to herself. "Maybe she does need more medication. We can't watch her twenty-four hours a day, and we can't lock her in. Though I suppose she'll be locked in when she goes to Rose Point—"

"Rose Point?"

She glanced at Tangi. "Rose Point Nursing Home. They're building a new wing. Dad's reserved one of the new private rooms for her."

Tangi looked horrified a moment, then made a noise of con-tempt, folded her arms, and hissed something under her breath.

"What?" Wim demanded.

The girl shot her a look of scorn from under dark brows, and in a moment transformed into her original unpleasantness. "Maori would never do that. Stick their old people away in a *home*. Only *Pakeha* do things like that."

Wim put the truck in gear without a word and headed back onto the road. Kia was still out there walking somewhere, blinded by the headlights of traffic, surely exhausted and frightened by now. She quelled the urge to turn on the radio as a way of preventing any further conversation. She had reached the lights on Route 6 when Tangi spoke again. "Don't mind me, eh," the girl apologized, contrite. "Mum always says I don't know when to keep my big gob shut. Reckon she's right. Though Uncle David says it's 'cause I'm a born artist and I'm just outspoken." She shot a sideways look at Wim and contin-ued, "Uncle David's meant to be rescuing me, you know. From myself. That's why he brought me with him to America. To get me away from bad influences, Mum says. It's 'cause I told her I was getting a *moko*. That's a traditional tattoo. Here." She gave a throaty chuckle, ran one finger in a looping line over the side of her face, and made a self-mocking grimace at Wim. "Mum wants Uncle David to straighten me out. Crikey, you'd think she'd know her little brother better, eh. He's hardly what you'd call 'straight' himself. He's not above coming home with a *moko* someday, for all he's Mr. Big-Shot lecturer at university. Wouldn't Mum just have *kittens!*"

"What?" Wim was so disconcerted she almost stalled the truck when the light turned green.

The girl giggled. "Oh, I don't mean 'straight' *that* way," she said with a grin, misunderstanding Wim. "No worries about *that*. Mum says Uncle David's been a magnet to women since he was a tot in primers." She screwed her face up in disgust. "Yeah, right. So if he could have his pick, why'd he go and marry that *Pakeha* bitch, I'd like to know. Thank God she took off—anyone can see he's heaps better off without her."

The conversation had become so disorienting to Wim she'd forgotten to watch the road for several miles. It was now completely dark, she was driving too fast, and when she jammed on the brake, the truck slued. Tangi chortled in delight. "Whoo-ee! Now you're driving like everyone in Pukemoana. That's up where my Nana lives." She cocked her head, studying Wim with sudden calculating curiosity. "Come to think of it, you *look* like you come from Pukemoana, too, eh. You don't look *Pakeha* anymore'n I do. You adopted or something?"

Wim had no idea how this incredible monologue, which was

tumbling her along like the undertow of a wave, had come to this question. All she could do was gulp and say, "No—no. Of course not." But she could hardly hear her own words. There was a roaring in her ears. *David . . . married?* But she'd taken off. *Pakeha. Moko. Tattoo?*

"Hey!" Tangi cried out. "Hey, look!"

She leaned out the window, pointing enthusiastically down the highway. As the cars rushed past, each set of headlights illuminated a small figure wandering unsteadily down the breakdown lane ahead of them.

Wim gasped. "Aunt Kia!" She eased the truck slowly along the side of the road until she was a few yards away, then put on the hazard lights and got out. "Get in the back of the truck!" she hissed at Tangi. "She doesn't know you. You'll only spook her. And *be quiet!*"

She walked quickly toward the old woman. "Aunt Kia!" she called gently. "Hi, Aunt Kia. You want a ride home?"

Kia turned. Her hair, blown loose, hung crazily over her face. Over a dressing gown she wore a sweater pulled on backwards, and she had only slippers on her feet. An expression of tired relief came over the old woman's face as Wim came up to her. "Why, Charlotte," she said. "What a nice surprise. I *am* going home—but how did you know?" She came closer to peer at Wim in the darkness. A truck roared by and Kia faltered in the wind of its passing. She took Wim's arm. "I don't want to be a trouble, Charlotte, but I really am so tired—"

"It's no trouble, Aunt Kia. Really. I was on my way home myself," said Wim, putting her arm around the old woman's thin shoulders. Her eyes blurred unexpectedly with tears.

Kia looked bewildered. "You are?" she asked, hesitant. "*My home?*"

Wim nodded and swallowed hard as she helped Kia limp slowly to the truck. The slippers, she could see in the headlights, were shredded. The dressing gown hung partially open, revealing a nightgown—wet, Wim realized, remembering the wet bed. The old shoulders trembled under her arm and she pulled Kia closer against her. "Dad's going to be happy to see you," she said, keeping her voice cheerful. "Sam. He misses you."

Kia shook her head ruefully. "That Sam," she said. "He is such a *good* boy." She spoke in a conspiratorial whisper. "He's always bored me a bit, I'm afraid. I do love him dearly, of course. But he just won't *burst out.*"

Wim managed a smile. The idea of her father *bursting* in any direction was ludicrous. Kia raised her eyebrows at her as if to say: *Yes, we do know, don't we?* Suddenly she stumbled on a stone and sagged against Wim. "My feet. My feet, Charlotte," she moaned.

Wim opened up the passenger door of the truck and tried to guide Kia in. To her annoyance, Tangi was standing a few feet away. She shifted to block the girl from the old woman's sight, but Kia was too observant. Her body stiffened with alarm and she balked, pulling sharply away from Wim. "Who is that girl?" Kia demanded.

"That's—"

Before she could continue, Tangi stepped closer. "*Tena koe, e Kui. Tena ra koe.*" She gazed down, avoiding looking directly at Kia, but the old woman stared intently at Tangi for several seconds. The girl did not look up, but her manner was strangely deferential.

Kia frowned. "Who are you?" she snapped.

"Tangi Te Aniwa, *e Kui,*" answered the girl, still respectful, but her voice barely audible.

Another truck thundered past, rocking the pickup and buffeting the old woman. But she did not appear affected this time. An uncanny stillness seemed to surround them. An electric current of apprehension thrilled down Wim's arms and legs, and she was not sure if she any longer had the power to interfere. "Aunt Kia?" she whispered.

"I'm here, Charlotte," the old woman answered. Her voice broke the stillness, and she turned abruptly away from the girl.

Wim took Kia's arm, hissing fiercely to Tangi, "I *told* you to get in the back of the truck. And keep down. It's not legal to have passengers in the back."

Tangi grumbled, "Geez. If it was illegal to ride in the back of a ute at home, none of us would get anywhere, eh." She peered into the truck bed. "It's grotty in there," she protested. "What's all that muck?"

Wim shrugged. "If you don't like it, walk. It's not far." She hoped the girl really would, but from the corner of her eye, as she finally persuaded Kia to get in, she saw Tangi climb over the tailgate and crawl down to sit with her back against the cab.

Wim was rattled and exhausted, and she fumbled so much trying to attach Kia's seat belt that the old woman began to squirm. "Let's go home and get something to eat," Wim suggested in as bright a voice as she could muster.

"Don't talk to me like that, Charlotte," Kia said testily. "I'm not a child. I'm sixty-seven years older than you, as a matter of fact. Just take me home."

Wim was astounded and dismayed to discover how far she had driven. Kia must have been walking for hours, she realized. She drove slowly, conscious of Tangi riding unbelted in the back, but Kia began to fuss, craning her head around to look at the girl through the rear window of the cab. Wim gripped the steering wheel, and in grim silence cursed the huge camper ahead of her.

"I don't like that girl here," Kia complained uneasily. "Let me out, Charlotte. I don't believe you're taking me home." The thin fingers clawing at the seat belt were stronger than they looked. Wim gave up begging her to sit quietly and just clamped her hand around the old woman's arm with all her strength to keep her from opening the door.

But she had to let go to shift gears at the lights and Kia twisted violently, slipped out of the seat belt, and got on her knees to face the girl through the window. Ahead of Wim, the camper laboriously headed left toward town, and after a moment's hesitation, Wim swung right in the direction of the barn. In the rear-view mirror she could see Tangi, too, kneeling to look in at Kia. She reached over and slammed the cab window open. "I told you to keep *down!*" she yelled.

"Charlotte," Kia remonstrated, shocked.

Wim resisted the temptation to accelerate suddenly enough to topple the girl back into the bed of the truck. Instead she glared at her in the mirror and said nothing. All at once the girl began to sing.

She had a low, husky voice and she drew out the notes at the end of each line with a weird little undulating drone. The tune, fluid and repetitive, was like a chanted lullaby. Kia visibly relaxed. Yet despite the sound of the girl's voice, Wim immediately felt the peculiar stillness surround them again, holding them all within it, as though no one else but they were meant to hear this eerie, foreign song. Kia seemed mesmerized, and it took all of Wim's willpower to concentrate on the road. By the time she had slowed to turn up the drive toward the barn, Kia was calm enough for Wim to drop her hand away from the old woman's arm. She pulled up in the dark yard and leaned her head for a second against the steering wheel. The physical relief was as sharp as pain.

"What is that song, girl?" Kia murmured through the open cab window.

Tangi sat back on her heels. "My Nana used to sing it to me when I was little," she said softly. She smiled at Kia without looking at her directly and added shyly, "I still ask her to sing it, when I stay up at the farm in Pukemoana." She hesitated, then asked, an unidentifiable note in her voice, "Do you know the song *e Kui*?"

Kia drew back, suddenly confused. "I don't know. It sounds like something . . . it sounds like . . ." She shook her head. Then she demanded, "Where are we, Charlotte? This is not my home. Why have you brought me here? It smells like horses."

"We're at the barn, Aunt Kia. The barn where I work. Remember I told you about it? You said you wanted to see where I worked. You said you loved horses." She was easing out of the truck as she spoke, hoping that Kia would remain calm. Through the window of the house beyond she saw the flickering light of the television, envisioned Tammy and Evelyn sitting in their chairs, cats on their laps, Tammy with her mystery novel and Evelyn smoking and repairing worn tack. She felt a pang of longing. It was such a familiar, comfortable vision; she wished desperately that she could ask them for help. But they wouldn't have heard the truck, and Wim was unwilling somehow to involve them in this strange and uncanny drama.

"I'm going into the office to call Sam," she told Kia through the window. "Sam will come take you home, Aunt Kia. I promise. You wait here." She glanced back to Tangi with dislike, angrier than she could remember ever being. She never yelled. Not at a horse, or a dog, not even at her sisters. She fought to control her voice and said, "Please watch her for a few minutes. And don't do anything to upset her." She flashed a warning scowl at the girl. "I mean it. Watch her."

"Okay, okay. No worries," muttered Tangi, subdued.

Wim ran to the barn, switched on the light, and called Sam. "I wonder if it would be better if we both come—your mother, too," her father said slowly, thinking aloud.

"Oh, Dad, it doesn't matter. Just *somebody* come." She tried not to slam the phone down; thought sarcastically, *yeah, no worries*, and turned to find a silent Tangi standing at the door of the office.

The girl's eyes were unreadable. "I tried," she said. "She was too fast."

"What!" Incensed, Wim pushed past Tangi and hurried through the barn. "Why didn't you hold on to her!" she said through clenched teeth.

Trailing behind Wim in the darkness, the girl answered sullenly, "You wouldn't understand. She is—well, it would be wrong for me to touch her."

The skin on Wim's arms prickled. She ignored the girl and tried to think. Which way would Kia go from here? She paused at a loss in the yard, straining her eyes to see through the darkness. "Aunt Kia?" she called softly. And softly, from behind the barn, came a low nicker. At the same moment, she remembered the photograph of Kia on the beautiful black horse. Stunned, she thought, *the Kid!*

The horse was standing near his shed at the far side of the corral. The light from the moon, just rising above the pines, spilled over his dappled coat. The white sand and his white mane and tail all glowed with the same cool light. He might have been dozing, so relaxed did he appear. But the horse's ears were pricked forward, the way they did when he was listening intently, and as Wim came up to the fence, she saw his hide quivering slightly.

She moved along the fence until she was closer. Carefully, carefully. Stood motionless, just breathing. Called finally in the gentlest voice, "Hey. Hey, Kid. Hey. Aunt Kia?"

On the other side of the horse stood the old woman, leaning against him, stroking him with both hands.

Wim had given the horse his name on the day the Animal Control officer had gone with a warrant to take possession of the neglected animal and release him into Evelyn's care at Dune Forest Stables. The officer had barely escaped the lethal hooves. Evelyn had been lucky, she admitted later, to get away with a few bruises. As the horse grew healthier, he practiced his deadly kicks alone in the corral, as if in sheer joy of their potential.

But the Kid, impossibly, was standing quiet under Kia's hands. The horse who could not be touched without heavy sedation seemed to be pushing slightly against the woman as she caressed him. Kia gave no sign of noticing Wim's presence, but the Kid started a little and blew sharply through his nostrils as he caught the tension in her. Wim closed her eyes. Took a deep breath, released it slowly, folded herself within the darkness until she was calm. When she opened her eyes, the Kid was once again relaxed.

She had half forgotten the girl, but all at once Tangi spoke. "He can help her find what she is looking for," she murmured. She moved up beside Wim and gazed across at the horse. "Greetings, *kaitiaki. Tena ra koutou, e Kui, e kaitiaki.*" Her voice seemed to have no more substance than the air through the pines, but somehow the old woman and the horse heard her, and both stirred. Kia turned, as if noticing them for the first time. The horse shook his head.

"Don't!" Wim hissed under her breath.

"It'll be all right," said Tangi.

The Kid began to walk toward them, slowly enough so Kia could walk beside him with her hand on his neck. The darkness blurred all distinctions between them, and Kia appeared to move as gracefully as the horse. The Kid approached Wim and stopped a few feet away. Kia continued on alone. For the first time, her step faltered. "Charlotte?" she said, her voice frail. "Charlotte?"

"I'm right here, Aunt Kia," Wim answered quietly. She slipped under the rail fence and, keeping her eye on the Kid, guided the old woman toward the gate. As she opened it, she saw the Kid start, throw up his head as if released from a spell, and skitter off with a quick slash of his hooves to stand trembling once more at the far side of the corral. But she had no time to try calming him. With renewed resentment, Wim turned to Tangi and muttered, "Go meet my dad in the yard. Tell him he's going to take Aunt Kia in the truck and I'll drive the van back—she hates the van. And *you*—" She couldn't bring herself to say more. The girl's eyes were glittering enigmatically in the pale moonlight and she seemed deliberately to wait a moment in silence before turning on her heel and going off around the barn.

At Kia's limping pace it took Wim several minutes to get her back to the yard. She was grateful the sound of her father's arrival in the van was muffled behind the barn. Kia brightened as soon as she saw Sam. "You've come at last," she said. "I have been trying to get home for hours. Charlotte wanted to help, but she apparently doesn't know the way."

Sam gave Wim a wan smile as he helped Kia into the truck. She sat in passive dignity and did not struggle at all when Sam fastened the seat belts.

"Sorry, Dad," Wim muttered.

Sam shook his head. "I'm the one who's sorry, Wimmie. I knew I shouldn't have let you go out to deal with her alone. I should have—"

"It's okay, Dad. Let's just get her home."

She waited until the taillights of the truck had disappeared down the drive before starting up the van with a savage twist of the key. She refused to acknowledge Tangi, sitting silently beside her, but she was aware the girl was giving her sideways glances. When the van roared into life, it seemed to jolt the girl into speaking. "Geez. This thing sounds like my cousin Hemi's car," she commented, her voice bland. "He didn't get a warrant of fitness last year and Nana was going to make him take it to the rubbish tip, but he said what the hell, he might as well drive it till they got him for it. The fine'd be less than buying a new car, eh. He had to tie the petrol tank up with fencing wire, it was that bad. Mr. Tauroa down the road showed him how to do it. Nana says Mr. Tauroa's going to tread the edge of the law once too often and . . ."

Wim struggled desperately to shut her out. She was tired to her bones. Hungry. And angry, when she remembered with a sick little jolt in her stomach that David Te Makara would still be at the house. Kia would probably be restless and wakeful after her ordeal. Almost in despair, Wim realized she had two trail rides scheduled for the next morning. There would be no time to spend with the Kid until late in the day. She set her mouth grimly. Her progress with him would be seriously compromised after this evening's agitation. Trust was earned painstakingly with horses, each day built on the day before; with a horse as wary as the Kid, a single breach of that trust could cost weeks of work. If that girl had only managed to keep Kia in the truck . . .

" . . . so that's when Uncle David reckoned his grant wouldn't be enough for us to live on here for the whole six months and we'd have to go home, but now your dad's letting us stay in the cottage and we can— "

Wim braked so sharply they were jerked against the seat belts. *"What!"* she cried.

Tangi's eyes were unreadable. "Uncle David's grant," she repeated. "His research grant. What I was saying. It was supposed to be enough to support him for six months while he worked here, but the hotels are so pricey he can't—"

"What do you mean, you're staying in the cottage?" She couldn't seem to get her exhausted mind to accept what the girl was saying.

The girl gave her a level look. "Yeah. We're going to stay in your dad's cottage," she said with faint impatience. "I told you. Your dad invited us. So Uncle David can finish his research on Cape Cod."

Wim continued home stunned. *It couldn't have been Dad's idea,* she thought wildly. *Dad wouldn't just ask them, just like that.* Somehow, she was sure, David Te Makara had maneuvered Sam into offering the use of the cottage. Sam was easily influenced, led by his enthusiasms to make impetuous decisions he later worried incessantly over. Usually Carol could temper this inclination in her husband with her blunt common sense. But even her mother, Wim realized, had become enveloped in David Te Makara's spell. And now this stranger and his niece had *purposely* intruded into her family. A shiver of something more than dismay ran through her. Something harder to identify, and unwelcome: *Excitement.*

Wim parked the truck on the road and went quickly in the front door of the house without waiting for Tangi, hoping to slip unnoticed up to her room. But her mother met her in the hallway, where she was gently closing the door to Kia's room. "She's already asleep, thank God," she said softly. She looked with concern at Wim. "You're exhausted, Wimmie. You haven't even eaten." She brushed the hair out of Wim's face in a rare caress, shook her head with a little frown, and said, "She gave you a pretty hard time, didn't she? I think it's really time for Sam to—" But she didn't finish. She smiled instead and added, "You look like you're getting one of your headaches, sweetie. Do you want some aspirin?"

Wim returned the smile. Thought: *Aspirin. As if aspirin could fix this. Absurd.* And she couldn't even say, exactly, what *this* was. "I'm just tired," she said. "I just want to go to bed."

"Well—" Carol glanced toward the kitchen. "Well, your father and I need to talk to you about something. It can't really wait."

David's laugh came to her down the hallway. "But *he's* still here," Wim protested.

Her mother looked slightly surprised. "You mean David? But that's okay—it happened while he was here. He's actually been helpful." She laughed a little. "Funny, isn't it, how you can sometimes feel like you've known a person forever after just a few hours? But you know, he's had a lot of experience with elderly family members, so when the agency called . . ."

Wim followed her reluctantly toward the kitchen. "The agency?"

Carol paused before opening the door. "The home-health agency. It seems we're on our own with Kia until the room at Rose Point is ready. Apparently our aide found Kia too much to handle, and she told the agency she wasn't coming back."

Her mother went into the kitchen. Wim stood in the doorway. Even knowing David would be there did not prepare her for the overwhelming impact of his presence once again. Unexpectedly, she felt a rush of heat to her face. Furious, she turned away to cut a slice of cold pizza from the box on the counter. She dallied as long as she could before going to sit down. She had no appetite now but stubbornly took a bite and stared at the pattern on the tablecloth.

"So how would you like a job?" Sam asked.

Wim said numbly, her mouth full, "Job? But I have a job."

"You know I'm not at all convinced this is a good idea," Carol interposed, addressing Sam. "She isolates herself enough at the barn as it is."

"It's only temporary. It should only be a few weeks till Rose Point is ready," Sam pointed out.

Carol continued as if he hadn't spoken. "It's the daytime meds I'm worried about, Sam. Wimmie isn't trained for that. It's a lot to ask of her. I still think we need to find another agency, or a temporary facility. Kia's just going to have to get used to people she doesn't know looking after her." She smiled sympathetically at Wim and put a glass of milk in front of her. "Here, sweetie."

A worried frown creased Sam's thin face. As if in apology, he commented to David, "Still, I have to agree with you. It's better for families to look after their own. Besides"—he glanced at Carol but continued speaking to David—"Wim is great at taking care of things. You should have seen her with that sick old dog she dragged off the street last winter. She was up every hour with him for weeks. Unfortunately, she was so good the dog's still with us." It was a feeble joke and no one laughed. Sam continued with determination, "She's a lot more responsible than that home health aide was, that's for sure."

The conversation rose and fell around her. She felt power-less, caught in an undertow and inexorably, invisibly, silently swept out to sea. She stared at the tablecloth, felt the weight of David's eyes on her, forced herself to take bite after bite of cold pizza. *In the cottage. He's going to live in the cottage.*

But he reached out and plucked her from the swirling water. "Maybe Wim should be the judge of whether she wants the job or not," David suggested smoothly.

"What do you think, Wimmie?" Sam asked.

"What?" she mumbled.

Her father gestured impatiently. "Could you do it? Look after Aunt Kia? You could still work at the barn, too. You'd just have to make sure and come back a few times during the day to check on her, get her lunch, give her medication. You know she won't run off if she doesn't get upset. She just didn't like that health aide, that's all." When Wim did not answer right away, Sam added, almost cajoling, "It would be a real job, Wimmie. I'll pay you exactly what I paid the agency, and I can deposit it right into your account. You could actually save a little . . ."

She was so intensely embarrassed she was sure, if she an-swered, she would burst into tears. Her face burned. She was humiliated for her father and wished in a rage that he would shut up, that her mother would change the subject. Under David's gaze, she felt utterly exposed and somehow— impossi-bly— *known.* He had breached the space of solitude around her in a fundamental way. She gulped her milk. Almost choked.

David spoke again, his warm voice neutral. He leaned toward her slightly, his hands braced apart on the table. Wim stared at them, distracted; they were beautiful, brown, supple despite their bluntness. She clenched her own hands in her lap. "Of course you know already that your auntie needs you," David commented. "But have you ever thought that *you* might need *her?* It's such an easy oversight, when dealing with old people."

There was no possible resistance. She said harshly, "I'll look after Aunt Kia if you want, Dad. It's all right. I don't mind."

In the brief silence she heard the echo of her words and despised herself. She had, finally, to look up, and it was David who met her eyes immediately. His own were at once unreachable and yielding. When he smiled at her, she thought she could not bear the ache of it within her.

Then Sam said, relieved, "That's great, Wimmie. And don't worry, honey—it won't be for long. And of course Mom and I will help."

But she knew there would be no help. She was alone with this stranger, completely trapped.

Five ෬

*A*ঔ unexpectedly as they had come, they were gone. Wim did not see David Te Makara or Tangi for a week. She did not ask about them and, oddly, even Sam did not mention them. They might have never been; she was tempted to believe it had all been her imagination. But on Saturday she once again saw the great white heron sail across the grasses of the salt marsh, and she knew they were real. And that they would be back.

It had been an especially busy week. She was able to do her job at the barn and look after Kia, but it left her no time to work with the Kid or to ride alone out into the dunes. On the days she knew she would be working in the office, Wim brought Kia and settled her on the sagging couch with a library book. Kia had developed a grudging affinity for Tammy, who shared her passion for mystery novels. "Where is she?" Kia would grumble if Tammy did not appear within a few minutes of their arrival. "That tall, bony one. Not the one with the loud voice."

"Oh, she'll be here soon," Wim would assure her and surreptitiously call the house from the office phone and whisper, "Tam. We're here. Bring something to drink." As often as not, Tammy would also bring a mystery from the seemingly endless store of books stacked around the house.

Wim quickly devised a routine for Kia. It involved several quick trips back and forth between the barn and home daily; the old woman was happier with a ten-minute visit than she was with longer ones, which tended to leave her agitated or exhausted. Wim often came home to find her contentedly reading or watching the Discovery Channel on television. Carol noticed an immediate difference in Kia under Wim's care, but she was reluctant to believe all was well. "You sure you're doing okay with this, Wimmie?" she asked more than once. "It's true Kia is happier, but you're having to run around so much. And she gets you up so early. I'm a little concerned—"

"I'm fine, Mom," Wim insisted. "Really. I don't mind it."

What she wished for primarily was to be left alone. To go unnoticed about her days. Not to have to explain anything. Most conversations irritated her like burrs under a saddle blanket. Only Kia, for some reason, did not intrude. Wim was as comfortable around the old woman as she was around the horses and dogs. What they needed from her was integral to her nature, so she did not experience their needs as demands. With Kia, with Angelo, with the Kid, her world remained as intact as when she was alone. She herself needed nothing.

But everyone else, it appeared, was worried about her. On Friday afternoon, the sun summer-hot overhead, Wim was hauling brush with the tractor from the area Evelyn had designated for the new riding ring. Tammy came across the yard to stand in front of her, hands on hips, blocking her path so Wim had to throttle the tractor down to idle. "Wim! I called you half an hour ago to get in the house—I'm not telling you again, kiddo. You're going to get dehydrated in this heat."

Wim pushed the hair from her sweaty face and protested, "But I'm almost done. I just wanted to get this bit cleared before—"

"Before nothing," said Tammy. "Get down and go inside."

Evelyn met them on the porch with glasses of lemonade. "That mangy Bart dog of yours has left another rat *right here*," she announced, gesturing with her cigarette to a dead animal on the ground by the steps.

Wim grinned tiredly. "One less rat to eat the grain. Be thankful," she countered.

They sat in a row, three pairs of booted feet propped on the porch railing. For several minutes there was a companionable silence. Then Evelyn nudged Wim's leg with the toe of her boot and demanded, "So. You gonna tell us what's up? You're either staring off into space half the time or working like a fiend. Haven't had a word out of you for days."

Tammy shot her an exasperated glance. "You sure have a real inviting way about you, Ev."

Evelyn ignored her and eyed Wim. "We worry about you, girl," she said.

Wim traced a spiral pattern through the condensation on the glass of lemonade. "Why?" she muttered, embarrassed. "I'm okay."

Silence again, before Tammy blurted, "Evelyn and I have been talking. You *do* work all the time, Wim. You never do anything fun. You need to make some time for yourself. Look, kiddo—you really need to find some friends or something. It's been a year since—"

"I have you guys," Wim said quickly.

Tammy gave her a kind smile. "Oh, Wim. We're not enough —two old ladies like us. That's not what I'm talking about. I mean friends your own age, someone to hang out with."

"Like a boyfriend, for instance," suggested Evelyn, and Tammy kicked her. "What!" protested Evelyn. "I'm not teasing her. I was serious."

Wim looked down and said nothing, staring at the spirals she had drawn through the moisture on the glass and thinking unwillingly of David Te Makara. She gulped the lemonade so violently it burned her throat.

Tammy put an arm over her shoulder. "Come on. Don't go all quiet on us, Wim. If we *are* your friends—"

Tammy's touch brought her dangerously close to tears. She retorted, "I said you were, didn't I? That's why I don't *need* any other friends! What's the point, anyway? You only end up losing them. They can't be there forever. They . . . they die, or they live on the other side of the world or something." She said the last with vehemence and wiped off the pattern she'd drawn so abruptly the lemonade sloshed out of the glass.

Tammy and Evelyn glanced at each other. Evelyn said carefully, "Well, I don't know about forever, but you don't always lose people, Wim. That just isn't true. I know that . . . that Jilly died, but she was only one person out of a whole world full of people." She paused, but when Wim refused to respond, she set her glass on the railing and stood up. "Well, girl, you just gotta slow down, is all we meant. The last thing we need around here is for *you* to kill yourself as well." Tammy gave her a shocked frown, but Evelyn ignored it and continued. "Let me tell you—the one thing I've learned in life is this: You can't live without friends to love. No way. And that *is* the truth. No matter how long forever is, or who you lose, it's still the truth." And with that, she turned and strode off down the steps and across the yard toward the barn, stopping to pick up the dead rat by the tail and sling it into the trees.

Wim was crying now. Tammy murmured, "Oh, Wim—"

"I don't know *how*," whispered Wim savagely. "I don't know *how* to love."

Tammy said nothing for a few seconds. When the phone rang they both jumped, and Tammy got up. "You did know how once," she reminded Wim softly and went inside.

That night, wrapped in her sleeping bag on the dunes, Wim sat gazing out over salt marshes barely visible in the cool glow of the moon. Jilly had loved sleeping out here, had craved the escape to this vast, magical space of wind, sea, and darkness. Sometimes they'd spend half the night talking, and other times they would nurture the silence between them like a precious secret. It had been a long time since Wim had slept out on the dunes—more than a year. It was the first time since Jilly's death.

Old Angelo and Sue were curled asleep at her side, and Bart had crawled deep into the sleeping bag and was buried warmly at her feet. He stirred when the sudden *yip-yap* of a coyote broke the predawn stillness, but Wim quieted him with a word. The moonlight filtered through the ground mist. The physical world appeared diaphanous, a curtain she could brush aside to reveal an unknown universe, if she simply put out her hand . . .

She stretched out one bare arm and twisted her hand slowly in the cool air, her fingers slipping from shadow into the pale, washed light and into shadow again. She almost whispered aloud: *David*. But she caught herself quickly, corrected herself, and thought: *He's a stranger*. The girl, too. Strangers. This was a fact, but somehow the form of that fact was no more substantial than the moon's breath drifting across the sand. Knowing them as though they had always been in her life was a *truth*, a solid certainty she could somehow touch. She couldn't explain it; she knew only that they fit inexplicably in the world with her, perfectly, the way the breeze fit among the scrub pines in the gully below, the way the rhythmic thud of far-off waves fit the beach.

The way Jilly had fit. Wim caught her breath in sudden panic. She realized she could no longer remember Jilly's voice or picture her face clearly. She shut her eyes. *"Come back,"* she begged in a whisper. *"Come back."* Angelo whimpered. Wim squeezed her eyes tight, concentrating until her head ached, but all she saw were spiraling flecks of light etching the darkness. Her eyes flew open. She looked around swiftly.

Dawn had begun to seep up along the horizon. The salt marshes took on dimension. Gulls wheeled, catching the new light on their undersides. Then she saw the great white heron. It came on slow wingbeats, luminous and silent, flying over her and gliding down to land in the shallows of a creek. The blue herons had arrived, too, hardly more than smudges against the dark grasses. But the great white heron glowed like a wedge of light through a partially opened door.

She ran toward it. The cold sand cut into her bare feet as she slid down the dune. She didn't feel it or the sharp needles of the pines as she pushed through thickets and descended to the muddy creek bank. A kingfisher rattled loudly away. Two blue herons nearest her lifted into the air and flew off. But the white heron remained. Wim stood as motionless as the bird, sunk to her shins in mud. The heron studied her.

She kept still although she could hardly bear the pounding of her heart. *Jilly Jilly Jilly*. The name pushed against her throat and she tried to get it out, but no sound would come. The heron stalked closer. One step. Two. The door opening wider, the light blinding. Something would surely burst within her.

But it did not. The white heron suddenly stabbed the water, lifted its dripping head to reveal a silver fish held in its beak, and swallowed it. Wim swallowed. The pressure subsided. The bird lifted its wings and rose a few feet, drifted delicately across a sandbar to another section of the creek, landed. Wim turned then, made her way back to the dogs, gathered her sleeping bag, and trudged across the sand to the truck.

It was shortly after five when she pulled up in front of the house. Kia would be awake, she was sure, and she hoped the old woman was quietly reading and not trying to make breakfast as she'd done a few mornings earlier. Wim had arrived in the kitchen to find pancake batter dripping down the counter and syrup puddled on the floor. "A slight accident, I'm sorry to say," Kia had remarked dryly. "I was trying to help you out, Charlotte. I'm afraid I didn't succeed, did I?" Their voices, when laughing, sounded remarkably alike, Sam had observed when he'd come downstairs to see what was the matter.

Wim kicked her boots off in the hallway by the front door and heard Kia singing softly in the kitchen, the haunting little tune she sometimes hummed to herself. Wim relaxed. She opened the kitchen door and there, sitting across the table from Kia and busily drawing on a pad of paper, was Tangi.

"Oh, hey," said the girl brightly, without pausing in her work. "Wondered when you were going to show up, eh. Thought it was only your aunt who went walkabout. But your mum said you woke up early."

Kia added, "This girl is drawing my portrait, Charlotte. Otherwise I would help you with breakfast. But I'm very hungry. I've been waiting for you for hours."

The old woman's dressing gown was open and the morning fog gave the air an edge. Wim pulled the gown closed and gently wiped a line of spittle from Kia's chin. "I'll fix you something right now, Aunt Kia," she said. It took a great effort to retain her composure. "Scrambled eggs, right? And toast?"

"And tea. Don't forget my tea," Kia reminded her. Wim put the kettle on. When she turned again to Kia, the old woman was leaning forward, her dressing gown open again, and was gazing intently at something outside the door. Without thinking, Wim kicked it shut so abruptly that Tangi looked up. Their eyes met.

Tangi commented conversationally, "My Nana sees things like that, too. Some *kuia* have the Sight. Uncle David says he's never known a *kuia* with the Sight like Nana has." She resumed drawing as though she'd only commented on the weather.

"What are you doing here?" Wim's anger flared.

The girl put her pencil down and leaned back in the chair. "Hoo-ee," she retorted. "Don't get your knickers in a twist, eh. We got in late, and your dad told us to make ourselves at home, and I couldn't sleep so I came in to make a cup of tea, and here was Auntie Kia."

"She's not your Auntie Kia," Wim growled.

Tangi gave her a condescending stare. "It's a title of respect," she said gravely. "I call lots of older women 'auntie.' Maori are raised to respect their elders, you know. Especially elders with *mana*."

The kettle whistled on the stove and Wim yanked it off the burner without answering. She plunked a mug in front of Kia, poured water in a cloud of steam. Kia looked at it for a moment. "Charlotte," she said, "I don't want hot water. I want tea."

Tangi had deliberately returned to drawing. Wim dropped a tea bag in Kia's mug and Kia added testily, "And milk. You've forgotten the milk. What is the matter with you this morning, Charlotte?"

"Nothing," muttered Wim. She glumly stirred eggs in the frying pan. From the corner of her eye she watched Kia. The old woman seemed once again to be staring intently at something outside. Surreptitiously, Wim followed her gaze. But there was nothing. Through the window she could see the early morning light beginning to pinken the fog over the harbor. The rose hedge appeared to glisten with blooms of diffused light. It was only six o'clock, and already there was warmth in the new sun. It would be another hot day. But Wim felt the touch of the fog on her skin and shivered, once again glancing in the direction of Kia's gaze. Sometimes the man with the tattooed face would appear from the shadows in these transition times, in the dawn mist, or the twilight, or the shifting light before a storm . . .

A thought struck her, coming so swiftly and with such shocking clarity she stood unable to move, holding the pan of eggs above Kia's plate. At the same moment, Tangi announced with great satisfaction, "There," and sat back, dropping her pencil with a flourish. "Done." She pushed the pad of paper across the table toward Kia. "Like it?"

Kia held it up and studied the drawing a moment. "What is this, girl?" she asked sternly. She tilted the pad slightly, and Wim could see now what Tangi had drawn.

The old woman's face was mirrored on the page. But around her mouth and over her chin, following the contours of her face, the girl had drawn a pattern of dark parallel lines and interlocking spirals. Kia tapped the page and stated, "This is not me."

"But it *could* be, *e Kui*," Tangi insisted respectfully. "You'd look like that if you had a *moko*, eh. If you lived in the old days. You'd have been a powerful *kuia*, I reckon." She took the pad back and inspected her work, looking pleased. "Yeah. It suits you. Like you *should* have one, eh."

"I should *not*," Kia contradicted, and turned her attention to the eggs Wim had spooned onto her plate.

"Can I look at that?" asked Wim softly, putting down the frying pan. After a moment of pointed hesitation, the girl handed her the pad.

She thought she must be dreaming. She could only be dreaming. Otherwise, it didn't make sense. On the margins of the page, surrounding the more finished drawing of Kia, were other sketches—a clump of fern fronds in the first delicate stages of unfurling; a sailboat, visible from the kitchen window, bobbing at anchor in the harbor; a series of the same intricate, spiraling lines that formed the *moko* on Kia's face. And in the upper corner of the paper, rising from the dark mass of pencil shading that constituted Kia's hair, a great white heron! Unmistakable. Long pale legs trailing, wings luminescent, white neck tucked in.

She could not bring herself to speak. She could only hold out the pad and point to the sketch of the heron. Tangi answered her look cheerfully. "*Kotuku.* Yeah, I like it, too. Did it from memory. Not bad, eh?"

"*Kotuku,*" breathed Wim.

"That's the Maori name," said Tangi. "*Pakeha* just call it a white heron. Supposed to be real good luck, if you see one. They're quite rare. Uncle David saw one, though—right before we left to come to America. He was out with his mate, the one who's always tramping around in the muck studying birds— Ian something-or-other—they went to university together. Totally daft bloke. Anyway, I promised Uncle David I'd try to draw it for him." She studied the sketch with a sudden critical frown. "I don't know . . . maybe it needs something more."

"No, it's perfect," said Wim. They looked at each other in surprise. Kia smiled at them. "These eggs are perfect, Charlotte," she said graciously. "Thank you for making them."

Wim worked all day at the barn in the dream that had been holding her since she'd woken before dawn on the dunes.

Sometimes she could not be sure any of it had happened. But her legs were scratched from her climb down the dunes to the marsh. And Tangi's drawing was propped up against the dresser mirror in Kia's room.

"You're jumpy today," Evelyn commented.

It was because she was expecting *him*. At every moment, she was sure *he* would appear, watching her with his fierce, yearning eyes from a dark face etched with lines. She had never before expected him. He'd always just come. She'd never looked for him. He just *was*.

Evelyn made her leave early. "No buggy rides tonight," she said. "I can do the barn. Go home and get some rest."

It was too early to wake Kia from her afternoon nap. She put the dogs out in the back yard and Bart immediately growled, tail erect, nose pointing at the cottage. Sue dashed toward the open door, stupid and eager. "Come here, Sue! Get over here!" Wim hissed, mortified. But it was too late. David Te Makara came out.

"Thanks for calling off your wolves," he called over to her, grinning. He went to the rental car parked next to the cottage, leaned in, and pulled out a box piled high with books. "I'll have to hire a private plane to get all this stuff back home," he commented ruefully over his shoulder as he carried the box to the cottage. Unwilling, but unable to resist, Wim followed him to the door and stood looking in.

Her memory had played tricks. She'd remembered David as a large man, towering over her in her mind's eye. But she saw now that he was not very tall, and not so much broad as compact. He went about his task with an economy of motion that in some effortless way exuded authority. He was younger than she'd first thought, too; he didn't look anything like a university professor, dressed as he was in torn jeans and a tee shirt with the words RADIO HAURAKI: VOICE OF AUCKLAND in faded letters across the front. He gave her a sheepish smile as the box he carried spilled open onto the already cluttered cot. "Shocking, really, my filing system," he said. "Good thing Tangi's with me. She'll sort out this lot in a jiffy."

Wim hung in the doorway, reluctant to go, uneasy about staying. David moved around the cottage as though he'd always lived there. A pile of storage boxes had been pushed untidily against the far wall. Old games and toys poked out of some, and others, with the words GINNY'S STUFF — DON'T TOUCH or BEA — HIGH SCHOOL scrawled across them, were taped shut. There was the wonderful, gaudily painted puppet stage someone had made for her sisters before Wim was born, which she had played with during her secret forays into the cottage as a child. Crushed in among the boxes, the velvet curtains were torn and one corner of the stage had been mashed, and she felt a pang of protectiveness. David said, "We tried to shift everything as carefully as we could. Looks like this place was your playhouse."

"It was my sisters'," she corrected quickly. "I never played much, anyway. My sisters are a lot older than me."

He was watching her intently as she spoke, his head tilted forward a little so she felt the full impact of his focus on her. She stopped, self-conscious. He appeared not to notice her discomfort but turned away to fiddle with a laptop computer on the makeshift desk near the window. "You know anything about these?" he muttered at last, holding up a couple of un-attached cables. "I can never work out where any of these things go. Have to use an adapter, too—different voltage here. Doesn't take much to confuse me about technology."

Again, the self-effacing grin. When he turned to put the cables on the desk, the vines growing over the outside of the window cast a shadow pattern of lines across his face. Wim could not move. His eyes had already caught hers. *As always.* And as always, she knew that he wanted something from her with such a terrible need he could not bring himself to speak it aloud. She had learned long ago not to reach out for him. Her touch, too, would be more than he could bear. He would only disappear.

She had never been able to withstand more than a few sec-onds of his gaze. "I have to go," she gasped, and spun away.

"Wait. Wait. Don't go," David said swiftly.

She stopped, bewildered for a moment because he'd spoken. They looked at each other. Finally he said, "Please, *hine.* Come in. Come sit down," in the same kind of voice she would have used to soothe a frightened animal. Her body moved of its own accord, and she sat on an upturned crate near the cot. David busied himself again with the laptop, and she wondered if he was giving her time to compose herself. "Tangi'll have to deal with this," he mumbled at last, dropping the tangle of cables on the desk in disgust. He glanced at her. "Unless you know anything about computers yourself?" She shook her head, not trusting her voice. David smiled. "You see why I brought Tangi with me. Couldn't have hired a better research assistant."

Wim took a deep breath. "Oh, is that . . . is that why she's with you? I thought she said . . . I mean, she didn't say she was working for you." It didn't matter. She just had to say something, to release herself from the spell.

"Well, she isn't officially, of course," he said. "I'm meant to be keeping her out of trouble. Giving her time to sort herself out. Her mum's idea. My sister. She doesn't like how much time Tangi spends hanging out on the streets, and she's worried about her mates—she thinks they're all in gangs. Tangi keeps threatening to leave school." He gave a disarming chuckle. "She might do, too. She's on her own path, that girl. Artist, activist, who-knows-what. Boring her to tears by making her work as my research assistant isn't going to change that." He shook his head. "Poor kid. I left her at the library to copy a couple hundred pages on that old Xerox machine they have there. It'll take her ages. I'll have to make it up to her—take her out for pizza or something. Do you know a good pizza place?"

Gently, gently, David was drawing her into conversation. But Wim still found it difficult to speak. It gave her a peculiar feeling to be with this stranger in this place. The cottage had never lost the air of being forbidden territory, alluring and unknown. She was perched uncomfortably on the edge of the crate, and she picked up one of the books off the floor so she would have something to look at instead of David. But he came to sit on the cot near her.

He was too close. Her face grew hot. She stared at the book blindly until he reached down and took it from her. "Your father was very generous to let me use his material," David said, running his hand over the binding of the book. His skin matched exactly the color of the leather. "This journal, for instance. It's a fantastic primary source. He's got some real treasures here."

Irrationally, she wanted the book that he had taken from her, although there were plenty of others around her on the floor. She felt that there was some secret she was being left out of. She could sense it as surely as she had as a child. She said, a little desperately, "He's got tons of papers and books like this. Mom wants him to donate it all to a museum. But he's going to . . . he wants to write a book himself." She hesitated. "I really don't think he ever will," she added without intending to, and felt immediately like a traitor. She frowned. "Let me see it," she demanded, reaching for the journal. To her surprise, he gave it back to her willingly.

She opened it and carefully turned over the damp-swollen pages. The ink was faded and brown, the words in the cramped handwriting unreadable. She peered closer. "Is it in another language?" she asked, curious despite herself.

David said thoughtfully, "Your father said it was in some sort of code. He told me it had been forgotten for decades in the home of a very old member of the historical society and when she died, it was given to him. It's too bad he never had time to work on it." He reached over to turn the pages back and his arm brushed hers. "There may have been instructions once for reading this, but I expect they've been long lost. I'm hopeless at this kind of thing, but Tangi's terrific at figuring out puzzles. Here, take a look at this."

He was indicating the first page of the journal. She had to turn slightly for more light and felt better to have moved a bit farther away from David. To her surprise, although the handwriting was tiny, she could read it.

This being the private journal of Emmanuel Dart, Age 17,

on his maiden Voyage to the South Seas on the trading vessel
Agatha Anne, whose Master is Capt'n Chas. Wm.son Thorpe of
Provincetown in the Year of our Lord 1834, in October, in ap-
prenticeship to the surgeon of this ship, Dr Robert Kendall. I
leave my excellent Mother and two sweet sisters to the Mercy
of God and our neighbors, whilst I learn the trade of doctoring,
for which purpose Dr Kendall has kindly asked leave of his
good friend the Captain that I be allow'd to accompany him. I
fully expect much practice at this trade, for Capt'n Thorpe deals
in Guns and God with the Heathenish peoples of the remote
South Seas islands, most esp. with New Zealand, of which I have
heard many a Horrific tale told of the native habit of eating
Human Flesh."

She looked at David, astonished, and he smiled. "Oh, yes—
it's true," he said. "Unfortunately, most of the 'native habits'
that Emmanuel Dart actually did see are as yet undeciphered.
For some reason, he began to keep the journal in code soon
after they set sail. I can only read the first three pages."

She ran her hand over the worn leather cover of the journal. "He sounds so real," she said in wonder. "Emmanuel Dart.
It's a nice name. He was my age." No one in Sam Thorpe's
family had ever shared his passion for family history, but there
was such a difference between this journal and the dusty genealogical chart that had been on the wall of her father's study
all these years. Although he'd barely been mentioned, the Captain Thorpe of Emmanuel Dart's journal seemed much more
alive than when her father talked about him. She glanced at
David with sudden comprehension. "You're looking for *your*
ancestor, aren't you? The one who got a job on an American

ship and never went home again? Henry Cooper." She hesitated. "Do you think he sailed on Captain Thorpe's ship? Is that why you've come . . . to ask my father?"

Wim had begun to notice how changeable David's eyes could be, how they could run deep as a shadowed sea, or open into her own, clear as a night sky. How they could go blank and flat, as they had now, the way the surface of the harbor looked before a storm. He took the journal from her hands without a word and put it in a box. But as she was about to make an excuse to leave, he seemed suddenly to come to a decision. He reached into the pocket of his jeans and took out several small white objects and held them out to her on the palm of his hand. "This is why I've come," he told her softly.

Mystified, she stared at the objects. They were a few inches long, narrow and cylindrical like tiny bones or broken pieces of a white pencil. She could see that each had once been hollow, but the cavities were filled with grit. "Take one," he said, and when she did, he continued, "That's a little piece of Cape Cod earth—Martha's Vineyard white clay, to be accurate."

She rolled one between thumb and forefinger. It was very smooth. Without thinking, she put it to her nose to smell, then tasted it with the tip of her tongue. It was faintly salty. But then, embarrassed, she gave it back to David. He didn't smile this time, just nodded and said, "That was the sea you tasted—the saltwater from the port of Russell, in the Bay of Islands, near where I grew up in Pukemoana."

"You found these in the sea, in New Zealand?" she asked, incredulous.

"Many times," he said. "Whenever we'd go into Russell

when I was a kid, we'd run off straightaway to the beach, to see if the tide had washed any up. They weren't easy to find. The museum would give us fifty cents for each one." He leaned toward her intently. "They're broken bits of clay pipe stems—the pipes that American sailors smoked—made from the white clay of Martha's Vineyard, and they've been rolling around in the bay for more than a hundred and fifty years, since the days when Russell was called Kororareka."

Wim recalled suddenly, "They threw their pipes overboard for good luck. The New England sailors. Whenever they left a foreign port to head back home." It was David's turn to look startled. Almost apologetically, Wim added, "It's just something we learned at school. When we studied Cape Cod history."

"Well, you had a good teacher." David smiled. He held the pipe stems in his hand and studied them, touched them lightly with one finger, reverent. "I was nine years old when I picked the first of these up from the beach at Russell. I don't think I knew it then, but I had claimed my *turangawaewae*," he told her quietly. "And it is a demanding and difficult standing place. It has roots in two lands, a whole world apart. It's very hard sometimes, trying to keep a foot in both. Sometimes I am not sure which story is mine to speak."

She was taken aback by the sadness in his voice and did not know what to say. He still held the pipe stems on the open palm of his hand, and she wanted to put her own hand over his. She moved restlessly on the crate, but his mood changed again, and he asked swiftly, as though he wanted to keep her from leaving, "Enough about me. What about you? What do you like to do?"

It was so unexpected, she blurted the first thing that came to mind. "I watch things," she said, and felt immediately foolish.

"Yes, I've seen you watching," he replied. "You touch everything with your eyes."

She squirmed. He was looking at her with such seriousness. She said defensively, "I just watch birds. And animals. Horses. Things like that."

He nodded, smiling, but his eyes remained serious. "So all your watching now is outward. I understand. Inner watching requires such tremendous courage," he said. Then quickly, as if to forestall any questions, he continued in a lighter tone, "So you watch birds. Tell me about the birds you see around here."

"*Kotuku*," she answered. "A great white heron. I saw one this morning. I didn't know they ever came this far north." She spoke as casually as she could and studied her hands so she could avoid his gaze. "Actually, I saw it this morning for the second time. The first time I saw the white heron was the day I met you."

His words about courage had stung her, and she'd meant to startle him by mentioning the rare bird by its Maori name. But when she glanced at him, she was completely unprepared for his reaction.

David's eyes were filled with tears. He stood up slowly and faced the window. As he drew himself straighter, he appeared to grow larger until his presence filled the small room. He began to chant softly, *"Kokiri te manu . . ."* His voice deepened into song. *"Takiri ko te ata. Ka ao, ka ao, ka awatea."* Then he turned to look at Wim and sang it again, softly and in English. "The bird has awoken. Dawn breaks. Oh, it is daylight, it is daylight. Oh, it is morning." There was something so heart-breaking in the chant, Wim's own eyes blurred with tears.

After a moment of stillness, David said, "I didn't mean to upset you. It's nothing to be upset about. I am just very . . . happy." He spread his hands wide and gave a little shrug, smiling. "Really. It's okay. Just keep watching, *hine*. Watch everything. Your birds, your dogs, your auntie—"

"Oh! Aunt Kia!" Wim jumped up, stricken. "I've left her in the house for *hours!* I forgot about her. She's probably been awake for . . . oh, I have to go—" And she ran outside and across the yard in a panic.

She had no idea how long she'd been in the cottage. Her sense of time had dissolved. She slammed through the kitchen door and ran down the hallway.

The door to Kia's room was open. Her aunt was gone.

Six ⊚⊙

This time she did go to the police. She flooded the truck engine in her haste to start it, ran back to the house to leave a message for Carol at work, and finally had to accept David's offer to drive her. She sat in the passenger seat struggling to keep from crying, until he reminded her gently, "You need to tell me where to go, Wim."

Pete Alva, on duty at the station desk, squeezed his bulk from behind the counter as soon as she ran in. "Slow down, slow down, Wim. We found her already. Don't worry—she's okay. I just sent a guy down to the wharf a few minutes ago to pick her up."

"How—?" she began.

"One of the crew off the *Dolphin* called. Cripes, Wim, when did your folks say they were going to get her in a nursing home?"

She was grateful he wasn't making any of his usual jokes. Painfully aware of David standing beside her, Wim mumbled,

"Dad says a few more weeks. What was she doing, Pete? She was all the way down the wharf?"

The officer did chuckle then, and he gave a jovial wink. "She was all set to buy passage on a ship," he told her. "That's what she called it, too — 'passage.' Had her coat an' handbag an' all. Got kinda belligerent when they told her the *Dolphin* was just a tourist excursion boat." He shook his head, included David in the conversation with a good-natured glance, and continued, "My granny was like that. Man, what a time we all had with her! She'd be up at three A.M. wantin' to get to work an' all. Got so my mom couldn't handle her, no way. She's at a nice home now, up in Hyannis." He gave Wim a kind, concerned frown. "Your dad have any idea what a tough job you got takin' care of her, Wimmie? Ain't like takin' care of a dog."

Wim flushed defensively. "He knows that. And it isn't that bad, Pete. This was my fault. I left her alone in the house too long."

She was grateful when the door opened and a young officer came in, giving Pete a wry smile and nodding. "Hey there, Wim," he greeted her. "She's okay. She's a little damp, though — "

"Thanks, Jim," she said tiredly, remembering that the sheets on the bed had been wet. She followed him outside and saw Kia struggling to free herself from the hand of another officer. She faced Wim, outraged. "I am being arrested, Charlotte," she announced, her eyes blazing. "I have not broken the law. Tell this man to take his hand off me. You know I have to go, Charlotte. The ship is sailing with the tide."

"They're not arresting you, Aunt Kia," said Wim. "They just want to help you."

Kia snorted and, with a violent jerk, she managed to twist

herself free. Wim took her hand and led her a short distance away from the others. Kia's hand was trembling. "Oh, Aunt Kia," Wim whispered. "Look how cold you are. Can't we go home so you can get out of these wet things? Please?"

But Kia stamped her foot. "You're not listening again, Charlotte!" she snapped. "I have to get to the sea. You *know* that."

Wim had almost forgotten David. But now he came toward them, his eyes deep and unreadable, and bowed his head slightly at Kia. And Kia, to Wim's startled surprise, stopped trembling and stood motionless, staring at him. "*Tena ra koe, e kui.*" David greeted her softly, so only Wim and Kia could hear. "*Tena koe, e Kui* Kia. I greet you with the greatest gladness."

The formality of his manner did not seem out of place. A stillness had grown between the man and the old woman, as if the very air were watching over them, as if the earth had set apart this space for them alone.

And all at once Wim recognized this space. A shock ran through her. Then Kia spoke. "It's *him*, Charlotte," she murmured excitedly. "I've been trying to tell you. I *see* him. I always have. I thought . . . I thought you did, too." Her voice faltered and her body followed, and Wim had to catch her arm to keep the old woman from falling. She did not feel very steady herself. A car pulled into the lot behind them and she heard a door slam.

"Your mother is here, Wim," said David quietly.

Carol Thorpe had been a nurse for thirty years. She was efficient and unsentimental and, Wim knew with a sense of hopelessness as she listened to the discussion between her parents, she spoke with reasonable common sense. "You're going to have to face this, Sam. Senility doesn't go away," her mother was saying, interrupting Sam's protests. "Your aunt is eighty-four years old. She may appear healthy physically, but she's got blood pressure problems, she's dangerously delusional, and she's combative. Wim can't handle her; I don't *want* Wim trying to cope with her. You need to find Kia an interim place until Rose Point is ready for her, Sam. She needs it and *we* need it."

Wim thought about the nursing homes she had toured with her father earlier in the year. She could not imagine the old woman living in one of those places, with their colorless walls and austere hospital corridors, where the pervasive smell of tasteless food and disinfectant couldn't quite mask the odor of stale urine. Even thinking of Rose Point, the private facility that Sam had mortgaged his business to finance for Kia, filled her with anguish at the memory of its hushed and sterile atmosphere. She watched her father struggle to combat her mother's sensible words. "You know Kia is like a mother to me, Carol," he said at last. "I don't remember any other. She's a strange, wonderful, independent woman and I will not stick her in some dump just because she's difficult to deal with. I'll stay home and take care of her myself, if it comes to that."

Carol made an exasperated gesture, but Wim said quickly, "It *was* my fault, Mom. Really. Dad's right; Aunt Kia wouldn't survive being shut away just any old place. And besides . . ." And besides, could she explain how she had come to love Kia? Could she possibly explain how she needed every last minute with her? Searching for the right words, she gazed outside beyond the kitchen window. A man was standing by the gate in the rose hedge, looking out over the harbor in the deepening twilight. *David.* Her eyes flew back to her parents. "Let me try again," she begged. "Mom? Don't make Aunt Kia go yet. I know she has to go to Rose Point. I know that. But let her stay here a while longer."

Carol reached across to her with a smile and brushed the hair from her face. "Oh, Wimmie. I know you. But sweetie, Kia isn't one of your abandoned dogs. Believe me—we're not abandoning her and it's not that we don't care. We're trying to find what works best for her. And best for *you,*" she added, giving Sam a look. "Anyway, I thought you'd be relieved. I know you care about Kia, but this way you could spend all day at the barn without having to worry about her, and you could visit her—"

"Maybe you could just take her to the barn more often," suggested Sam, still hopeful. "I thought she liked it there. She always loved horses. She had horses all those years I was a kid. She was an amazing rider, too—used to do show jumping, won dozens of ribbons."

Kia appeared in the doorway. "Don't you go on about horses, Sam," she said impatiently. "You always thought my horses were a waste of money." She looked at Wim. "There you are, Charlotte," she said. "You haven't come to bring me my tea. You know I can't go to sleep without my peppermint tea."

Wim jumped up. Carol said firmly to Sam, "You see? That's exactly what I'm talking about. It's just too much. I want Wim to *enjoy* her summer. Next summer she'll be getting ready to go to college, and then—"

"I'm not going to college." She said it automatically, knowing it would go unheard.

Sam gave Kia a hug. "You're looking great," he exclaimed in a hearty voice. Kia pushed him away.

"Sam, if you think I don't know what you're trying to do, you underestimate me," she snapped. "I may be old, but I'm not stupid. Don't assuage your guilt by treating me like a child." She looked again at Wim, more sharply this time. "Is the ship ready to sail yet, Charlotte? I must book my passage."

Carol rolled her eyes and slammed the kettle on the burner. Sam said, "Oh, Aunt Kia, you know there's no ship. Don't you know—"

"The voyage has been postponed," Wim said, interrupting. "The sails need repairing. Don't worry, Aunt Kia. I'll make sure you get to the sea."

Sam sighed and reached for the keys to his van. "Well, I guess I'll go check on the store. Late-night closing tonight." He gave Kia a peck on the cheek.

Carol said, "You have to make some phone calls tomorrow, Sam. I've made a list of possibilities. We'll talk about it more later."

Wim slumped in her chair. The man by the gate had gone. An evening mist had rolled in and she could not see beyond the dark yard. Kia asked suddenly, "Where is that man, Charlotte? That man with the ta—"

"David," said Wim quickly. "You mean David. You just met him today."

"I did *not* just meet him today," contradicted Kia, her eyes narrowing in suspicion. "Why did you say that, Charlotte? You know it isn't true."

"Are you talking about David?" asked Sam, pausing in the doorway.

Kia opened her mouth to answer, but Wim cut in, "David was here, so he drove me to the police station to get Aunt Kia. The truck wouldn't start."

Carol put a cup of steaming tea in front of Kia. She lined the saucer with three small cookies. "And that's another thing we need to talk about," she commented to her husband. "Renting the cottage out to those people—David and his niece. Quite apart from the fact that they're complete strangers, have you asked him how long he plans to stay? Because I would like to know."

"He was on a six-month leave, and he's already been working on his grant for several months. That's all I know," said Sam vaguely, looking beleaguered. "We can talk about that, too. I'll be home around ten." He gave Wim a tight little smile and kissed Kia's cheek again. "See you two later. Go to bed soon, Aunt Kia—don't tire yourself."

Kia snorted. "You're more tired than I am, Sam, and I'm practically twice your age. You're asleep in your heart. I can hear your soul snoring."

The look of sheepish bewilderment that crossed her father's face cut Wim to the bone. When he left the kitchen, she buried her face in her arms on the table. Carol rubbed her shoulders briefly. "You need to go to bed, too, Wimmie," she said. "You've had a long day." To Kia, her mother added testily, "And don't wake her up so early, Kia. She needs to sleep the same as you do."

Carol left. Wim couldn't be sure, with her head buried, but she thought she heard Kia mutter, "Old *bat*."

A cool breeze drifted the mist through the window screen,

smelling of the night and the sea, and Wim rubbed the goosebumps on her arms. The light from the cottage fell with a
muted glow in squares across the dark grass. The cottage
seemed a great distance away, as if a vast sea lay between it
and the house. She imagined David in there, his head bent
over a book. Over the mysterious journal, perhaps, working to
uncover the secrets of Emmanuel Dart's coded entries, working to make his own the stories of her family . . . the family
she'd never felt part of until Katherine Irene Thorpe arrived.
Aunt Kia, who would soon be gone. She raised her head.

The old woman was watching her over the rim of her teacup. The steam swirled up around her lined face. "Charlotte,"
asked Kia, "what are you so afraid of?"

"I don't want to lose you," Wim answered, her voice hardly
audible even to herself.

The old woman was silent a moment. Finally she nodded.
"It's a worthwhile fear. I have lost many people. Almost everyone," she said.

Wim looked down. "That's why I'm afraid to love," she
whispered.

Kia reached out and urgently grasped her hand with strong
fingers. "That is *not* a worthy fear. That is cowardice." She
dropped Wim's hand abruptly and took her teacup to the sink.
"I am going to sleep now," she announced. "I will be leaving
early tomorrow, as you know."

Wim took the dogs to the beach. They raced happily ahead
of her, disappearing at once into the mist. She didn't walk far
before the loneliness came over her again so profoundly it
sapped all her strength. She stood waiting for the dogs, re-

membering how she had found each one of them abandoned and alone in the world. The sorrow cut so deeply it seemed her very flesh and bones had become grief, had become the memory of Jilly. Jilly, alone during those last days and hours. And gradually, as she stood there, she knew the grief was no longer for Jilly, but for herself, for what she had lost and what she could not find. The damp mist made her shiver, and she felt sure that nothing waited on the other side of this barrier of loss except an even deeper cold. She wrapped her arms around herself and waited, and when the dogs returned, knew she was still waiting. She strained her eyes through the milky darkness, but no one broke through the mist to come toward her. She called the dogs and turned back.

Across the yard the weathered cedar shakes on the cottage gleamed silvery under the stars. The building did not appear quite solid; she was viewing it through a haze that seemed more than mist, more like a dream. To go there would require a journey of immeasurable length. Yet, as in a dream, without effort, she found herself knocking on the door.

There was nothing *not* solid about David Te Makara. When he opened the door and stood backlit a moment before moving aside to let her in, it was no longer possible for her simply to dream of him. He was too substantial, too real, and Wim was tongue-tied. She mumbled, "I know it's late . . ."

He laughed. "Not when you have a deadline breathing down your neck. Then it's early."

"You're busy. I shouldn't interrupt," she said desperately.

She wasn't sure if he actually took her by the arm to propel her into the room or if he just willed her to come in, but the door closed behind her before she could say more. Tangi was sitting at the laptop, the journal of Emmanuel Dart open next to her on the desk. The girl made an involuntary movement of her arm across the pages, hiding them. The sense of interruption was almost palpable. The girl shot an inscrutable glance at David, then perused Wim with an equally unreadable expression. "Oh, hey," she greeted her. Then, bluntly, "Uncle David says you can't handle your auntie and you're putting her in a home."

Wim, stung, flushed hotly, but before she could speak David frowned at his niece. "Be quiet!" he snapped at her, and the girl looked down immediately. To Wim, he said with sympathy, "It's a painful decision for your family. But when both your parents work—that's the way things have to be. Your aunt is a powerful person for you to look after all on your own."

"Don't make excuses for me," muttered Wim.

David was silent a moment, gazing at her. Then he agreed softly, "All right."

Tangi went back to her work on the computer as though nothing had happened, tapping on the keys and scowling in concentration. Wim stood uncertainly in the middle of the room. David was searching for something in a box. When she could not endure the silence any longer, Wim stepped closer to Tangi, indicated the journal, and said politely, "I guess you figured out the code. What is it?"

To her amazement, Tangi shut the laptop lid with a snap, looking startled and—Wim thought—afraid. "It's too complicated to explain," she muttered, then swung around to face Wim directly and demanded, "How do you know about it, anyway?"

Annoyance overcame unease. "I know about it because it belongs to my father," retorted Wim. "He lent it to David to work on. It's been in my family for generations." She knew this wasn't strictly true, and it felt peculiar to say so possessively "my family," but she had to restrain herself from snatching the journal from under Tangi's protective arm.

David moved smoothly between them. He picked up a sheaf of pages from the laptop printer and, without glancing at his niece, handed them to Wim. "It's truly wonderful material," he said. He gestured toward the crate he used as a chair and she sat, feeling trapped, and forced herself to read. At first she was just grateful to focus on something other than David or Tangi, but within a few words she became caught up in the fascinating world Emmanuel Dart opened before her.

January 13, 1835. We are on the Open Sea and have not been in sight of land now since the New Year commenc'd. I do not understand the Grand Romance of sailing upon the sea, of which sailors sing, for I have been sick in my Bunk for many days and unable to consume anything but the weakest Broth. The Doctor Mr Kendal my Master reassures me in his Kindly fashion that I will soon get my sea legs under me. It is a Blessing he has required no work of me yet, but he is much closet'd with his great friend the Captain, who appears to be sorely Troubled, and I do not see him oft'n.

January 20. Much better, God be thank'd. Spent much of today with young Willie, Capt'n Thorpe's only Son and Heir, to whom he dearly wishes to Teach the arts of sailing a trading vessel. But I fear he wishes in Vain. My good Mother would chide me for making so Free as to call the captain's son Willie,

*whose Christian name is Wm.son Alexander Thorpe, but altho'
the boy is grown to 19 yrs and looks to be a man, he is such a
Simple soul that he is more like to a babe of 5 years. Willie seeks
my company oft, for the sailors are a rough lot, while I am content to watch the birds and Strange fishes of the Sea by the hour,
which is the Occupation he most loves. He claps his hands with
such Delight like a child when he spies me. No manner of
prompting on the Captain's part can compel Willie to learn the
simplest task of Sailing or navigation. So far by the Grace of
God there has been little sickness aboard the* Agatha Anne *but
my own, and the only doctoring I am doing at present is to care
for poor Willie's happyness.*

Wim was smiling without realizing it, and David, meeting
her eyes when she looked up from the page, smiled in agree-
ment. "He was the kind of person who would have been a
good friend," he said.

"I would have liked him," she added, surprising herself. Unexpectedly, the loneliness she'd felt on the beach washed over
her again. She dropped her eyes to hide what she knew must
be there, but David said nothing. A strange quiet seemed to
have crept into the room, like the presence of another person.
Tangi pushed her chair back noisily and stated, "I'm going out.
Can't bloody breathe in here." She flashed Wim a look. "Hope
I can say goodbye to your auntie before they take her away."

"It's not going to happen tomorrow," said Wim as calmly as
she could, embarrassed that the girl might elicit another repri-
mand from her uncle. "It might not happen at all. At least for
a while. They're only worried that she could hurt herself—"

"Well, so what?" flashed Tangi with contempt, going into

the back room where she slept and grabbing a denim jacket off the cot. She called out, "Yeah, I mean it, eh. So what if she hurts herself? She's *looking* for something. It's important to her. She has to find it before she dies. Don't you get it? Her safety isn't anyone's bloody business but her own!"

The girl was pulling on her jacket as she spoke, and Wim could see beyond her into the room. The walls, normally bare, were covered with pictures taped or tacked to the plaster. Wim stared. Although the light was off, the watercolor paintings created their own luminescence. Some appeared to be abstract swirls of brilliant color, but several depicted a powerful, sinuous figure, a snakelike woman with long, flowing hair swimming under water that shimmered with electric blues, greens, and golds. Transfixed, Wim rose slowly and came to stand in the doorway of the room.

"Did you paint those?" she asked.

Tangi paused. "Yeah—" She buttoned the jacket. "You like them?"

"They're really . . . incredible," breathed Wim.

Tangi pushed past her and addressed Wim in words that seemed intended instead for her uncle. "Painting is my *life*," she said vehemently. "I want to leave school because I'm an *artist*, not because I'm some kind of hard case. School's just a bloody stupid waste of time. I read, don't I? And Nana's taught me more *Maoritanga* than any damn school ever could, eh." Now she turned to face David squarely. "You keep telling me that the most powerful Maori voice today is in the arts. You said it's the one voice in New Zealand that the rest of the world could hear! Well, *I'm* an artist. *And* I'm Maori. I need to be out in the real world, not wasting time in some useless school." She stalked past him to the door of the cottage, paused, and said to Wim with a short laugh, "You see what happens when people worry that you're going to hurt yourself, eh."

She left without closing the door. Wim edged after her, feeling like she'd been dropped abruptly from a whirlwind. But the whirlwind within her would not quiet. "I'm sorry. I better go," she said in a low voice.

To her dismay and wonder, David followed her out the door, standing close. "You don't have to go. You don't want to, do you? Come on. Couldn't those wolves of yours use another run?"

It was impossible to refuse him. She did not want to. She went with him through the gate onto the beach, the dogs happy at the chance to be out again. The moon had risen, a hazy orb of light in the mist, just enough to see by. David walked beside her, so close she could feel his warmth. She scuffed her feet through the sand, nervous, and cast around for something to say. "Aren't you going to look for Tangi?" she asked finally, glancing at him.

He gave a little grimace. "No. She can suit herself—stay out all night, if she likes." After a moment, he continued thoughtfully, "She revealed quite a bit to you. More than she's let on to me in several months."

"Why is she so angry?"

He shrugged. "Oh, it's mostly her personality. She was born that way, I think. Although she would say she has plenty of reasons to be angry."

"It's a waste of time," Wim said. "Anger. It doesn't change anything."

David gave her a brief look but made no comment. After walking a few more seconds, he said, "You know, I think your Auntie Kia reminds Tangi of my mum. Nana. She loves her Nana. You see, my mum's the only one who could ever keep Tangi in line. Trouble is, Mum's been getting more confused herself lately. It scares Tangi. And when Tangi is scared, she gets angry."

They were walking slowly along the water line, and the wavelets in the harbor lapped over Wim's boots. Bart dashed at the water, then scampered back around Wim's legs. She sidestepped, bumped into David, and stumbled. He caught her and laughed. It was a natural extension of that movement, then, to brush her hand against his and for him to take it. She looked down so he could not see her face. He did not acknowledge their touch but held her hand and continued talking in his quiet voice. "I promised Tangi's mother—my sister—I promised her I would try to be a steadying influence for Tangi. Her father's never been much good at that. But Tangi's not an easy kid. She's complicated and contradictory. And I'm not sure I'm the—" He shook his head. "Maybe I'm just not the right candidate for this kind of task."

They had come to a low cement wall that ran out into the water and David sat, disengaging his hand from Wim's. She felt utterly bereft. He smiled and patted the wall beside him, and she sat too, but a little distance away. After a moment Wim said, "Maybe she doesn't want to be influenced. Maybe she doesn't want people to expect anything of her before . . . before she's figured out who she is."

The fog had deepened without her noticing, muffling sound

and shape. The only thing she could see at all was David, a few inches away. It was strangely comforting, like being wrapped in a blanket, but the intimacy almost paralyzed her. The lap of water against the shore and the slap of sail lines against the masts of boats bobbing invisibly at anchor in the harbor were more sensation than sound. Out beyond the breakwater, the light of a late-arriving fishing boat was no more than a diffused, unearthly glow as it advanced slowly toward the wharf. The moon was all but obscured. Motionless, Wim gazed into the mist. David shifted a little, asked, "Are you cold?" and his shoulder touched hers. She shook her head. She did not want to speak, even to breathe; it might break the spell.

"Does it make you angry, that people expect things of you?" asked David softly.

"No," she whispered.

He said nothing for a long time, and she felt no disbelief from him, but she amended finally, "Yes."

"Because you want to be something different from what they want you to be?"

She did not take her eyes from the milky night. "No," she said. "Because I don't want to be anything at all."

Angelo came up to them, and Wim put her arms around him gratefully, burying her face in his fur. He smelled of sand and seaweed. He thumped his tail and nudged against David, too, and David stroked his knobby head. Wim wondered what it would feel like to have that broad hand stroking her hair. David murmured, "I thought you were a watcher."

"That's not *being* anything," she replied, her voice muffled by Angelo's fur. "That's just what I do. I don't want to have to *be* something. People make themselves miserable by wanting to be something."

"You mean — people make themselves miserable by dreaming?"

She nodded, waiting for the inevitable argument, wishing she could express what she really meant. If she could just tell him about Jilly, whose dream of being a great dancer had killed her . . . but she would not allow herself to say the name. And when David still did not answer, Wim said slowly, "Yes. Dreams. They get too big for people. Dreams are always *out there*, where you can't reach. No one's ever big enough for them. Dreams can . . . can kill people."

She realized with shame that she had begun to cry, and he put his hand on her shoulder, then drew her close against him with one arm. Angelo lay contentedly at their feet. "Dreams kill people?" David asked gently.

She held herself stiffly until she was no longer crying. "They die inside," she said. "Like my father. He wanted to be a writer. It was always his dream. Except when he finally got time to work at it, *I* came along. Now he just talks about writing, and it fools him into *thinking* he's a writer." She tried to mask the bitterness in her voice with a small smile. "It's an understatement to say I wasn't planned," she said. "Everything fell apart because of it. My mother — she always wanted to be a doctor and she'd already been accepted at medical school, but—"

"You came along," he repeated for her with an answering smile.

She was uncertain of his tone, but his eyes as they looked into her own were serious. Suddenly he asked softly, "Who died?"

"What?"

"Who died?"

She tensed, pulling away from him. "No one died. I didn't say . . . I only meant—" The name was pushing insistently against her throat. She swallowed. She didn't know what would happen if she spoke it aloud. She whispered, "Jilly."

Nothing happened. She was not even sure, after all, if she had spoken. David gave no sign. With his arm still around her, she felt the resistance within her dissolving at an alarming rate. But her throat no longer hurt. She let her breath out slowly. "Jilly was my best friend. Since we were eleven years old." It felt absurdly easy now, to talk. She grew almost reckless. "Actually, I never really had other friends . . . just Jilly. She was a dancer. It was all she ever wanted to do. She danced all the time, and she was determined to be famous. Everyone wanted her to be famous . . . mostly her mother. Her mother was always worried Jilly was eating too much. You have to be really thin to be a dancer, and Jilly thought she wasn't thin enough—" Unexpectedly, she clenched her hands into fists in her lap. "She *was*, though. She was perfectly fine. She was *beautiful*. But she hardly ever ate anything, and it got worse and worse until—"

"Until she stopped eating and died."

She twisted to face him directly, but he did not drop his arm from around her. His eyes seemed to have gathered what light there was from the misty darkness. "I didn't know how to help her," she continued in a low voice. "Everyone told me that all I had to do was be her friend. They said that would be enough. They said she'd pull out of it. And I *was* her friend. But it *wasn't* enough." She spit the last words out bitterly.

Why was she was telling this stranger everything? He had not been in her life more than a moment. But the heart she felt beating against her was not a stranger's heart. It was more familiar to her even than the heartbeats of the dogs or the great thumping hearts of the horses. Pressing against him, she thought her own heart might stop if he let her go. "Who are you? Who are you?" she whispered fiercely.

"You know who I am," he answered, almost breathing the words into her.

In the darkness, and so close their faces almost touched, Wim asked, "Does Aunt Kia know who you are?"

"Yes. She does."

She took a deep breath. His body felt very still against her own. "Are you who I . . . who she sees?"

He seemed to pull himself out of a spell, and his voice was stronger. "In Aotearoa—in New Zealand—Kia would be a respected *kuia*. Her natural *mana* is tremendous. She is a very unusual person; she was born with it. It was not bestowed on her, and it has not been trained. But perhaps . . . perhaps it was inherited." His voice trailed off. After a long moment, he murmured, "Why is her name *Kia*?"

Startled, Wim answered, "Kia? I don't know. I think she said it was her Grampy's name for her, or something. I thought it was just short for Katherine Irene. Why?"

David stood abruptly. "Oh, it doesn't matter. Let's go back, *hine*."

She followed him, stunned. He had shut her out as surely as if he had closed a door in her face. But Wim had learned many times that it did no good to pound and yell at doors. It had never worked with her sisters and it had not worked with Jilly in those last terrible weeks when she was shutting herself down before Wim's eyes. As they walked back along the beach toward the house, she busied herself with the dogs so he would not think anything was wrong. When he got to the gate, she lingered on the sand on the pretext of throwing one last stick for Bart. David watched, seeming troubled, then came back.

"I can't explain anything right now," he said.

She shrugged. "That's all right." She threw the stick again.

He started to say something and stopped. But after a few seconds he commented thoughtfully, as if continuing their earlier conversation in the cottage, "You know, come to think of it, I know several people who spend their lives *watching*. My friend Ian, for instance—he works for the New Zealand government researching endangered birds. *Kakapo, takahe, kokako* . . . not much he hasn't studied. Basically, that's all he does. Slogs around in the bush watching birds. Well—" he conceded with a quick grin, "I guess sometimes he writes things down in a little notebook."

Bart danced on his hind legs, begging her for the stick again. Wim gave it to him without throwing it. "Is the white heron . . . is the *kotuku* endangered?" she asked, letting David draw her back into his sphere.

"Oh, yes. Very, very rare."

They had wandered back to the gate. Wim paused. "It was so incredibly beautiful," she breathed.

She had meant the great white heron. But she wondered, as his eyes met hers, if he thought she'd meant their walk together. She wondered if perhaps she *had* meant that. Neither said goodnight; they just parted at the gate. She walked toward the house and David toward the cottage. But at the same moment she turned to look back at him, he paused too. "Keep watching," he called softly, and later, as she was falling asleep in bed, his words still swam sweetly through her.

Seven

In the rush of the next few days, when Wim was busy at the barn or sharing Kia's care with her mother, only an elusive memory of that night remained. It intruded on the everyday world as an ephemeral scent tantalizes with its intoxicating, indefinable promise. For many days, as she came and went, Wim caught no more than a passing glimpse of either David or Tangi. Once she drove up just as he was driving away, and she caught his eye. But he only gave her a cheery wave and left.

It was now deep summer, the July air hot and still, with no relief except the early morning fogs that rolled in off the water. But the sun burned through by eight o'clock. Wim was sticky with perspiration one morning as she worked Kia's hair into a thick braid.

"Please try not to yank my head off," commented the old woman dryly, sitting straight-backed in a chair before the mirror on her dresser.

"Sorry," muttered Wim.

Kia tucked a loose strand of hair behind her ear. "You miss him, don't you, Charlotte?" she asked.

"David?" She spoke before she thought.

Kia glanced at her impatiently in the mirror. "Oh, that isn't his name," she grumbled. "Why do you call him that?"

The sweat that trickled down Wim's neck was suddenly cold. "Aunt Kia—" she began, and gathered her courage. But the old woman stopped her by taking Wim's hand and holding it against her wrinkled cheek. "Charlotte, Charlotte," she murmured, rocking slightly in her chair. "You are so very afraid, aren't you? Oh, yes. I know. Believe me, I know how it is. Too awesome, too wonderful . . ." She seemed to be reassuring herself as well, her eyes half-closed, pressing Wim's hand to her face. Then she leaned forward and peered at Wim's reflection. "You must look so much like her," she mused in a whisper. "That's why *he* comes, you know, Charlotte. He's looking for her."

Wim glanced at herself in the mirror. This is what David sees, she thought glumly. Unruly dark hair frizzing loose from the same kind of braid she'd just done for Kia. Heavy, straight brows, eyes too black in the dim room for her to read her own expression. "Such sad eyes," her father often said, puzzled. "Sad beyond your years." There was nothing in Wim of the ruddy brightness of the Thorpe family. Ginny and Bea sparkled; Wim brooded. She turned away from the mirror abruptly.

"You look like that other girl," Kia remarked suddenly. "You could be her sister, Charlotte. Have you noticed?"

Carol appeared in the doorway. "Still here, Wimmie? Good morning, Kia. You seem rested."

The old woman snapped, "I'm far more rested than I need to be."

Carol caught Wim's eye and chuckled. "I'll call you at the barn if there's any change of plan, but otherwise just make sure you get her back here by three. Her doctor's appointment is at four." She hesitated. "Honey, Ginny's going to call you later this afternoon. I told her you'd be here."

"What does she want?" Wim asked, wary.

Carol gave her a hurt frown. "She just wants to talk, Wim. She didn't see much of you the last time she was here." She hesitated. "Actually, you know Mark, her new boyfriend? His daughter is your age. Loves horses, Ginny said. She spends weekends with her dad, and Ginny wants you to come up and—"

"No."

She stubbornly avoided her mother's troubled gaze. "Wim," said Carol, annoyance tinging her voice, "you can't go on like this forever. You've got to make an effort. This just isn't healthy. I can't go through another summer like last—"

"*You* don't have to go through anything!" Wim cried, incensed. "And I don't want to talk about it, Mom. I'm fine."

Kia had begun to stir uneasily. "Are you going away, Charlotte?" she asked.

Carol said firmly, "Wim might go visit her sister Ginny in Boston, Kia. You remember Ginny, don't you? Ginny wants her to meet someone. And—" she persisted, addressing Wim again, "Mark is starting his postgraduate work in the fall at Tufts Veterinarian School, and he's offered to drive you over for a tour of the campus."

"Charlotte isn't going to be a veterinarian," announced Kia in disdain.

"Wim has to start thinking about her future, Kia. She's going into her last year of high school."

If it hadn't been so horrifying, Wim might have laughed at the way her mother and Kia were tugging her back and forth between them like two dogs with a stick. She heard a car start up outside and her stomach jumped. "Are you ready to go yet, Aunt Kia?" she asked desperately. "I need to get to the barn." She ran to the front door in time to see David's car backing slowly out onto the street.

Kia came down the steps after her while Carol watched from the doorway. Wim paused on the path, her heart in her throat. *David. David.* But she did not wave or go toward him.

The car stopped and the window was rolled down. "Air-conditioning," called David, grinning at her from behind large reflective sunglasses. "I'm hermetically sealed into this machine. Almost didn't see you."

She made herself walk calmly to the car, although her heart was dashing ahead of her like silly Sue. She felt her mother's eyes on her and knew that Kia was suffering in the sun. But she went up to the car. "Hi," she said. She could see only herself, mirrored in his glasses.

"I'm off to the Brewster Historical Society archives today," he said. "Dry as toast, I'm afraid. Tangi's still asleep, lazy thing. She made me promise to get donuts for her before I left." He was chatting as if nothing had ever happened between them. She could have been anybody standing there. He did not take off his sunglasses. "How's your auntie this morning?"

"Fine," Wim croaked.

Nothing. There was nothing. She'd dreamed it all. He drove away, and Kia said in a quavering voice, "Charlotte, are we going? I don't want to stand here."

At the barn, Wim could not concentrate. After she got Kia settled on the sofa in the office with a mystery novel and the television on, she switched the fan to high and tried to sort through the pile of mail and phone messages Tammy had left on the desk. She couldn't make herself focus. The fan blew the papers around. She propped her chin on her fists, sighed, and forced herself to study the week's calendar of events. She had to fit in one more trail ride, three more lessons, and a change in the blacksmith's scheduled visit. When she looked up, Kia was gone.

She rushed from the office and heard Tammy's voice coming from a stall halfway down the barn. "Hey there, Kia," Tammy was saying. "Giving us a hand?"

Wim reached the stall in time to see the old woman jab energetically at the hay with a pitchfork. "This stall is a mess," Kia said. "Don't you know it can rot a horse's hooves?"

Giving Wim an amused grimace, Tammy herded Kia gently from the stall and took the pitchfork. "Well, sure we know," she said amiably. "And we're getting to it. See those girls there?" She pointed at two girls mucking out stalls at the far end of the barn. Kia reluctantly let herself be taken back to the office.

The next time Kia escaped, Wim was on the phone trying to negotiate a new appointment with the blacksmith. She was sure she'd been keeping half an eye on Kia during the conversation, but the old woman was silent, cunning, and quick. This time, Wim didn't realize she was gone until she heard Evelyn bellowing for her. She spun around, dropped the phone, and ran outside. Evelyn vaulted the fence of the riding ring. "Damn it, Wim!" she yelled. "Get her out of there. Your mother'll sue me for all I'm worth. *Damn.*"

They reached the Kid's corral at the same time. The horse was standing quietly in the midday sun. Kia faced him, stroking both sides of his head, brushing back the tangled white forelock from his eyes. She was crooning her strange, lilting song. "Wim," hissed Evelyn under her breath. "*Do* something. The Kid's gonna kill her."

"No, no. She's done it before," whispered Wim. Evelyn stared at her. Wim nodded, shamefaced. "The other night—I didn't tell you. But it's okay. See? He isn't scared of her. Just wait. Let me talk to her."

She spoke first to the horse, but he did not answer with his usual nicker. He did not seem to hear her. Then Kia stopped singing and stepped back. The Kid followed. Kia took another step back, and again the horse followed, nudging her with his muzzle. Wim smiled, relaxing. "Hey, Aunt Kia," she called. "I need to get the Kid some water. Will you help me?"

"Charlotte," said Kia. "You don't need my help to get water. Stop treating me like a child." She squinted at Evelyn and demanded, "Why does this horse have such a ridiculous name?"

Evelyn barked, "The Karate Kid? Because he kicks like a black belt, that's why. You're lucky he hasn't kicked your head off."

"Nonsense," Kia snorted. "He has no need to kick me. If he kicks, it's because he's trying to tell you something and you aren't listening. Charlotte doesn't listen, either."

Evelyn looked in exasperation at Wim. "Are you going to get her out of there, or what?"

"Aunt Kia—" Wim began, without much hope.

The old woman was stroking the horse again, running her hand along his neck and down his back. But the Kid only switched his long white tail. "This horse should not be kept back here alone," Kia stated. "What is he being isolated for? Horses don't like that. You should be spending time with him, Charlotte. Every day."

The injustice of it stung deeply. "I can't," retorted Wim. "I'm spending all my extra time with *you*. There isn't any more time."

To her surprise, Kia, with a look of sudden chagrin, said nothing. The Kid threw up his head and trotted off to the far corner. The old woman let herself out through the gate. She paused to say to Evelyn, "If you treat him like he's dangerous, he'll be dangerous. Move him closer to the house so he can watch what's going on. Feed and water him out of your hand— give him a reason to trust you." To Wim, she continued, "Poor Charlotte. I didn't mean to be thoughtless. You're being pulled every which way, aren't you? Your heart is all in a tangle."

Evelyn turned to go. "I've got to go to Orleans for the grain. Tammy's around somewhere if you need her. Try not to let your aunt take over the whole establishment, okay?"

"Surly creature," Kia commented as Evelyn walked away.

Wim said nothing. All at once she was exhausted, and she went back to the office without even checking to see if Kia was following. Out the window, she was startled by the sight of David's car just pulling into the yard. She hesitated, ambivalent, then went to the doorway of the barn and stood there. David rolled the window down and called over to her, "I tried phoning you, but no one answered. My plans have changed. I'm off to New Bedford instead and I didn't want to leave Tangi alone for so long. I thought it might be more comfortable for her to hang out here."

The light glinted off his sunglasses. His bare arm lay across the car's window frame. It seemed unimaginable to Wim that she had been held by that arm. He turned away to speak to Tangi, and although Wim could not hear them, it was obvious from the length of time that the girl was unwilling. Eventually Tangi got out, slammed the door, and leaned sullenly against the car. David asked, "Is this all right, Wim? It'll be a few hours."

"I don't care," said Wim.

There was a silence, impossible to read. Then Kia appeared beside Wim, looked sharply at David, and went over to Tangi. "Why have you come, girl?" she demanded peevishly. Peering closer, she added, "How do I know you?"

Tangi had immediately straightened at Kia's approach. "*Tena koe, Kui* Kia," she said, her eyes lowered.

"What is your name?" Kia barked.

Wim said, coming forward, "She told you the other—"

"Tangi, *e kui.* Tangi Te Aniwa."

Kia stood very still for several seconds, her gaze at the girl never wavering. Strangely to Wim, Tangi did not seem at all disconcerted by this but rather appeared to be waiting with patient respect for whatever Kia did next. Finally the old woman spoke, her voice firm. "Yes, that *is* the name. I remember. Te

Aniwa. Te Aniwa." She turned to Wim with triumph. "I told you I knew her, Charlotte. Te Aniwa. Yes. It was *hers*, you know. It was Annie's. The necklace Grampy gave me, that I lost in the sea. He told me it was hers." She suddenly leaned closer to Wim. "That's why I *must* get to the sea, Charlotte! You didn't believe me, did you?"

"Aunt Kia, that isn't—" She stopped, helplessly.

David Te Makara took off his sunglasses and got out of the car. As before, and at once, the air seemed to gather around him and the old woman. He greeted her quietly. *"Tena koe, Kui Kia. Tena ra koe, e te rangitira."* He bowed his head slightly with respect. Then, *"E kui,* please—who is Te Aniwa?" he asked. His voice remained quiet, but Wim could sense the force coiled beneath that calm, a focused purpose whose expression he was controlling with great effort.

"What are you talking about?" Kia grumbled. She pointed at Tangi. "That girl said she was Te Aniwa."

David persisted, even more softly, more deferential, "How do you know Te Aniwa?"

Kia wavered under his spell. She clutched Wim's arm. "Charlotte, why is he asking me these things?" she moaned. "That girl is not Annie. Why does she say she is? Annie is gone. She was gone long before I was born, Charlotte. How could *she* be Annie?" She looked accusingly at Tangi. "I was the only person Grampy ever talked to about Annie. He said so. He said he cried and cried after she was gone, but he was only a little boy and they would not allow him to talk about her. He gave me the necklace because I looked like her."

David lowered his head. So quietly his voice was hardly

more than a breath, he asked, "Please, *e kui*, why did your Grampy give you your name? Why did he call you Kia?"

The old woman could not escape his questions. She gasped, "It was a word from her song . . . it was pretty, a pretty word. Grampy said I was pretty, like her." Tears were running down the creases of Kia's face, her voice broken as a sobbing child's. Still David did not move, and still he appeared to be waiting. Wim put her arm around Kia and pulled her away. Over her shoulder she said to David roughly, "What are you bothering her for? Can't you see you're upsetting her? What do you *want?*"

David turned and got back in the car. He put on the sunglasses. "I'm sorry," he said, expressionless. "I didn't wish to." To Tangi, he said, "Are you staying? Or coming with me?"

Tangi hesitated. Inadvertently, Wim caught her eye. The girl lifted her chin. "I'll stay," she said decisively and sauntered into the barn with deliberate nonchalance.

"Suit yourself, then." David spoke to her receding form, then he nodded at Kia. "*E noho ra, e kui.* I hope we may speak again. Stay in peace." He said nothing to Wim, just closed the window and drove off.

Kia said in a conspiratorial whisper, "That was *him*, you know, Charlotte."

She was too heartsick to respond. Kia plucked insistently at her arm. "He likes you better than he ever liked me," she observed jealously. "He speaks to you."

"He spoke to you, too, Aunt Kia."

"Only because you were there," retorted the old woman in a slight huff. "I am very hot out here, Charlotte. I want to sit in front of the fan." She hesitated, frowning. "Is that girl still here? I don't want her here. She makes me . . . she makes me—"

"I don't want her here, either. But she is and that's all there is to it. I can't do anything about it," Wim said, more irritably than she'd intended. Kia looked at her in surprise, and then, somewhat subdued, she turned and went into the barn.

Wim caught Tammy watching her from the doorway and was immediately contrite. "I'm just in a bad mood," she muttered, embarrassed.

Tammy was straightening out the straps of a bridle. "You're allowed," she said. "Looks like you've got your hands full. First your auntie, and now—who's the girl?"

She mumbled a short explanation and Tammy didn't comment further, just reminded her, "I've got six people going out in half an hour. Can you tack up for me? God, it's hotter'n dickens. Wish they would've canceled. I'll have to take them on Beech Forest trail." She paused. "You look beat, Wim. Any reason other than the usual?"

"I'm fine," Wim answered shortly. "Aunt Kia's just . . . difficult sometimes." It felt like treachery to say this; she knew it had nothing to do with the old woman. But she did not want Tammy or Evelyn to grow curious about David and Tangi. The world of the barn was *hers;* it offended her deeply that David had intruded, that Tangi was at this moment sitting in the office.

As she followed Tammy into the barn, the woman commented, "I sure wish your dad would find a temporary place for your aunt, like your mom wanted. It'd make things a lot easier for you."

She felt as though she was being torn apart. Contradicting her own words, knowing she was unreasonable, she cried, "It's not *her!* I don't *want* her to go! Don't you understand?"

Tammy paused. Shrugged. "I'm trying to, Wim," she sighed. They tacked the horses in silence. Neither Kia nor Tangi had emerged from the office, and Wim could not imagine what they were saying to each other. The group arrived for their trail ride and Wim helped Tammy bring the string of horses out into the yard. "There's nothing else scheduled for the day, thank God," Tammy said. "Why don't you just hang around until Ev gets back and then go home?"

Wim found Kia dozing on the couch and Tangi watching a television talk show with the fan blasting on her. It was such an ordinary, peaceful scene she was taken aback. But Tangi gave her a wary look. "Reckoned you wouldn't object to me watching the telly, eh."

"You reckoned right. But I need my chair."

The girl scooted quickly to sit at the far end of the couch. Wim pulled the chair up to the desk and, deliberately ignoring the girl, began to work on some unanswered mail. After several minutes of listening to the jabber of the talk show, she reached over and turned the volume down. Tangi stirred uncomfortably. "It wasn't my idea to come over here, you know," she muttered at last. "It was Uncle David—he just wanted an excuse to see you."

Wim dropped her pencil. "Oh. Yeah."

The girl growled, "You don't have to believe me. Just so you know it wasn't *me* that wanted to come, okay?" She lifted her face to the fan. "Is it always so bloody hot here?"

"It's actually much cooler in the cottage," said Wim pointedly.

The girl stood up. "Right, then. I'm off," she said. "And look — I really don't give a flip if you believe me or not about Uncle David. I just thought you'd like to know, eh. But I got my own life to worry about, so suit yourself." She started out the door.

Wim sighed, resigned. "You can't walk all the way back home in this heat," she said.

"I'll manage. No worries." But Tangi hesitated a fraction of a second, long enough for Wim to catch a fleeting look cross her face. It was a look she recognized, and it twisted her heart.

"Don't leave," she said softly. "I don't mind if you stay."

Tangi leaned against the door frame and pretended to consider a decision, but her dark eyes stayed on Wim hungrily. Kia woke and sat up. "Charlotte," she announced. "It's time to go to the sea. I want to ride. Please saddle a horse."

Tangi giggled in delight. "Whoo-ee! That's the ticket! Let's do it, eh. Better'n sitting here melting."

"Don't be absurd," said Wim, turning back to the desk. But she could feel them watching her. She knew they were testing her, but she was afraid to turn around, to face again in Tangi's eyes that lonely, defiant hurt she herself was so familiar with. And she was afraid to face the compelling power of Kia's haunting need. She rustled aimlessly through papers on the desk. The barn was drowsy in the afternoon stillness. Outside in the pines, a cicada trilled abruptly once and was silent. There was no one around. The Kid nickered softly from his corral behind the barn. Wim started. "Okay, why not?" she said. Reckless suddenly. She looked at Tangi. "Can you ride?"

The girl snorted. "I can ride anything you got here, that's for sure."

"Then take Betsy—stall six. Down there on the left. Get her ready. The bridle's on the rack with the saddle."

She would take Macho, a tall, rawboned horse rarely used by anyone but the most experienced riders, and little Muenster for Kia. She could take them at a pleasant walk around the Upper Loop Trail, where they took children. Fifteen minutes at the most. It would be something to do until Evelyn came back.

She kept Kia in sight while she got Macho ready, but there seemed no danger now that the old woman would wander off. Kia's eyes burned with excitement. Wim left Macho saddled in the stall while she got Muenster out. At the far end of the barn, Tangi was leading Betsy into the yard. "You should saddle her up inside," Wim called to her.

"What is *that?*" Kia demanded, pointing at the pony.

"This is Muenster. This is who you're going to ride," said Wim, pulling the pony's thick forelock from under the bridle headstall.

"A child's pony?" Kia frowned in disbelief. "I won't ride a child's pony, Charlotte."

Wim paused as she buckled a strap. She looked Kia in the eye. "I am the boss here, Aunt Kia," she said firmly. "You'll ride Muenster or you won't ride at all. I shouldn't even be letting you do this."

She turned abruptly and went into the tack room for Muenster's saddle. When she came out, saddle over her arm, she froze in horror.

Kia was riding Macho in the yard. And beyond her, clinging bareback, using only a halter and lead rope, was Tangi on Betsy. The mare was dancing uneasily, unused to being ridden without a saddle, but Tangi dug her heel in and forced the horse to turn in a tight circle. Kia backed Macho expertly out of the way and snapped, "Don't be stupid, girl. Treat the horse with respect. You're not a cowboy."

Wim dropped the saddle and sprinted the length of the barn. Kia, hands adept, seat balanced and confident, sidestepped Macho out of reach as Wim grabbed for his bridle. "Aunt Kia!" gasped Wim.

"Aunt Kia nothing," said the old woman calmly, looking down at her. "I want to *ride*, Charlotte, not fall asleep in a rocking chair. You ride the pony."

Tangi cantered Betsy in a circle around the yard. "Come on, then!" she cried. "What're we waiting for? It's heaps cooler in the bush." And with that she headed the mare sharply away and plunged down the trail leading into the pines. Kia reined Macho in a perfectly collected turn and followed. Wim was left listening to the receding thud of hooves.

Numbly, she threw the saddle on Muenster and tried to urge him immediately into a canter. The pony resisted, shaking his head. "Get *going!*" cried Wim. She gritted her teeth and kicked his soft sides. With a grunt of surprise, the pony broke into a clumsy canter. The trail curved down through the pines and out across a swampy meadow before rising gradually toward the upland forests. She could smell the sea on the warm breeze. For one wild moment she considered escaping away over the dunes. Then, as the pony labored along the soft ground of the meadow, Wim saw the other two horses disappearing ahead of her into the woods. She did not bother shouting. She just followed grimly.

She caught up to them ten minutes later, but only because they had stopped and were waiting for her. Macho, dark with sweat, was throwing his head nervously up and down, and Betsy was blowing hard. Wim faced them across the small clearing. Muenster's sides heaved under her. "Satisfied?" she asked them finally.

Tangi looked mutinous, but Kia raised her hand in an imperious gesture before Wim could say anything more. "Charlotte," she commanded. "Just be quiet and listen."

For several long moments the three faced each other in the clearing. Except for the stirring and breathing of the horses, it was utterly silent. Tangi was gazing off into the shadow-dappled thickets, and a strand of sunlight fell across her cheek so her brown skin was washed with gold. *She's beautiful*, thought Wim, first in wonder, then bewilderment, and all at once she was terribly afraid. *Jilly!* she cried in silent panic. *Jilly! Come back!* But Tangi was too vivid, too alive; Wim couldn't see around her.

"Now are you listening?" Kia asked softly.

She was furious, and she wanted to cry. She felt something precious had been taken from her, something she nevertheless could hardly remember. And the struggle to remember no longer even seemed so important. The old woman's eyes rested briefly on her, then looked past her to the tangled undergrowth of ferns and vines among the trees. Helplessly, Wim followed her gaze. She knew what she would see.

From shadows fractured by sunlight the man with the tattooed face looked back at her. She waited. An intricate fern frond, a looping tendril of wild grapevine . . . was he really there? Or was his form only the stuff of light and shadow, his substance the stuff of longing and loss? Then she could not help herself; she reached toward him. Immediately, only the ferns and vines remained, quivering in the seaborne breeze.

Kia made a sound, full of grief. "I didn't mean to lose it!" she called to the shadows. "I didn't want to lose it! Grampy gave it to me. It was so beautiful. Oh, it was lovely. Green stone . . . green and shining, and Grampy showed me how to hold it up to the light to see the tiny, dark heart inside. But I was a little girl, and I lost it. I lost it in the sea." The old eyes focused back on Wim. "Oh, Charlotte. I miss Grampy so much. He sang to me and told me stories and walked with me by the sea every single day. He said I looked like her. It was hers, you know. The necklace. That's how *he* knew who Grampy was, when Grampy was a young man. But Grampy was afraid of him, Charlotte. He told Grampy terrible things—he tried to make Grampy come away with him." Kia's hand was at her neck, as if feeling for the polished green stone, and after a moment she whispered, "I never even wore it. Not once. I was playing, and I threw it up in the air, and it went into the sea, and that's why *he* comes. *He* wants it, Charlotte . . ."

Wim sat motionless, mesmerized by the old woman's keening voice, but Tangi suddenly moved the mare alongside Kia and reached for Macho's reins. *"Kia kaha, e kui. Kia kaha tonu,"* she said softly. "Don't be afraid. Be strong, eh. I know it's hard, but there must still be farther for you to go. Today isn't the day. Let's go back now, *e kui."* She pulled at Macho gently and nudged Betsy around the way they had come. To Wim she muttered, "Don't scold her. She had to do this. It's part of her story. She has to live it in her own way. I know you don't understand, eh. Just ask Uncle David." She flung the last words over her shoulder, a condemnation and a challenge, as she rode past leading Macho.

Wim managed to get Kia home before her mother arrived. The old woman was subdued during the drive back in the truck, and Tangi, glowering in her old way, went immediately off to the cottage without a word. When Carol got home, she peeked in at Kia dozing on the bed and wrinkled her nose. "What did you do—put her to work mucking out stalls?" she asked Wim. "Well, there isn't time for her to change. I'll just tell Dr. Andrews you've hired her at the barn."

She hardly heard them leave. She sat on the steps staring at the street, swept into a fluid, formless world. Her thoughts were disconnected, flickering through her like fragments of light through water. Farther below, indistinct shadows eddied by deeper currents, were questions she could not shape with words. She was adrift in this sensation with no means to pull herself out. Even the threatened phone conversation with her sister later that afternoon left barely a ripple on the surface. "Wim?" Ginny asked. "Are you okay?"

"Of course I'm okay," said Wim. The words came from far away, from some distant shore.

"But why don't you want to come to Boston? We could have so much fun. I really want you to meet Mark's daughter. She's so cool—really, Wim. You'd like her."

"No," said Wim.

Ginny made an exasperated noise. "Why are you being so stubborn? You don't even have a reason."

"Yes, I do. I just don't feel like telling you."

Ginny was angry in the end; it was inevitable. She was making an effort at being friendly and sisterly, and Wim was making no effort in return. But Wim couldn't bring herself to care; it would have required an effort she could not summon. She gazed out the kitchen window as Ginny talked. David's car pulled up in front of the cottage. "I have to go, Ginny," Wim said.

"But we haven't—"

"I have to go." She hung up without waiting for a reply and ran outside. But the car was already backing out into the street again, this time with Tangi inside. David's head was turned away. Suddenly, the drifting ended. A vast wave crested, dropped her hard onto the sand, and receded. Bruised and dizzy, she stood in the yard a long time. The dogs wagged around her. She hardly responded to them, but they seemed to understand where she was going before she did and dashed ahead of her across the yard toward the cottage. She left them outside and went in.

Immediately she was a child again, an intruder, sneaking into a forbidden place. Instead of her sisters' things, Tangi's denim jacket was hung over a chair and David's books and papers were piled around on the floor. The cot where he slept was rumpled, covered with more papers, and after a moment, she knelt next to it and embraced his pillow, pushing her face into it to find his scent. Then she was crying; she clutched the pillow against her and hoped fiercely that it would still be wet from her tears when David returned.

Finally it grew hot and difficult to breathe, and she sat up, hugging the pillow against her. Her eyes fell on the laptop computer and the cardboard box next to it on the desk. She got up slowly. In the box, on top, was the old journal. Under it were the printed pages Tangi had transcribed. She grabbed the whole sheaf and went back to sit on the floor by David's cot.

She scanned the pages quickly at first, nervously, almost gulping at words. She flipped through until she reached where she had stopped reading before, keeping her ear open in case David returned. The first words of the new page caught her like a hook.

. . . except for Willie, I find myself much alone, which I prefer above all. I have made no other friends, and am sailing with strangers to a far-away Land I know nothing of. Dr Kendall is a most undemanding Master. He is often closeted with the Captain in private conversation, which leaves me to many welcome hours of solitude. I question what I am meant to be, and what I must Become. I know that by my Nature, I am compelled to take care of any Creature I find weak or hurt. It may be that a doctor is something more than this, however. I wish I could voice these questions to my Master.

But there is some trouble weighing Heav'ly on Dr Kendall's heart, for as this journey progresses he is more and more given to Drink and when he sees me, which is not Frequent, his tongue is oft more loose than I would care it to be. He insists we shall have no Secrets between us. Apprentice and Master, he tells me, is an ancient and sacred Covenant of trust. But tho' I am fond of the Doctor, I am uncertain of his sensibilities when he is drinking, and so I have devised a code for my Journal, that no other eyes but mine can read it.

Tho' I protest, Dr Kendall insists I hear his Thoughts on the obligations of a Doctor's life and work. These thoughts, I do fear, are some of them close to blasphemy. My boy, he says to me, a doctor must look after more than the Earthly body of man. He must attend to all the Woes and Suffering of the human Soul as if he was God himself. Boy, he tells me, you must prepare to hear tales of misery that would cause the martyred Saints themselves to quiver in anguish. I assure him that I am ill-equipt to bear these burdens, for who am I to receive such stories? You are my Apprentice, boy, he admonishes me, and I would do you a vast disservice did I neglect this aspect of your education in the oath-bound trade of healing. And he proceeds to tell me of things in his Mind which I think would be far better kept Secret. It is no small Relief to unburden myself in the pages of this Journal that only I will ever read.

Oh, before God, in all sincerity of my Heart, I do desire only to go Home! I am sick with missing all that is Familiar. I am passionately unfond of Exploration into unknown places, either dark Heathen lands or the dark regions of the human heart.

Wim found herself nodding as she read, as if Emmanuel Dart were speaking to her directly. She turned the page and came to the last entry Tangi had transcribed.

February 12. My great solace on this journey is Willie, who all the others view as a Tragedy. I do not view him as such. But he is the cause of profound sorrow, anger and shame to Capt'n

Thorpe, for the boy is his only Heir and it is obvious Willie will not continue the shipping trade. Neither will he carry on the Thorpe name. Dr Kendall tells me Willie had the Smallpox at the age of 6 yrs. and his brain was subsequently Diseased and will remain always as a child's. Dr Kendall confides in me that the Captain's Wife was rendered barren by this Illness, and for the same reason is Willie incapable of fathering offspring. These Misfortunes, Dr Kendall says, have greatly altered the Captain's character. Never underestimate the Evils of illness, the doctor admonishes me. Death is not the only enemy of Man.

But Willie knows nothing of Evil. He is a happy child and delights in any New Thing of wonder. I do not understand Capt'n Thorpe's anger. Can Willie be who he is not? It is the Captain who Dreams that the Thorpe name and shipping business will carry on into the Future, and he pays no heed to Willie's desires. So great is the Captain's disappointment in Willie he at times seems barely able to acknowledge him as his son.

The sound of a car made Wim jump. She scrambled up swiftly, put the pages back in the box, and peeked out the window. But it was not David returning. It was her mother, bringing Kia home from the doctor. Wim came out to meet her as she was opening the door on the passenger side.

"Oh, good. I was hoping you'd be home," Carol said wearily. "We've had quite a time. Kia's going to need a little help getting into the house. She got badly agitated at the doctor's and he gave her a new medication. I think it's going to be more effective in the long run, but right now she needs a nap. So do I, for that matter."

The transformation in the old woman shocked Wim. Kia's

head lolled to the side. Her eyes were open but opaque. Gone was the fierce vitality, the magic. Kia's mouth hung slack and there was a dark patch on her blouse where she had drooled. Carol reached in with expert hands and shifted the unresisting woman to the edge of the seat. "Just put your arm under her there," she directed Wim. "She can walk—she's just a little disoriented."

Nothing that Wim knew Kia to be remained. "Mom . . . Mom," she whispered, anguished.

"It looks worse than it is, Wimmie," said Carol as they lay Kia gently on the bed. "The meds will help. Really. All this turmoil . . . all these escapes, the agitations—it just isn't doing her any good. And the dementia seems worse. She kept babbling about riding a horse to the sea. Her blood pressure was off the chart. She has to be kept calm."

Wim sat by Kia's bed for a long time, listening to her uneven breathing. The sun slanted low through the tree outside the window. Evening came. A breeze from the harbor stirred the lace curtains. But the man with the tattooed face did not appear. Wim knew he would not come. This would be too sad for him to bear.

Eight ಄

Wim stayed at the barn for several days. Carol had taken time off from work to look after Kia. "I need to see how the new meds are working," she said. "Don't look so worried, Wim. It doesn't have anything to do with you. You've done fine with her. But Kia really does need full-time professional care."

In the end, she felt only relief in being at the barn. She was too busy to worry, surrounded during the day by the bustle of familiar activity. In the late evenings, a delicious peace settled over her among the contented horses, the dogs, the barn cats mewling around her legs. She slept on the sofa in the office despite Tammy's protests that there were beds enough in the house. Evelyn said, "Oh, leave her be, Tam. She doesn't need us fussing over her like mother hens." Later that night, Wim wandered to the house for a drink of water and found the two women laughing and hugging affectionately in the disheveled comfort of the kitchen, and she felt embraced by the same happiness. At the barn, the world was always simple and right.

Where could she ever go that would be better than this? She did not want mysteries in her life, or the dreams other people thought were so important. She was content with the soft nickered greeting of a horse, with the love of old Angelo, with the straightforward tasks of each day.

One evening, as she leaned on the fence of the Kid's corral gazing up at the emerging stars, she thought about Emmanuel Dart, the young man her own age who had lived over a hundred years ago. *"I am passionately unfond of Exploration into unknown places,"* he had written, and the words resonated in her now like an affirmation. She sighed and looked across at the Kid. They'd spent hours together like this each evening, she leaning on the fence, he standing languid at the far side switching his tail. Only his ears, responding to the sound of her voice, ever betrayed that he was aware of her presence. She never asked for more. She was content just to be near him. This evening, on the edge of night, the Kid was no more than a pale blur against the dark pines. But at her sigh, the horse suddenly shuddered as if she'd touched him, shook his head, and began to walk slowly across the space between them.

Wim hardly breathed. Tried not to think, tried not to feel tentative or bold or happy. She tried to be Kia, to meet the horse as the old woman had. She slipped under the fence and he came up to her. Without hesitation she put out her hands to touch his face. Soon she was leaning against him, breathing in the warmth of his dusty coat. She pressed her head against his side and heard the heart deep within. Only her mind told her she had never touched him before; otherwise, she knew him utterly. She reached her arms around him and he supported her weight, shifting a little so he could stand more solidly.

It was full dark by the time Evelyn called to her from the fence. "Hey, Wim," she said softly. "Hey there, Kid." Then she ducked under the fence and came across to sit on an upturned feed bucket a few feet away, watching them. Her head was within easy striking range of the Kid's hooves. But the horse stood steady against Wim and did not even quiver. After a moment, Evelyn murmured, "So old Aunt Kia was right. He just needed a reason to trust you."

"I haven't done anything," Wim whispered.

"Sure you have," Evelyn chuckled. "You're leaning on *him*. See? We've been trying to fix him. But he didn't want to be fixed. He wanted to be *trusted*." She got up and, in one smooth motion, ran her hand down the Kid's neck, along his withers, and let her arms drape as if by accident over his back. Now they stood, Wim and Evelyn, one on either side of the horse, and talked about barn business in low voices. The Kid's head drooped. His ears relaxed. His eyes half closed.

"If Tammy would take that group out tomorrow morning, I could finish clearing the brush from the new ring," Wim said. "The bulldozer guy's coming on Thursday, remember."

"Yeah, you could," Evelyn agreed. "Or I could. What're you hiding from, Wim?"

Startled, she muttered, "What do you mean?"

Evelyn rested her folded arms on the Kid's back. "Well, I *mean*—you've been hanging out here for days. You know we don't mind. But you keep looking for more and more work to do. It's making me nervous." She laughed. "Not that there isn't plenty to do. But come on, Wim. Give me a little credit for knowing you, okay? You're avoiding something." She paused, appraising Wim shrewdly. "Something's going on at home, isn't it? Like maybe those people staying in the cottage? That girl and . . . what's his name? The guy?"

"David." She blushed and looked away, furious with herself.

But Evelyn just said laconically, "Yeah. Him. And your aunt—what's up with her? You used to bring her over here. I kinda miss her turning the place upside down."

Wim took a deep breath. It was safer talking about Kia. "I can't now, Ev. It's horrible," she said. "She's on a new medication. She just sits around all day staring at the television. I don't even think she recognizes me half the time." She fiddled with the tangles in the Kid's mane. "I can't stand it. Really. I can't stand seeing it. She wasn't like this before, and I—"

Evelyn nodded. "You miss her."

Oh yes, I do. Jilly Jilly Jilly. But no, they weren't talking about her. They never did. No one ever spoke about those last months when Jilly was in and out of the hospital, growing thinner and weaker and whiter, acknowledging no one, staring day after day at the flickering television while doctors tried to pump nutrients into her collapsing veins. "I do miss her," Wim whispered, and the anger came without warning. "It's my own fault." She heard the words being spit out as if they were someone else's. The Kid shifted, his ears twitching uneasily. Wim lay her face against his neck and continued in a low voice, "I know it's stupid of me to feel this way. I do, really. Aunt Kia's old. She was going into the nursing home anyway. I knew that when she came here. She's going to die. What's the point of getting attached?"

"No point," Evelyn agreed blandly.

Wim glowered. Evelyn raised her eyebrows but said nothing. Wim cried, "It's easy for you! You've got Tammy! There *is* a point in being attached to her—*she* isn't dying or . . . or going away."

"Oh, I see. It's like Jilly all over again, huh," Evelyn said softly. Wim flinched. Evelyn continued, relentless, "So. Aunt Kia, and . . . what's his name? David? He's going away, right?"

She spun back in fury. "What do you know about him! You've never even met him!"

The Kid, strangely unperturbed this time, took a step so that once again she was leaning on him. Evelyn followed. "I don't know anything about him," she admitted, thoughtful. "Tam just mentioned about him coming by here the other day. I trust her insight, that's all."

Wim had seen Evelyn teach riding students for years, knew the way she goaded and prodded them toward excellence. She never let her students get away with being sloppy or careless with themselves or the horses. At times it seemed to Wim that Evelyn tormented her students, but somehow they all wanted to work harder for her, even as they glared at her the way Wim was glaring now. She knew she'd get nothing kind or comforting from Evelyn when Evelyn was in pursuit of the truth.

"I was really okay before," Wim said at last. "I was, Evelyn. I was looking forward to the summer. I was still sad, but I had the Kid, and the dogs, and I don't mind being alone. I know everyone thinks I need to find another friend, but I . . . I can't just *make* it happen, you know. I just wanted to work at the barn and—" Evelyn's eyes had softened, and the Kid, dozing again, warmed Wim in the cool night. She struggled to explain. "But suddenly all these people just . . . *arrived.* Aunt Kia. And Tangi and David. I didn't want anything to do with them. Really. I didn't want any of them around. But then . . . I don't know what happened. And now it's—"

"Now it's too late?"

"Yes," whispered Wim.

Later, she lay restless and awake on the sofa in the office, unable to still her mind. Her thoughts turned to Emmanuel Dart again, as to a kindred spirit. Tangi had not transcribed more than a quarter of the journal, but Wim was certain that, wish as he might, Emmanuel would not be able to avoid the "Exploration into unknown places" he so passionately disliked. Into his life, too, people had *arrived;* he would not be able to avoid them any more than she could. She reached down and stroked Angelo's head, listening to the soft stirring of horses in the barn. It was a fleeting reassurance. Like Emmanuel, she was on a ship with strangers sailing toward an unknown land.

She was dragging brush with the tractor the next day when she saw David's rental car pull into the yard. First Tammy and then Evelyn came out to stand talking with him. He leaned casually against the car, arms folded and obviously at ease, enjoying himself as if he'd known them for years. Wim couldn't see inside the car, but she wondered if Tangi was watching her suspiciously through the tinted glass. David glanced toward her. Flustered, she almost stripped the gears backing up the tractor. Evelyn bellowed, "Cool it, Wim! I can't afford to fix that thing! Come over here!"

She was sweaty and caked with dust. Her hair was frizzing loose from its braid; she yanked at it with one hand and slapped twigs and leaves from her clothes with the other. Her arms had long scratches from hauling brush. She walked reluctantly across the yard. "Sorry," she mumbled in Evelyn's direction, without looking at anyone.

"Good lord, Wim. You're as red as a beet," Evelyn said. "You trying to see what'll burn out first—my tractor or yourself?"

"Evelyn," Tammy pointed out, "she's cleared the whole ring for you. You might at least say thank you." To Wim, she added, "You better get something to drink before you go."

"Go?" she repeated dumbly.

David said apologetically, "No, look—it was only a suggestion. It doesn't matter. You look like you're busy . . . ."

"He wants to ride out into the dunes. You could show him around," Tammy said.

Strangely, David seemed almost flustered himself, now. "I thought you could show me some of those birds you told me you watch."

She began, "It's too hot. Birds won't be out—"

But Evelyn spoke over her. "You could take Pat and Sassy. They haven't been ridden for a few days. They need a good run."

The tractor's roar still seemed to be in her ears. She couldn't think straight. She asked David, "Can you ride?" and immediately realized what a stupid question it was.

"No worries," he said, laughing. "I grew up in the back blocks, remember? Bunch of wild kids, wild ponies, no gear. All we cared about was going fast. We had miles of beach and nothing much else to do. Wonder we weren't killed. My mum said we were totally *porangi*—just crazy." He grinned at her.

"Well, try not to wind the horses, that's all I ask," Evelyn commented dryly. "C'mon, Wim. I'll help you tack up."

Tammy said to David, "So this book you're writing—what's it about? You're researching birds?"

David laughed again and shook his head. "Well, no, not exactly. Though it'll be helpful to learn something about the natural history of Cape Cod."

"Wim's sure the right one for that," Tammy asserted. "She knows every bird's nest, every fox den, every otter run and deer trail around."

"The book is actually more of a mystery story—"

"That's it, then," said Evelyn as she turned and propelled Wim ahead of her toward the barn. "If it's a mystery, Tam'll be asking him questions all afternoon. She's nuts about mysteries. You'll have to get him away from her."

The roaring was still in her ears as they got the horses ready. "You're awfully quiet," Evelyn remarked at last. "Don't you want to go?" It was an innocent-sounding question, but Wim caught a smug glint in Evelyn's eye and refused to answer. "It's only an excuse, you know. About seeing birds," Evelyn continued blandly. "He just wants to spend time with you."

Wim frowned, acutely embarrassed, and pulled Sassy's girth-strap tight in silence. Evelyn chuckled. "Yep," she said, unhooking Pat from the cross-ties and slapping the mare's rump to move her over. "You don't have to be a rocket scientist to figure *that* out." And she led the two horses into the yard.

David rode tight and hunched, as though he expected the

horse to buck at any moment. *Like he's riding a half-wild pony,* Wim thought, and imagined a brown, barefoot boy on a shaggy pony plunging through salt spray and waves on a faraway shore. Ahead of her on the narrow trail, David looked back and smiled, and her stomach flip-flopped. He slowed Pat until Sassy crowded up on the mare's hindquarters, and Wim reined her horse sharply to the side to avoid having her leg brush against David's. "What do you want to see?" she asked, guarded.

He waved his hand in an encompassing gesture. "Anything you want to show me. It's all new," he said.

Suddenly she hated how calm he always was, how easy he was around her, when a look alone from him could unsettle her. She wanted to cry out, *Where have you been? Why did you take that walk with me and then avoid me! What do you want from me?* Instead, she dug her heels into Sassy's sides and galloped ahead without waiting to see if David was following. She chose the trail that would lead through a pine woods past a boggy pond and into the uplands. It had long, straight stretches where the horses could run. She urged Sassy on and thought fiercely, *Let him keep up!*

He did. He rode aggressively, and when the trail widened briefly, he pushed past her at a gallop, flashing her a look she could not read. Finally he drew up where the trail dipped toward the road and waited for her. He was breathing hard, his face flushed. "Feel better?" he asked her.

She was shocked by the roughness of his voice and couldn't meet his eyes. "I don't know what I feel," she mumbled.

He looked immediately abashed. "Oh, *hine.* I know. I'm sorry."

"It's not your fault."

"I think it is," he said slowly, but he did not elaborate. The horses shook their heads, mobbed by flies. "How far is it to the sea?" David asked.

Subdued, she took him across the road and traversed a patch of low dunes broken by spikey grass, bogs, and thickets of stunted pines that had grown no higher than the horses' bellies. The horses picked their way slowly, and for a while neither Wim nor David spoke. She was afraid to look at him, and she wished desperately that he would talk to her about what had just happened. But he only asked, "Where are you taking me? It's beginning to look like another world." His voice was light, purposefully breaking the mood.

The dunes had become steeper, the trees confined now to the hollows from which white flanks of sand swept up into sculpted crests against the blue sky. "I want to show you the beach down from Race Point," she said. "I love it there. It's like another planet, or the moon or something. The sky feels bigger." She glanced at him momentarily, still self-conscious.

"There's a place at home that feels like that," he answered. "It's called Ninety Mile Beach. It's way north of where I grew up in Pukemoana. I used to dream about it—all that endless sand and sky and sea." It seemed to Wim that David's smile was faintly sad. "When I was a boy, I dreamt of running away to live there. All I'd take was my horse, and a blanket to sleep in, and a pot to cook in. I'd fish, live on food from the sea . . . what we call *kai moana*. That's when I first began thinking about how Maori lived before the *Pakeha* came . . . in the days when Maori remembered all the old stories and knew all the pathways through the stars." He closed his eyes a moment. "I'd imagine that sky over me, and imagine making my way by the stars, and how I'd be all alone — "

"*Yes,*" she breathed.

He glanced at her, almost shyly. "I still dream of running away there. Silly of me, eh," he said softly.

She said, "It's not silly. I don't think it's running away, either — wanting to be alone sometimes. It's just . . . it's just part of being alive."

The horses had been laboring side by side up the rise of a dune, and at the top, in the rippling dune grass, they stood with the offshore wind full in their faces and the Atlantic breakers filling the air with spray. In accord, without hesitation, David and Wim gave the horses their heads and they plunged down the slope and onto the hard-packed sand of the beach. This time they galloped together, racing along the edge of the foaming, broken waves. David urged his horse deeper in, and they leaped into the waves with reckless joy. Head thrown back, sun shining on his face, water streaming off him, his laughter spinning behind him in the wind — Wim watched David in envy and amazement. She could not take her eyes off him. How could he abandon himself so willingly to joy? But joy was bursting through her as well, unfamiliar and terrifying; she clenched her teeth, tried to pull Sassy in. Then David was beside her, laughing, and in mid-gallop he reached out to touch her hands on the reins. "Let her go!" he cried. "Let her go!"

And it was impossible not to. Joy rose in her, wave after wave rising and crashing and spreading through her until she could not tell if she was crying out with laughter or in pain. She was soaked with spray, her hair whipped across her face so she could not see, the wind roared in her ears. A sharp ache was digging so hard into her chest she struggled to breathe, and she gasped, "Wait! Wait! I have to stop!"

David pulled his horse around in a wide circle and trotted back. With the sun behind him and his eyes burning with excitement, he seemed charged with an electrical energy as vital as light itself. Even before he took her hand, she could feel the force of it. They stared at one another. Only when her horse danced beneath her did she pull her hand free, and David whispered, "Thank you."

"For what?" she muttered.

He threw his head back as if to drink the wind. "For bringing me here. For giving me this. Oh, Wim, you have no idea!"

She felt, suddenly, the weight of a whole history she knew nothing about, and for a brief, bewildering moment, she saw only a stranger beside her. She turned and rode down the beach. When they reached the estuary, she tethered both horses and led the way on foot along the creek into the salt marshes. And even though it was David who followed *her,* Wim felt all along that it was the stranger who was leading her someplace she had never been. And even though she pointed out an osprey's nest and showed David the mud flats where the red-legged oyster-catchers hunted, she felt sure every moment that this stranger would show *her* something she had never before imagined. By now the sun hung low over the marsh, melting the grasses to gold. The wind had died to intermittent gusts. She and David were sitting side by side on a sand bank, and beyond them, the great blue herons stalked the shallows.

David seemed content not to speak. He had been watching the herons intently for a long time, one hand shading his eyes. Wim drew a spiraling line in the sand with her finger, looping farther and farther outward from a center mark. "Don't you have blue herons at home?" she asked finally, trying to sound calm and conversational.

He didn't turn but answered, "Not nearly this large."

She had extended the spiral to the limit of where she could reach and stopped, leaving the line incomplete. "I don't know if I'll ever see the white heron again," she said in a low voice. "I think it just got blown up here in a storm by accident. I've never heard of anyone seeing one on the Cape. It came from Florida."

Like Aunt Kia, she realized with a start. *Don't expect magic twice in the same place.* She glanced at David from the corner of her eye. He had not responded and was still gazing out at the hunting birds. A little desperately, she said, "When it's hot like this, a lot of birds go out to the islands. That's why there aren't many around. But you could get some good bird guides at the visitor's center. For your research, I mean. There's probably more in them than I could show you."

David lowered his hand and turned toward her. "This is just fine," he said quietly. He began to draw a spiral in the sand to meet up with hers. She watched spellbound as his finger moved in a perfect curve to connect the two patterns. "Wim," he said. "What is troubling you?"

She opened her mouth to say "Nothing," but burst out, "I don't *know!* I feel like I don't know *any*thing anymore."

He smiled ruefully. "Well, join the club."

She focused on the spiral pattern, took a deep breath. "I was fine before, you know. Then all these people came—Aunt Kia, and you, and—I don't know. Everything feels connected somehow, but when I try to figure out how, my mind just gets muddled. I feel like I'm supposed to *know* something, but I don't know *what*. So I just work all the time at the barn, and I'm really tired—" She expelled her breath and cried, "I just want this summer to be the way I thought it would be, before everyone came."

"Yeah—life does have a way of dragging you in, doesn't it, whether you want to go or not," David nodded.

"I *don't* want to go," she said vehemently.

David laughed. "Sure you do," he said. "You wouldn't have all these questions otherwise. Questions take courage."

"I don't have courage."

He reached for her hand. She jumped, but he held her hand between both of his firmly. "You have more courage than you think," he said.

"I don't," she whispered. "Really. I'm afraid of everything. I don't ever want to leave the Cape. I don't want to do anything different. I just want to stay here with my dogs and the horses. I'm afraid of *everything*."

"Of me?"

"Especially of you," she whispered.

He sat for a while, head bowed, cradling her hand as if it were an egg he'd found rolled from the nest and he was warming it into life. She waited for him to ask why. Because you look like *him*, she would answer. Because you have claimed my family for *yourself*, when I don't know how to claim them for *myself.* But instead she spoke the words that were brimming over in her eyes. "Because I like you so much and you're going to leave."

He pressed her hand to his cheek and said nothing.

Into their silence, the great white heron came flying from the west, sailing toward them on slow wingbeats over the golden marsh grass. At first, silhouetted as it was against the setting sun, Wim thought it was another blue heron coming to join the ones already there. But when it banked to land, dropping its long legs and lifting its wings, the heron's plumage caught the light and burst into white flame.

David caught his breath. *"Haeremai, haeremai,"* he called softly. *"Haeremai, te kotuku rerenga tuarangi.* Welcome! Welcome, *kotuku."*

The white heron seemed to arrive as a gift, binding them with a rare magic so palpable Wim cried, "Oh!" full of wonder. David's hands tightened around hers. They watched together as the heron fished the tidal creek until it grew dark. Still the bird's plumage glowed with the remembered light.

The ride back at twilight was not difficult; she took the shortcut, and the sand trails showed clearly in the dark woods, but it required enough concentration that they did not speak. In the barn, though, as they brushed the horses down before putting them in the stalls, David's silence seemed to have a tension that had not been there before. Now it was he who seemed troubled, and Wim asked cautiously, "Are you worried that Tangi will be wondering where you are?"

"She won't care a fig where I am, but she'll swear a bloody blue streak at me for being so late." He grunted as he heaved the saddle over the rack. She did not follow him from the barn. He hesitated in the doorway. "What shall I tell your mother?" he asked.

She stared at him, stung. "My mother? You don't have to tell my mother anything. I'm not a child. I often stay here."

"Right, then," he said abruptly and went to the car. He gave her the briefest wave and drove off without saying goodbye. She was left standing alone in the dark barn.

The lights were on in the house. Supper would be kept warm in the oven for her. Tammy and Evelyn would be sprawled in the living room, cats on their laps; Sue would be curled on the sofa and Bart would be sniffing for crumbs among the newspapers and books and dirty supper plates that cluttered the floor. She longed suddenly for their simple company, for the easy comfort of their home, and for the lingering, unacknowledged presence of Jilly. She didn't understand why it seemed so unattainable now.

Instead she went into the office and sat on the sofa in the dark, bewildered. In a moment, there was a hesitant nudge against her hand. "Oh Angelo, Angelo," she murmured. She stroked his head and he crawled up beside her, his body pressing against hers.

"Hey, kiddo." Evelyn stood in the doorway. "You fall asleep sitting up?" She came in and plunked herself next to Angelo, slapping him affectionately. "This mangy mutt of yours refused to leave the office all afternoon. Couldn't move without tripping over him," she said. When Wim did not reply, Evelyn leaned back on the cushions, arms behind her head. "Wow. You sure got it bad, don't you?" she asked.

"Got what?" Wim asked warily. She could not make out Evelyn's expression in the darkness.

"Love. You got love bad. Do you think I'm blind?" Evelyn peered at Wim suspiciously. "Are you crying, Wimmie?"

"Don't call me Wimmie!"

"Oh, good Lord," Evelyn said. "You think I don't know what's going on? I couldn't do anything *but* cry for weeks after I met Tam. I was hopeless."

Despite herself Wim asked, "Why?"

"Same reason you're crying," chuckled Evelyn. "Couldn't stand the feelings. Too intense. Didn't know if she loved me. Didn't know how to tell her I loved her." She shook her head. "Yep. Love is just *impossible*."

"But it wasn't impossible for you and Tammy."

Evelyn twirled a piece of hay between thumb and forefinger. "Sure it was. Took me ten years before I got up enough courage to tell her I loved her, and she never knew in all that time."

Wim jumped up and slapped the dust and hay from her jeans. "I don't know what you're talking about," she said shortly. "I'm not in love. How could I fall in love with anyone in such a short time? It's ridiculous."

Evelyn snorted. "Are you kidding? It can happen in an instant. Hits you like a ton of bricks. That's what it feels like, too—bricks. Nothing romantic about it. Painful as hell." She got up and pushed Wim out the door. "Go in the house and eat something. And call your mom—she's been pestering me all afternoon."

A shiver of apprehension ran through her. "Mom's been calling here? She hardly ever—is Aunt Kia—"

"I believe she's just a *little* concerned that her seventeen-year-old daughter spent several hours out alone with an older man she doesn't really know," said Evelyn dryly.

Wim flushed with anger. David must have said something to her mother after all. In the kitchen, slumped over a plate of spaghetti she had no appetite for, she muttered into the phone, "What are you so worried about, Mom? We just went for a ride. What did he tell you, anyway?"

"*He* didn't tell me anything," Carol said. "That's what I don't like. The girl told me. Tangi."

"I'm not a child!"

Carol sighed. "I know you aren't, Wimmie. That's what worries me." She paused. "Why don't you come home tonight? Kia misses you. Dad's found a possible place for her—he'd like you to go look at it with him sometime tomorrow."

Exhaustion overcame her, and she wanted only to end the conversation. "Okay, Mom," Wim said, resigned. But she put off going as long as she could, sitting in the doorway of the barn and staring up at the night sky. She wished fervently that David Te Makara would finish his research in Provincetown and go back to New Zealand. She wished Rose Point Nursing Home would finish building their new wing so Kia could move in and get settled. Then her life would go back to the way she wanted it, without these unfamiliar, unsettled feelings pummeling her, without these incessant questions rummaging around for answers in her head. "I *was* perfectly okay. I was perfectly *fine*," she whispered to herself now with fierce resentment. Before. Before life dragged her in, whether she wanted to go or not.

She wrapped her arms tightly around herself, frightened to discover that she had to concentrate to miss Jilly. But it *was* all she wanted: the barn and the animals, her own familiar solitude, and missing Jilly. She did not want love. She did not want courage. It would only make her dream of more.

Nine ⊙⊙

The harbor lay sluggish and heavy, a low sky pressing all vitality from the water. Wim lay on her bed in her room, gazing at the ceiling. The air was stifling and smelled faintly of rotting seaweed. Nothing stirred. The window curtains hung limp. A restless, edgy lassitude filled her. She rolled off the bed and went to the window. In the yard, the dogs had disappeared under the bushes around the cottage. The cottage itself appeared empty, as if no one had ever been there. The rental car was gone.

"Wim?" her mother called to her up the stairs. "I'm leaving now."

She came down slowly and went into the kitchen, the linoleum sticky under her feet. The only relief in the pervasive grayness of the day was Carol's white uniform. "Kia's still asleep," said her mother. "You'll have to wake her to make sure she gets her meds around eleven. And Sam said he'd call after lunch. Are you sure you're all right with this, Wim?"

"Why wouldn't I be all right? I can manage." Edgy. The coming storm prickling along her skin.

Carol hesitated, fiddling with the top to a Thermos of coffee, obviously wanting to say more. Wim sprawled in a chair at the table and absently traced a spiral design into a patch of spilled sugar. "I'm glad you're home, Wimmie," her mother said finally. "I miss you when you stay at the barn for days like that. But you seem so . . . distant. Are you okay? Even your dad noticed . . . and you know how well *he* pays attention." She was smiling, trying to keep her voice light.

Wim shrugged. "I'm sorry. I'm just . . . I don't know."

Carol sighed. "Maybe I shouldn't go back to work just yet. Should I take another few days off? I don't like the idea of you cooped up here with Kia by yourself. You really should go to Ginny's. Maybe you just need to get away. And I wish those people in the cottage—"

"What's wrong with them!"

Carol twisted the Thermos lid sharply and jammed two apples into her lunch bag. "Don't snap at me, Wim," she said wearily. "I'm going to get snapped at by patients all day long." She paused, pensive. "I didn't mean there was anything wrong with them. I like David—you know that. I just don't know him very well, that's all." She zipped up the bag. "And you're here all day alone."

Wim slammed her chair back from the table. "What does *that* have to do with *him!*" she cried. "Why don't you just get a babysitter for Aunt Kia *and* me, then. Since you don't trust me. Anyway, I thought you wanted me to make new friends. So what's wrong with Tangi?" She meant David and she had an uncomfortable feeling that her mother knew it. She knew she was overreacting. But the storm was building inside her; the thunder tingled up her spine and fluttered over the back of her neck. She slumped in the chair and glared out the window, refusing to meet her mother's troubled eyes.

Carol glanced at the clock, then sat opposite her at the table. "Wim," she said quietly. "Wim, look at me. I do trust you. I also know you. This girl—Tangi. She's a lot like . . . like Jilly." She withstood Wim's furious retort in silence, then continued, "I know you don't want me to mention her name. I haven't mentioned her name for a year. But Tangi—it's the same kind of thing. She'll latch onto you. It's an uneven relationship, Wim. You'll end up taking care of her somehow, just like you took care of Jilly. And David—I don't know. He may be a grown man, but I think it's the same thing. He seems very troubled—"

"I'll go see Ginny, Mom. I'll go." She was so desperate for the conversation to turn away from Jilly, from David, that she blurted out the first thing she could think of. She repeated wildly, "I will. I'll go see Ginny. Okay? That's what you want, right? You want me to meet her boyfriend's daughter? Okay."

Carol gathered her bag and interrupted Wim's rush of words impatiently. "Wim, stop. I don't want you to do it for me," she said. "Go if you want. Ginny would love it. I know it's been difficult for you to . . . to feel close to your sisters." Her mother looked away for a moment, hiding the old hurt, and Wim felt a sullen, unwanted remorse. "But Ginny's making an effort, and I do know she means it. It would be nice if you could, too."

Wim mumbled, "I know, Mom," but by then, Carol had left the kitchen.

The air weighed down on her in the still house, so she found it difficult to make herself move. For a while, she stared out the door at the cottage. Then she went slowly down the hall to the front door and watched the stillness that had settled over the street. Finally she peeked into Kia's room, where the old woman lay in sleep, her mouth open. So flat and motionless did she appear on the mattress, Wim thought for a panicked moment that she had died. But then she heard Kia's faint, uneven breathing.

She leaned against the door frame, feeling as heavy and breathless as the atmosphere. Any possibility of relief had diminished, as Kia had, to nothing. In this torpid oppression before the storm, the mystery she and Kia shared seemed nothing more than an airless hollow within her. Looking in at the old woman, Wim felt an emptiness that sucked everything vital out of them both. Kia seemed already gone, already lost to her. The cottage, too, was hollow, devoid of all its mysterious promise as it would soon be empty of David. And suddenly she knew that their only hope lay in the man with the tattooed face. He connected them all. But how was she to understand anything, if he never spoke and never allowed himself to be touched? If he wasn't even *real?*

Kia stirred. "Charlotte? Charlotte? Is that you?" She spoke weakly, twisting her head toward Wim.

Wim knelt beside the bed. "I'm here, Aunt Kia," she soothed her. "Are you thirsty? Do you want to get up?" She poured a glass of water, tapped the prescribed medication into her hand, held it out.

Stopped. Dropped the pills back into the bottle.

"I don't want to go yet," mumbled Kia. "Charlotte. Am I awake? Are you there?"

"I'm right here," Wim repeated.

Kia's eyes fluttered open. "Did you find it?" she begged. "Don't keep it from me, Charlotte. You didn't give it to *him*, did you?"

Thunder rolled in over the harbor. The first cold gust of wind whined through the screen door. "I didn't find anything, Aunt Kia," said Wim. She lay her hand on the old woman's forehead. The skin was clammy. Kia moaned, "I am so tired. Why can't I move, Charlotte? What will I do? I have to find it . . ."

Wim threw the bottle of pills savagely across the room. It clattered against the wall and rolled under the dresser. "I'm going to help you," she whispered. "I promise, Aunt Kia. I promise. I'll help you find what you're looking for."

"But I'm so tired . . ."

"I know. Just sleep a little more. I'll be here when you wake up."

Even before she finished speaking, Kia's head lolled to the side, her eyes rolled up, and she relaxed once more into sleep. Wim pulled a light blanket over her, shut the windows against the coming rain, and went quietly out, closing the door behind her.

The storm rushed across the water. The wind shredded the rose bushes, scattering the yard with leaves and pale, broken blooms. On the beach, sand whirled up in miniature tornadoes and the wispy dune grass flattened. Above the wind, Wim heard a loud crash. She went to the kitchen and looked out. The door of the cottage had come unlatched and was banging violently. She hesitated, feeling the first spit of rain sting her face as she stood at the open window. The door swung open and crashed shut again. The storm swept in on a phalanx of thunder and lightning, churning the harbor to foam, and Wim dashed across the yard and inside the cottage just as the rain sluiced down.

She had always been afraid of storms, and ashamed of exposing that fear before her sisters' exuberant delight. They would rush out to dance, red-haired and bright, in the howling rain, while Wim would stalk away with what dignity she could feign to the shelter of her room. Now she stood unnerved, her back pressed against the closed door. Lightning lit the room a ghostly silver for an instant, then she was in darkness again, tensed for the next onslaught. She couldn't remember where the light switches were; she had never become familiar enough with this place. Suddenly angry with herself, she stepped forward abruptly and stumbled over a pile of books, falling to her knees. Lightning flashed again.

The man with the tattooed face stared fiercely up at her. She gasped. The room went dark. Another flash, and he was still there, his black eyes burning as though the electricity emanated directly from them. She reached out, groped blindly around on the floor. Grasped a book. When lightning split the darkness again, she saw that she was holding him in her hand.

Clasping the book against her, she scrambled desperately across to David's cot and ran her hand over the wall beside it until she found a light switch. The bulb flickered with each flash of lightning. She sat on the cot for several minutes without daring to move, her heart drumming against the cover of the book. Then slowly, she lowered it to her lap. The man with the tattooed face met her eyes from the glossy book jacket.

She studied the picture for a long time, until her heartbeat slowed and her breathing had calmed. This was not the same man she had seen all her life—she realized that almost at once. This man was much older, his expression more worldly and challenging, not yearning at all. The mouth was similar, though—wide and full-lipped above a strong chin—and the hair was much the same, thick and black, pulled back tightly in a high knot. Three white feathers were stuck into the knot. Around his neck hung a pendant in the shape of a grotesque, contorted figure with a huge head and round, staring eyes. Wim tilted the book toward the light. The pendant was green, a mottled, polished green. *Green stone,* she thought. She peered closer, but she could see no dark spot in the carved figure that might be perceived as a heart.

She held the book on her lap with both hands. This was not her tattooed man. This was almost certainly not Kia's green stone necklace. She frowned, ran her fingers tentatively over the picture, traced the dark parallel lines that spiraled over the contour of the man's face in a beautiful, intricate pattern. For the first time, she read the book's title. *Days of Revolt: Hone Heke in the Bay of Islands 1845–1846.* And the author: David Te Makara.

It was not the draft coming in under the cottage door that pricked the skin on Wim's arms into tiny bumps. She swallowed hard. Her hands froze around the book. At the next strike of lightning she flinched, blinded. A sudden blast of wet wind made her shiver. When her eyes focused again, David Te Makara stood in the open doorway.

When her sisters had caught her in the cottage, it had been hurt and humiliation; this was terror. She dropped the book. But David only grinned cheerfully at her, shaking water from his jacket as he came in and saying, "You gave me a fright, eh." He pulled some papers from his pack and piled them messily on the desk. "You missed Tangi again. I made her stay at the library to copy stuff for me." He shook his head and chuckled. "I guess she's right—I do overwork her. Well, it ought to straighten her out."

The book lay face down on the floor near her. She would have to step over it to get to the door, an almost insurmountable obstacle. David turned from the desk and Wim scrambled off the cot. He gave her a quizzical, penetrating look. "I have to go," Wim mumbled.

"You don't have to. You can stay, if you want. Weren't you reading? I don't mind the company while I work," David said. Again she caught the question in his eyes, but he spoke casually, adding, "You'll just get soaked if you go now."

"I can change." She sidled past him. "Aunt Kia's going to wake up any minute, anyway. I really have to go."

He opened the door for her and for a moment, as she hesitated, they stood very close. The rain still lashed the yard, although the thunder sounded more distant. "Here. Take my slicker," he insisted, and before she could protest, he wrapped it around her. It was still warm from his body.

She knew he stayed in the doorway watching her as she ran across the slippery grass, but she did not look back. In the house she took his jacket off immediately. Her stomach was so tense it hurt. *Who are you? Why are you here?* she cried silently. The image of the tattooed man on the book cover burned in her mind's eye. She felt as if the most private, secret part of herself had been breached.

He is real! She fought the impulse to run to her room and hide. *He is real!* It took her breath away. Had she not believed it before? But before, he had come to her out of the world of her solitude, hers alone. She stood in the kitchen, the storm battering against the house, and felt profoundly exposed. Betrayed. She went into the hallway, called softly, "Aunt Kia? Aunt Kia? Are you awake?"

She had been too afraid to question the old woman before; now she was so afraid, she had to. Kia knew something. The old woman had recognized David as Wim had. And more— *"Some kuia have the Sight,"* Tangi had said. Wim needed to know what Kia saw. She went quickly down the hall and pushed the door open.

Kia was gone.

The storm had only just begun to abate. In panic, Wim felt the bed sheets. Cold. She thrust open the front door and screamed into the street, "Aunt Kia! Aunt Kia! Where are you!" knowing it was useless. She ran back to the kitchen and grabbed at the phone, dropping it in her frantic haste. Hands shaking, she called Sam at the Provincetown store. But he had just left for the store in Hyannis. She left a garbled message with the clerks.

She called Carol at the medical center next, but her mother was assisting with an emergency and could not be reached. "Tell her . . . tell her to call Pete at the police station," Wim said. "I don't know where I'll be—tell her I have to go look for

Aunt Kia." She hung up, feeling sick. When she got Pete on the phone, she could barely speak.

"Come on now, Wim. Calm down," Pete said, all business, no hint of joking. "Get hold of yourself. Okay? Now. How long do you think she's been out there?"

She couldn't think. With David, time disappeared. "Maybe an hour. I don't know. Maybe longer."

"Wim, look—we'll find her. We always do, right? Just calm down. Do you have any idea where she might have gone this time?"

She whispered, "She keeps talking about the sea. She wants to go to the sea."

She was still clutching the phone, numb, when David came to the door, looked at her, and came in. He took the receiver from her hand and spoke briefly, listened, spoke again and hung up. "He said you should wait by the phone and he'd—" he began.

She cried wildly, "No! No! I have to go look for her!"

She stumbled back, tripping over a chair, and David reached for her.

"Wim. Wim—" But she pushed him away, crying so hard she could not catch her breath.

"*Hine, hine,*" David said, distressed. "Wim. Wim—come on, eh. Listen to me. *Kia kaha.* Don't give up—it's not time to cry yet. They'll find her. Come on."

His voice, compelling and soft, wrapped around her and pulled her into its warmth. Then his arms were holding her, too, and he was speaking quietly in words she only half understood, his mouth against her hair. She felt his heart beating against her cheek, felt his voice as if it was coming from the same place, steady and warm. Gradually she found her own strength and he sensed it immediately, holding her by both arms away from him so he could look at her. "Okay, *hine?*" he asked.

She nodded and gulped.

He smiled. "So let's go," he said. "Let's go look for her."

"But you don't have to—"

He said seriously, "Of course I do."

The helpless feeling threatened to undermine her again as soon as David pulled his car out onto Commercial Street and she stared blindly out the window. This was the way she always set out looking for Kia. Down the street, past the marsh, out toward the dunes. But today, the rain sluiced over the windshield so she couldn't see more than a few feet ahead. No people were out on the road. The wind careening across the harbor had flattened the grasses in the salt marsh to beaten pewter. There were no birds anywhere. No herons wading in the shallows, no kingfishers perched on telephone wires along the road, no sandpipers flitting along the narrow sandbars. Even the ever-wheeling gulls had sought cover, and the sky was empty of all but the ragged clouds.

"She's gone someplace to hide," said Wim suddenly. She sat foward and clutched the dashboard. "The barn," she gasped. "Maybe she went to the barn."

Evelyn came running out in the rain as they came up the drive, calling to them even before they got out of the car. She was soaked, her face and clothing streaked with mud. "The Kid—it's the Kid," she said rapidly, glancing once at David and then back to Wim. "She's here, Wim—your aunt. And the Kid's out. She must have let him out, and he won't let me near, and . . . look, I was just going in to call Joe Blair—" Without continuing, Evelyn turned and ran back toward the house.

Wim cried after her, "But where is she! Ev!"

Evelyn gestured toward the woods and Wim dashed across the yard and around the corner of the barn. The Kid's corral was empty, the gate open. She looked around wildly. His hoofprints showed up clearly in the wet sand, leading down the trail that curved away through the pines. Beyond the trailhead, almost invisible among the rain-darkened trees, she could just make out a gray shadow and below it a motionless lump on the ground. Wim stopped, paralyzed. "Aunt Kia?" she whispered. She hardly heard her own voice. She could not make herself move closer. But David came up beside her. "He hasn't hurt her," he said in a low voice without hesitation. "Tangi said the horse is your aunt's *kaitiaki*—her guardian."

He will help her find what she is looking for. Wim closed her eyes a moment, tried to feel the Kid, tried to listen for his presence within her. The rain had died to a fine mist. The wind brought the smell of the sea. She took a deep breath. Suddenly, she heard the Kid's shrill, furious cry cut through the last shreds of the storm. She opened her eyes and saw Tammy advancing along the edge of the trees, a coiled rope in her hands.

"No! No, don't!" cried Wim, but the Kid had already burst from the woods squealing with rage and was rearing over Tammy. His front hooves flailed the air and Tammy jumped back, fell, tried to roll away. The Kid swung his hindquarters around. By then, David had reached them.

He stepped up close to the horse and without hesitation put his hand on his neck. The Kid wheeled instantly to face him.

Wim whispered, "David. David," and the word came out like a prayer. David had not moved. His hand was steady on the Kid's neck. The horse flung his head wildly up and down, his entire body shuddering violently, but he did not lash out.

David spoke to him in the same gentle voice he had used to calm Wim, sometimes in Maori, sometimes in English, the continuous words forming a soothing chant. The Kid danced and shivered under his touch, but David's hand never left his neck. "Ah, that's it—*whakatata mai.* Come on, come on, *e kaitiaki,*" David crooned. "*He aha te mate,* eh? Can you tell me? That's right. I'm listening. Tell me what is wrong. Oh yes, I see. *Ka aroha ra, e tama* . . . you're guarding her, aren't you? Eh? *Ka pai. Ka pai.* You're a good one, eh. Good, *e tama.* But look—we have to work together here. Eh? *Me mahi tahi tatou.* Understand, *e tama?* So move along . . . there. Good. *Ka pai ra,* that's right. There . . . move, now. Good. Shh. Shh. *Ka nui tenei.* That's enough, *e tama.* You've done a good job. We'll help her now."

Slowly, slowly, with words and touch, David was moving the Kid away from where Tammy had fallen, away from the woods and Kia's motionless, huddled form. Suddenly from the yard came the sound of a vehicle roaring up, a door slamming, a shout. A moment later, Wim saw Evelyn and Joe Blair, the Animal Control officer, hurrying toward them. Joe carried a rifle. The horse squealed, enraged again, skittered away from David, and in an instant, Joe was on one knee, rifle aimed.

She didn't think. She flung herself at the Kid and threw her arms around him. "Wim!" bellowed Evelyn. But she clung tighter, hanging desperately from the horse's neck when he reared. Then David was there again, one hand on the horse, the other on her shoulder, crooning in his low chant. The Kid stood still. Wim cried in a frantic sob, "Make him go away! Make him go!"

David turned without taking his hand from the horse. "He'll let you go to her now," he said softly to Evelyn and Joe Blair, indicating Kia with a gesture of his head. "Don't hurt him. She needs him."

Joe barked, "What're you—crazy?" and sighted along the rifle.

David held Evelyn's eyes. She met them levelly. Then she put her hand on the rifle barrel and pushed it down. "Wait," she told Joe. She looked at Wim. "We need your help, Wimmie," she said softly.

David took his hand from her immediately and she let her arms slide off the Kid's neck. She looked at him once, he nodded, and she turned and walked into the woods. Tammy got up shakily, brushed herself off, and joined her. Wim heard another vehicle drive up in the yard as she and Tammy knelt on either side of Kia.

The old woman did not seem to be unconscious, although she did not move. Her eyes were open. Something flickered in them briefly when Wim spoke to her, but otherwise they were blank and unseeing. She clasped Kia's hand, shocked by how cold it was, and cried in a whisper, "I promised I'd take you, Aunt Kia. I promised. Why didn't you wait for me?" She rubbed the unresponsive hand, almost shaking it until Tammy said softly, "It's okay, Wim. The ambulance is here. Give them some room."

She watched numbly while the paramedics wrapped Kia in blankets and lifted her carefully onto a stretcher. She heard them speak into their radio. "Elderly female. Extreme exposure," said one man. "Yes. Yes. No, no sign of injury." She began to follow them as they carried Kia toward the waiting ambulance, but Tammy held her back. "They won't let you go with them, Wimmie," she said. "You have to stay here. She'll be okay now."

Joe Blair sauntered over, rifle still in his hand. "Geez, Wim," he said. "What the hell happened here? Ev didn't tell me much —just told me to get out here." He looked dubiously through the trees at the Kid, still quivering with rage but standing quiet under David's hand. "That the crazy horse we pulled out of the muck last spring? Cripes, Wim. You should've let me put him down. Kindest thing. You know that. Horse like that's no good to anyone." When Wim did not reply, he shrugged and added, "Well, I hope Ev knows what she's doing. Who's the guy, anyway? One of them new-age horse trainers—whispers stuff in horses' ears?"

She gave him an exhausted smile. "Yeah," she said. "Sort of."

Tammy and Evelyn walked away with Joe toward the yard, but Wim hung back. Everything suddenly was calm. She could hear the steady, soft *drip-drip* of moisture falling from the pines onto the sand. Overhead a gull cried. A wren, hidden deep in the woods, trilled into song. David was no longer talking.

They looked at each other mutely across the churned-up ground. The Kid stood with his head drooping to his knees, only an occasional spasm shaking his body. Wim whispered in agony, "She's going to die. She looked like she was dead."

David left the horse and came to her swiftly. "She was in shock," he said. "People look like that when they're in shock."

She was in the grip of something she could not control. "I

didn't watch her," she said in a strangled voice. "I told Mom I'd be all right with her, but I left her alone, and she ran off, and now she's going to die."

"Wim," David interrupted sharply. "Wim. Don't do this. It's senseless."

It wasn't because she was bold that she reached for him, but because she thought her legs would give out beneath her. He held her, and she wrapped her arms around him and cried fiercely, "I love you. I love you," because she felt she would burst if she did not.

He said nothing, and she felt him tense against her. After a moment she pushed him away. He sighed and muttered, "I'm sorry, Wim. I can't. I don't know what I should do."

"You just think I'm a child!" She spat the words out.

He shook his head emphatically. "Oh no, I don't. That isn't it at all—"

She stalked away toward the corral, intending to get the Kid's feed bucket, intending to fill it with grain in the barn so she could entice the horse back through the gate. Anything to get away from David, to keep from looking at him. She was seething inside, her face hot with shame, and she thought that if she saw him again, if he was still out there near the Kid, she would scream at him. But David was nowhere in sight when she came out of the barn, and to her amazement, the Kid had already entered the corral on his own and was standing, suddenly docile, at the corner where she usually fed him. She could not bear the sight of him, either, and she hung the bucket on the fence and left.

Evelyn found her in the office. "You better get home, Wim,"

she said. "Your mom's waiting for you there. Sam is already at the hospital."

"I want to stay here."

Evelyn gave her a troubled frown and said gruffly, "Well, you can't, kiddo. Your mom's worried sick and I don't blame her. Get going."

To her horror, she realized the only way to get home was with David. She walked stiffly to the car and got in, saying nothing. But as soon as he drove out onto the road, he pulled over to the side and stopped. "This is ridiculous, Wim," he said abruptly. "I can't stand it."

"I'm sorry."

He gave a short laugh. "For what?"

"For making you uncomfortable," she answered briefly, fighting to keep the dignity in her voice.

He asked enigmatically, "Is there something wrong with that?"

"You acted like there was," she muttered.

He looked away from her out the window for several seconds. Cleared his throat. "Wim, you know what I have to say. I know you do. This isn't fair. You're seventeen—"

"I'm almost eighteen." He wasn't looking at her, and she blurted recklessly, "And anyway, what does it matter! Age doesn't have anything to do with . . . with feelings."

He gave her a stricken glance. "I know it doesn't, *hine*. But actions *do* matter. *My* actions matter. I don't think of you as a child, Wim. Believe me. But—"

"But you don't have those kinds of feelings for me," she finished bitterly.

He frowned. "I didn't say that. I didn't say that at all." He gripped the steering wheel and turned to look at her with such intensity she shifted uneasily on her seat. "I'm just trying to explain why I can't *act* on my feelings."

She demanded, "But do you want to?"

"Yes, I want to," he replied, fierce. He started the car and they did not speak until they were less than a block from the house. Then Wim said abruptly, "I want to tell you something." David pulled over and stopped immediately, bowed his head to listen.

She hesitated, unsure how to begin. Finally she said simply, "I see a man with a tattooed face. I've seen him all my life— for as long as I can remember. He just appears. I've never told anyone. Not even Jilly. He wants something from me. At least I think he does. I don't really know. He's just always been there." She paused, bewildered that there seemed, after all, so little more to say. She took a deep breath. "I never imagined anyone else could see him, but I think maybe . . . I think Aunt Kia does. And David—" She had to look at him now. "You look like him. Almost exactly. Except without the tattoo."

He was listening to her with his eyes closed, rapt . . . as though, she thought, he was receiving a blessing. He gave no sign of responding. She studied him. Imagined the dark lines spiraling over his broad cheekbones, slashing tigerlike across his forehead, accentuating the strong line of his nose. She imagined his hair grown long, pulled back in a knot . . .

She watched him now as she spoke. "Today when the storm came, I went to the cottage because the wind was blowing the door open," she said. "I saw the man with the tattooed face on the cover of your book. It wasn't really him, it was just a lot like him." She paused, waiting. A meager evening sun was sifting through the last storm clouds and a pale, clear light washed over David's face. His eyes were still closed, but his cheeks were wet with tears. Wim leaned toward him. "Who is he?" she whispered urgently. "Who is he? You must know!"

But David only said in a soft, fervent voice, "Thank you, thank you, *e kotuku. Tena koe, kotuku.*"

She frowned. "*Kotuku.* You said *kotuku.* What do you mean? What does the man with the tattooed face have to do with the white heron?" When he still did not answer or open his eyes, she grabbed his hand, almost shook him, and demanded, "David! Why did you come here? You didn't just find my father by chance—I know you didn't! You came all the way here on purpose to find him! And why did Aunt Kia act like she knew you? Why won't you *say* anything!"

David sat back. Although he opened his eyes, his face closed down as if he'd shut a door. He pulled his hand away. "I can't answer your questions, Wim," he said stiffly. "I haven't had time to draw any conclusions from my research. That could take months of work." He started the car. "I should have had you home before this. Your mother will be worrying."

Her throat constricted painfully. He drove to the house and parked, still expressionless, and Wim pleaded, "Why are you angry? I just want to know!"

He was silent. She stared at him a moment, unbelieving, then got out of the car without another word. He got out, too, and came quickly around to intercept her. "Please . . . please, *hine*," he said in a low voice. "I'm not angry. I just can't . . . I can't answer you."

Stony-faced, she kept walking. "It doesn't matter," she said without looking at him. Her mother came out of the house and half ran down the steps toward her, smiling with relief. All at once, Wim wanted only her mother's voice, her own home, and she met Carol gratefully. Before going inside, Wim turned to David and said politely, "Thank you for your help with Aunt Kia. I'm sorry you had to take time away from your work." She meant it. After all, his work meant nothing to her. He was a stranger, and in a short time he would be gone from her life forever.

Ten ⊚⊚

K i a developed pneumonia overnight. By morning she had been placed in the intensive care unit at the hospital in Hyannis. Sam told Wim as he gulped down a cup of coffee in the kitchen before he left for the store. His face was haggard from lack of sleep and a thin frown creased his forehead. She could not bear the defeat in his voice; she knew he somehow considered this all his fault. She wanted to shake him into real anger, wanted him to yell at her and accuse her. She said harshly, "Aunt Kia's going to die, isn't she?"

Her mother set her coffee mug down with an impatient thump. "No, she's not going to die from this." She got up and, glancing at her husband, took the bottle of Kia's medication out of a cupboard. "I found this on the floor in her room," she said, holding it out to Wim. "Did she even get her meds yesterday?"

"No!" Wim said defiantly. "I didn't give it to her. She was drugged enough. I can't *stand* that she's all drugged up!" She stared out the window, refusing to acknowledge her father's bewildered gaze, and added with deliberate calm, "I know it's my fault. I didn't give her the meds and I wasn't watching when she woke up."

No one said anything. Sam fiddled with the newspaper, his thin shoulders slumped. With angry shame, Wim thought: *How could Aunt Kia have raised someone who turned out like Dad?* How could someone who had lived since early boyhood around Kia grow up to cast such an uncertain shadow as Sam Thorpe?

"Wim," said Carol at last, "I know you don't want to go up to Ginny's, but under the circumstances I've decided to take you up there myself this evening after work. I think you're trying to deal with too much around here."

Wim's gaze flew involuntarily to the cottage, nestled warmly among the roses in the early morning sun. Just there, across the yard, David was sleeping, his head on the pillow she had pressed to her face. A restless heat rushed through her. "I want to go see Aunt Kia," she said in a low voice.

They both looked at her. "No," said Carol. "Absolutely not. She doesn't need any visitors right now, she needs rest. And she just gets agitated when she talks about you, Wimmie—keeps calling for Charlotte, says you promised to take her somewhere. No. I don't want you seeing Kia for a while."

For a long time after her parents had gone, Wim sat on the back steps staring blindly out at the harbor. The dogs lay patiently near her. Lethargy crept over her again like a fog, bringing a loneliness that seeped with gray breath into the marrow of her bones. Even when the cottage door opened, she hardly raised her eyes, and when David and Tangi came out, she imagined she was no more visible than vapor. Certainly Tangi did not seem to notice her, but ran barefoot across the grass, leaned on the gate, and called back, "Whoo-ee! Choice day, eh, Uncle David! Smells like at Nana's, the sea and all. Makes me homesick."

But David walked directly to Wim, fending off the boisterous attention of the dogs. *"Ki'ora,"* he greeted her. "How's *Kui Kia?"*

She didn't answer, just shrugged and looked away. She didn't even care enough to call off the dogs. Tangi joined them. "Sorry about your auntie," she said, her voice uncharacteristically kind. "We say prayers for her."

With a momentary stir of surprise, she managed, "Thanks."

David said, in his curiously formal manner, "Please give her our greetings and our love when you visit her in hospital."

"I'm not visiting her," Wim answered.

Tangi stared at her with incredulous disapproval. "What do you mean, you're not visiting her?" she demanded. "You *have* to visit her. You're her family."

Wim shrugged again. "She'd only be upset if she saw me. Anyway, my mom told me I couldn't go."

Tangi began a furious protest but David silenced her with a gesture, his thoughtful eyes never leaving Wim. She got up abruptly. "I have to get to the barn," she said. "I'm going to Boston to stay at my sister's, and I have a lot to do before I leave."

She had already opened the door when Tangi called after her, "You can't go to *Boston!* Your auntie's sick in *hospital!* She needs you!"

David's quiet voice had the force of a slap. "Hush up." Tangi spun away across the grass. To Wim, David said more gently, "Come for a walk with me. There's a lot to talk about."

"There's nothing to talk about," said Wim.

David smiled, the private, warm smile that caressed her like his breath against her skin. "Oh, there is," he murmured. "Come on, Wim. Look—your wolf pack is restless. They need a good run, eh. We'll take them on the beach."

She was hardly conscious of following him until she found herself at the gate with Tangi blocking the way. "I'm coming, too," the girl said stubbornly. An inscrutable glance passed between her and David, but he did not forbid her.

They didn't walk far. Wim sat, suddenly exhausted, and lay her head on her drawn-up knees. David squatted near her, idly sifting sand through his fingers. After a moment, Wim whispered, "I don't know what's wrong. I feel sick."

"'Cause you know your auntie needs you," Tangi said smugly.

David glared at his niece. "Go away now and be quiet, if you can't speak with *aroha.*"

The Maori word struck Wim as funny. *Aroha.* It could mean anything. She tried to swallow her laugh, feeling a little hysterical. But David grinned. *"Aue,* that's good, *hine.* A laugh is good."

Blood seemed to flow again through her limbs. The numbness dissolved, like fog melting under the sun. "I don't want to go to Boston. I want to see Aunt Kia," she whispered.

"I know, *hine.*"

Tangi muttered, a wary eye on her uncle, "If it was my Nana, I'd go to that hospital and take her straight out of there without a by-your-leave, eh. Throw some gear in the ute, enough *kai* to eat for a few weeks, and off we'd go on the open road. You wouldn't *see* us for the dust!"

"I can't even look after her properly at home, let alone on the open road," said Wim bitterly.

Tangi cocked her head. "Don't you know your auntie doesn't *want* to be looked after?" she asked. She glanced again at David, but her uncle did not stop or correct her, just listened with his head bowed. The girl continued, "Don't you see, eh? I told you before: There's something important she needs to do. And she needs your help. You're like her *mokopuna*, her grandchild. You *have* to help her." She knelt next to Wim, intent. "My Nana could explain it, eh. Couldn't she, Uncle David? She'd tell you that *Kui* Kia's not afraid of dying. She's afraid of . . . of . . . ." The girl hesitated.

"Of not being able to complete her story," finished David softly.

Wim was silent. David got up and wandered down to the edge of the water, and although it appeared casual, there seemed something deliberate in his leaving her alone with Tangi. The girl sat back on her heels, arms crossed, watching Wim. "You still feeling crook?" she asked bluntly. Wim shook her head. After a moment, Tangi demanded, "You follow the rules, don't you?"

"Follow the rules?"

"Yeah. You know. You do what your mum and dad tell you to do. You like it safe, eh. Quiet." She paused, reflective. "Bet your auntie wasn't like that. Bet she wasn't much on playing it safe. You can feel it—nothing much quiet about *her*, eh."

Again Wim did not reply. She glanced at David wandering along the beach. It bothered her tremendously that he might think of her as "safe and quiet." She felt an inexplicable tugging within her and frowned, watching him; why had he suddenly relinquished control of the girl, leaving her to say whatever she wished? And then Tangi leaned close, giving her no room to think further. "Uncle David says you have the most penetrating eyes of anyone he's ever known," the girl said. "He says you only need courage to claim your power. He says the world needs your sight. He said you're like your auntie, and that she had the same power, but she never—"

"I'm not like Aunt Kia," Wim contradicted, her mouth dry. "I'm not anything like her. She's incredible. She's—"

"Of course. She's a *kuia*—an elder. She has *mana*," said Tangi impatiently. "That's why we need to listen to the elders. They teach us." She grimaced. "That's what my mates can't get into their thick skulls, eh. They think all the old Maori stuff is a load of rubbish—a waste of time. But they're idiots, the lot of them. If they knew my Nana—"

She half listened, watching David again. He had kept his back to them the whole time, walking slowly, stooping every once in a while to pick up a shell or pebble from the sand, contemplate it, drop it. But there was a strange, persuasive eloquence to his movements, as if he were choreographing something she couldn't quite see, and she was both curious and uneasy.

". . . and my Nana says that's what comes of living in two worlds—it screws him up. But *I* think it was that *Pakeha* loser he married—" Tangi paused in her monologue and grinned mischievously at Wim. "Hey! *You* should marry Uncle David! My Nana would love you, eh! Yeah, you even *look* Maori—"

Wim's attention jerked back to the girl. "That is totally ridiculous," she snapped.

"No, it's not," Tangi insisted with enthusiasm. "Don't you see him looking at you? He's absolutely *rapt*. It doesn't matter that he's old. My Nana married PopPop when she was sixteen, an' he was twenty years older than her, and she said that made them even 'cause men take so bloody long to grow up, and she said—"

"I don't want to hear what she said!" Wim burst out. "Don't you ever shut up?" David was walking back toward them. Wim scrambled to her feet. "I'm going to see Aunt Kia," she said fiercely.

"I'm going with you," announced Tangi. "I want to tell you more about—"

"Okay. Okay," said Wim, frantic. Anything to shut the girl up. She glanced swiftly at David, afraid she would see triumph in his eyes. But he was just nodding, solemnly thoughtful.

"Please convey my greetings to her," he said again, and followed her back across the beach to the gate.

She half wished the truck would stall as it had the day before, but it started up immediately with several loud backfires. Tangi giggled. "How do you get a warrant of fitness on this thing?" she asked.

Wim shrugged and pulled out onto the street. "Evelyn manages somehow. She gets it through inspection every year," she said.

"Probably sleeps with the mechanic at the garage," Tangi suggested. "That's what my cousin Hemi did, eh, and he got his warrant of fitness every year, just like that." She grinned at Wim. "'Cept of course, it was a *lady* mechanic at the garage. Boy, was he ticked off when she quit!"

"It would have to be a lady at the garage for Evelyn, too," said Wim dryly. "But Tammy would break a pitchfork over her head if she ever did anything like that."

Tangi hooted with laughter and all at once, surprised, Wim found herself laughing, too. Within moments they were both laughing so hard they had to gasp for breath, giddy, and talking as though they'd known each other forever. As though they were friends. When they got to the hospital they lingered, laughing and talking, until it grew too hot for comfort in the truck. "Let's go in, eh. I'm about to melt," said Tangi.

Wim hesitated. "What if she doesn't want to see me? It really is my fault she's sick—"

"Oh, don't be such a bloody *idiot*," said Tangi.

The only sound in the hushed intensive care wing was the steady *beep-beep* of monitors and the occasional muted buzzer. A nurse at the desk gave Wim an inquiring smile. "Could you come back during visiting hours?" she asked apologetically. "In ICU, it's better to keep disturbances at a minimum."

An uneven tapping came from a glass walled room behind the desk. From her bed, Kia was straining to reach the window with her hand. "Charlotte! Charlotte!" she called. Wim could barely hear her.

"She's already seen us," Wim pleaded with the nurse. "We can't leave now."

Tangi had already slipped around the desk and entered the room. Wim followed. *"Tena koe, e Kui,"* Tangi said softly. "It's good to see you. My uncle sends you his best wishes."

The nurse pushed between them to check the monitor. "Miss Thorpe," she said. "You need to stay calm. You remember what it does to your blood presure. I can only allow your visitors to stay a short time." She gave Tangi and Wim a pointed look and left.

Smiling, Kia reached out toward Wim with both hands. Wim realized with amazement that she'd never noticed how beautiful Kia was. The old woman's dark eyes were a rich, sparkling brown. Her thick hair had been neatly brushed back. "I'm so glad you came, Charlotte," Kia said, taking her hand. "I wasn't sure you would. Sam said he'd asked you not to. He thinks you upset me." She made a little grimace of impatience and said dismissively, "Your father is such a fool."

"Oh, Aunt Kia. He doesn't mean any — "

Kia brushed her protest aside with another flick of her hand. "I know, I know, Charlotte. He's your father. I love him too, you know. I raised him. It's just irritating that he insists on missing the point of everything so completely. He always has." The old woman turned for the first time to acknowledge Tangi. "Te Aniwa," she said, her voice startlingly strong and clear.

Wim and Tangi looked at each other, and Tangi, tentative, asked respectfully, "Why do you call me that name, *e Kui*?"

Kia frowned. "You told me it was your name, girl. Why else would I call you Te Aniwa?"

Tangi fell uncharacteristically silent. Kia stared at her, then clutched at Wim's hand, her eyes becoming troubled. "Charlotte. Charlotte, why did she come here? Did you bring her? Does she want her necklace back?"

Wim sighed. "Tangi is . . . she's my friend, Aunt Kia. She isn't looking for a necklace."

Kia pressed her lips together. "Oh yes she is. The necklace

was hers," she asserted. She glanced at Tangi and added slyly, "It was a very strange necklace. Ugly. Not pretty at all." Then she lay quiet for a moment, her eyes far away. When she spoke again, her voice dropped to a whisper. "I didn't mean to lose it. You know that, don't you, Charlotte? I told you. I was only a little girl, and I was playing, and I threw it up to see the way the light shined on it—" Kia's hand tightened and loosened convulsively around Wim's and her head twisted back and forth on the pillow. Wim glanced through the glass at the nurse and Tangi moved swiftly to block the line of vision from the desk to the room.

"Who gave you the necklace, *e Kui*?" Tangi asked.

Kia said grumpily, "I told you. I told you. *Grampy* gave it to me. He said I looked like her. Don't you listen, either?"

"But who? *Who* did you look like? Whose was it before?"

Frowning at Wim, Kia snapped, "Charlotte, this girl does not pay attention. It was Annie's of course. Grampy's mother, *Annie*. I told you." She sank back, exhausted, and closed her eyes. Wim shot Tangi a worried look, but before she could speak, Kia whispered insistently, "*He* wanted it, you know. The necklace. Oh, yes. *He* tried to take it away from Grampy. He tried to take Grampy away with him, too, when Grampy was a young man. But Grampy wouldn't have anything to do with him and called the police." Kia opened her eyes straight into Wim's. "That's why he comes, Charlotte. That's why he keeps coming. Because the necklace was hers, and he wants it, and he wants to take us far, far away . . ."

Her voice had become so weak Wim had to lean very close. She didn't think Tangi could hear now. The air-conditioned room suddenly felt clammy, and her skin broke into goose bumps. Kia said unexpectedly, "Don't be so afraid, Charlotte. That's very important. No fear. I spent too long being afraid. So did Grampy. It isn't a good way to live your life."

"What were you afraid of?" Wim whispered, although she was afraid to hear the answer.

"*Him*," said Kia simply. "I was always afraid of *him*. He would come, and he would show me things that I . . . I didn't want to see. Because it was just too hard . . . because all I wanted was to be safe, and quiet—"

Wim stepped back. She and Tangi stared at each other. The girl's eyes were very large. Beyond the glass walls, Wim saw the nurse at the desk check her watch, push back her chair—

"Who *is* he, Aunt Kia?" she cried in a low voice. "Who is he?"

Kia opened her eyes abruptly. "Why, he's Grampy's brother, of course," she said. "Who did you think I was talking about?"

The nurse came in. "Excuse me, Miss Thorpe. I need to check your blood pressure, so if you wouldn't mind . . ." She gave Wim and Tangi another pointed look.

Kia rapped her hand against the sheets. "What do they have to leave for!" she demanded crossly. "Stop bossing everyone around. It's no secret what my blood pressure is! It's going to drop out of sight soon enough anyway."

The nurse did not alter her impassive expression, but Wim suppressed a smile and chided, "Aunt Kia, she'll get fired if she doesn't do her job."

Kia looked resigned and held out her thin arm. Faintly sarcastic, the nurse murmured, "Thank you," and wrapped the cuff around it. When she was finished, Kia gave an imperious wave of her hand. "Now go. I'm not done talking with my niece and her friend."

"Miss Thorpe, I—"

"Ten minutes more," said Wim hurriedly. "I promise."

When the nurse left, Kia grunted at Wim, "Your promises aren't worth much, Charlotte."

"What do you mean!" she cried, stung.

Kia turned her head away. "You promised to take me to the sea before I die," she complained. "You did promise, Charlotte. I need to find the necklace."

Wim knelt by the bed so her face was level with the old woman's. "I promised, and I will," she said. "You aren't dying, Aunt Kia. You're getting better." She paused. "Why is it so important to find the necklace? What are you going to do with it?"

Kia looked at her, incredulous. "Why, I'm going to give it to you," she said. "What else? It's too late for *me*, you know. But you have your whole life ahead of you. If you are brave enough, you can give it to him and listen to him and maybe you will even go with him . . ." She turned her head suddenly and gave Tangi a long, level stare. Tangi averted her eyes as always but stood her ground. Kia pointed to her and said to Wim, "That girl—your friend. Don't lose her. She wants to help you."

The old woman dropped her hand on the bed and all at once she appeared small and weak. She closed her eyes again. "I'm tired, Charlotte," she whispered. "Go home. I'm too tired to talk." She coughed, her body arching slightly with each spasm. The nurse hurried in and, without a word, checked the monitor and adjusted the pillows under Kia's head.

"We're going," said Wim softly.

The nurse nodded, preoccupied, her fingers on Kia's thin wrist checking her pulse. "*Ma te Atua koe e tiaki.* God care for you, *e Kui,*" Tangi spoke softly. "*Ka kite ano. Kia kaha* . . . stay strong."

Wim paused in the doorway. Kia seemed so vulnerable and exposed in the glass room, bound to life by flimsy tubes hooked to a machine. She tried to imagine Kia as a young girl, whirling in a dance on the beach, twirling a green stone necklace on a cord around her head to see it flash in the sun . . .

She drove home pensively, and Tangi, for once, seemed content to sit silently beside her. *Grampy's brother?* Wim thought. Grampy had a *brother?* She squinted in the sun's glare and tried to fit together the fragments of information she already knew. Grampy was actually Aunt Kia's *great*-grandfather, Thomas Alexander Thorpe, the only grandchild of Captain Charles Williamson Thorpe. At least, according to her father's stories, Grampy had been an only child and Captain Thorpe's only heir. She struggled to remember everything Sam had told her over the years. As an old man, Grampy had lived with *his* grandson, Kia's father, and his family. When Kia was ten years old Grampy had died, and the Thorpe family moved from Cape Cod to Florida. For years after that, the old Thorpe house, built in 1820 by Captain Thorpe himself, was occupied by a succession of unreliable tenants, until the Historical Society took over its upkeep. Then in 1980, just before Wim was born, Sam Thorpe moved to Provincetown to restore his ancestral home and raise his family there.

She frowned, trying to recall details from the genealogy chart that hung on the wall of Kia's room, the chart that she,

Wim, was missing from. Was someone else missing from it as well? Did Kia's Grampy have a brother? But why would the brother have a face tattooed like the fierce-looking Maori pictured on the cover of David Te Makara's book?

"My name is really Melanie," announced Tangi suddenly.

Wim nearly swerved off the road. "What?"

Tangi drew her knees up and wrapped her arms around them, staring ahead through the windshield. "Yeah. True. I *took* the name Tangi Te Aniwa," the girl continued. "Tangi—it means 'tears' in Maori. The tears of Te Aniwa." She didn't go on right away, and Wim drove around the Orleans traffic circle twice before regaining focus enough to take the correct turn. "Te Aniwa is our ancestor," Tangi said then. "Uncle David discovered her through his research. He told me about her three years ago, when I was twelve—just after I ran away from home for the first time and the police found me. Te Aniwa lived a hundred and fifty years ago. She was captured in a raid and made a slave and then sold . . ." The girl stopped abruptly and seemed to be trying to decide something. Then she shrugged. "Yeah. Happened all the time back then—tribal wars, and whatnot. Maori had slaves, you know. Anyway. Te Aniwa. Uncle David said she never got back to her home or her family. She was on her own, like me. I took her name to honor her. So she'd know she wasn't forgotten. And I took 'Tangi' so her sorrow would not be forgotten, either." Again the girl paused and shrugged. "I just liked the name, eh. I wanted a Maori name. Didn't want a bloody stupid *Pakeha* name," she said with contempt. "My Nana says it's important to acknowledge the ancestors. She says our ancestors are always with us." She laughed a little. "It's more'n my parents ever manage, that's for sure. *They* can't be bothered to be around me for more than a few minutes at a time. Never have."

Wim could find nothing to say. Her mind was whirling like the translucent green stone pendant whirling around Kia's head, flashing green fire in the sunlight, a dark spot like a heart deep inside it. She drove slowly through the busy traffic of Provincetown. When she parked in front of the house, neither Tangi nor she moved for a moment. She felt strangely unwilling to part from the girl. There seemed to be something left unsaid. She glanced involuntarily toward the cottage, and Tangi said softly, "He won't have got back. He's gone to New Bedford again, to the museum. He'll be away hours yet." Then, as if she'd been struggling with a decision, she blurted in a rush, "I wish I had a sister. Someone I could talk to about *anything*."

"I have two sisters," Wim answered. "I can't talk to them about anything at all." She gazed at Tangi, seeing the girl's angular, squared shoulders, the defiant tilt of her head. "Have you ever had . . . a real friend?" she asked in a low voice.

The girl seemed to quiver slightly, the way the Kid quivered when someone got too near. She lifted her chin. "I'm an artist. Artists are always alone," she said.

They got out of the truck and went around to the back yard. The dogs greeted Wim with leaping enthusiasm. Tangi went to the cottage and stopped, holding the door open. "I want to show you something," she said.

She waited while Wim filled the dogs' water bucket from the hose by the cottage. "I'll take you out in a while," Wim murmured to them. "Settle down. Settle down. I'll take you out. I promise."

I promise. She coiled the hose and shoved it back under the rose bush by the cottage wall. *I promise.* The leaves cast a shadowy pattern against the gray shingles. She waited. But there was only light and shadow. No face appeared. Perhaps he would never come again, after all. She could take Kia to the sea, and Kia might even find what she was looking for, and she could give it to Wim—but the man with the tattooed face might have given up on her by now and left her to live her quiet, safe life.

"You coming?" Tangi called, and Wim followed her inside the cottage. The girl had changed into a sleeveless man's undershirt that hung nearly to her knees, and she grinned at Wim's expression. "Yeah, it's Uncle David's vest. Choice, eh. Comfortable, anyway. I'm going to expire in this bloody heat. It's never this hot at home, even way up in Northland." She rummaged around and pulled out another undershirt from a pile of books on David's cot. "Here. You wear one, too. He's got heaps." She dangled it suggestively in front of Wim. "It's real romantic, you know—wearing a bloke's clothes."

Wim blushed and muttered, "Shut up." But they were laughing again, and this time it was easier and came more naturally, and it didn't hurt at all. And she thought in wonder, *I'm in the cottage with a friend.*

"This is what I wanted to show you," Tangi said, and Wim went after her into the small back room where she slept. More of the brilliant, swirling paintings had been tacked to the wall. On the dressertop was a scattered mess of paint brushes, tubes of colors, a glass of water stained deep blue, a pad of drawing paper. From under her cot, Tangi drew out a large piece of cardboard with a sheet of watercolor paper taped to it, covered in newsprint. "It's a surprise for Uncle David," she explained shyly. She propped the cardboard up and flipped back the newsprint. "Think he'll like it?"

Wim was completely unprepared for what she saw. The image swept her up like a wave, taking her breath away. "Oh," she whispered. "It's beautiful. It's so beautiful."

The great white heron seemed to lift free from the paper, long legs barely brushing over the frothing crests of the green water it was soaring across. Through a break in the storm clouds, a single ray of sun struck the bird's white plumage. Light infused the whole painting so it glowed—the bird, the sea, the sky.

Tangi asked anxiously, "You reckon he'll like it? He told me he saw *kotuku* here, when he was with you—"

Kotuku. Kotuku. "He'll love it," Wim breathed. Then, cautious, she asked, *"Kotuku*—it seems to mean something really important to David. More than just . . . good luck. Is it . . . is it . . . ?"

She didn't know what she could ask. There was too much. The white heron, the man with the tattooed face, the old journal, David, Kia. Overwhelmed, Wim turned away and went to the window, staring out through a curtain of roses. "Why is it all such a secret?" she muttered.

But Tangi had already gone into the other room. From the doorway, Wim watched page after page come out of the printer hooked to the laptop on the desk. The girl said, "In Maori, *kotuku* is the name for the white heron, but it also means 'a rare visitor.'" She took the sheaf of pages from the printer and weighed them in her hand, considering something. At last she said, "People like talking to Uncle David. They tell him all kinds of stories, eh. Because he really *listens,* I reckon. Anyway, there's this story he heard—only, you have to understand *Maoritanga* . . . Maori culture—"

"Tell me," said Wim, urgent.

The girl leafed through the pages. "Okay," she said. She put the papers down and unselfconsciously, quite naturally, she stood straighter and held her head higher. Her voice altered almost imperceptibly, gaining a quiet authority that made her seem much older. She spoke with the same unobtrusive formality as her uncle. She began, "As soon as British and American ships started arriving in Aotearoa two hundred years ago, Maori people started disappearing. They died in the thousands from *Pakeha* diseases and many others had their spirit destroyed by *Pakeha* missionaries. Some sailed away, working on *Pakeha* ships. Some married with *Pakeha.* Maori began to lose their land, their fishing rights, their traditional knowledge and even the right to speak their own language. They were tricked and bullied by *Pakeha,* who considered them nothing more than happy children. Even if Maori did not disappear in body, they disappeared in here." The girl tapped her chest. "They lost the connection with their ancestors. They lost their *turangawaewae.* You remember Uncle David telling you about that? What it means?"

"Standing place?"

Tangi nodded. "Maori became exiles in their own land. They no longer had a place to stand. They no longer listened to the voices of their ancestors." She paused, and her eyes gleamed in the afternoon light. "But Maori have always been great fighters. Not everyone got lost. Not everything. There was once this powerful *rangatira*—that's like a leader, except he was bigger than that. He was seen as a prophet. He had such great *mana* people could feel it immediately and he commanded respect wherever he went. He traveled all over Aotearoa talking to Maori and gathering followers. He didn't care what tribe, or who was at war with who, or who was slave or chief. He said all Maori must stand as one people. He talked and talked, and he reminded Maori who they were. He reminded them to observe the old customs of the ancestors because that was the most powerful weapon against *Pakeha* influence." The girl stopped for a moment, seemed to gather herself. Then she continued, "So this *rangatira*, eh—he was called Kotuku. He was such a powerful *tohunga*—a teacher—they say he could change shape and become the white heron, and with his great wings he could cross time and space in an instant, and he would come and go all over Aotearoa and all over the whole world, bringing Maori home to their *turangawaewae*. Because of Kotuku's visions and dreams, people called him *matakite*—a seer."

"What happened to him?" Wim whispered.

Tangi smiled, a sweet, secret smile. "Who knows, eh. Some people say he never died. Some people believe Kotuku still flies across time and space, finding his lost people and showing them the way home."

Wim was silent a moment, strangely excited. "*The Lost People*—that's the name of the book David's working on . . ." She thought about Tangi's little smile. Her heart was beating fast. "Kotuku," she murmured. She looked at Tangi. "He lived at the same time your ancestor lived, didn't he? Te Aniwa? And she was lost, wasn't she? Captured? She's still lost . . . and David's looking for her . . ." Her voice trailed off.

But Tangi's manner had changed dramatically. "It's too bloody hot. I'm going for a swim," she announced. She hesitated, then thrust the sheaf of pages at Wim. "Here. Read this if you want. I just got this bit done yesterday, and I have to finish the rest this week. Uncle David's been on me about it 'cause we're leaving soon." She grabbed a towel, left the cottage, and ran across the yard to the beach.

Reading helped calm Wim, and very quickly, the journal caught her up.

Kororareka, Bay of Islands, New Zealand the Yr. of Our Lord 1835, in February of this Year. We have at last arrived safe and whole to this God-forsaken Land . . .

There was a break, as if some material had been lost, and the journal began again in mid-sentence.

. . . indeed a hell-hole, as I had heard, for the streets are deep to the knee in the foulest Mud and over-run with even fouler Men of every degenerate kind, speaking all manner of Languages. An evil smoke hangs over the huts in this never-ending rain. I do not doubt there is great Richness in this land, as is claimed, for the promise of Trade has lured Men from many lands. In the harbor are anchored to my count 93 ships flying the flags of 5 nations at least. But what Riches attract them is lost on me. I yearn only for my dear home in Massachusetts. Provincetown will have never seemed more truly named than when I set foot on her sweet shore again. I pray the Captain does not tarry in his Trading here, and that we will be leaving soon.

Wim heard Tangi's parting statement echoed in what she read. *"We're leaving soon."* And echo upon echo, Kia's words as well: *"I'll be gone soon enough."* The pages were trembling slightly in her hands and she resisted the urge to skim quickly, searching for a word, a passage, that would connect everything. She forced herself to read carefully.

But I am grateful to have been officially entrust'd with the charge of Willie, for he meets the world as a Child does, with great delight and trust. We are alone much of the time and can do as we please. Capt'n Thorpe spends hours in the filthy Huts where he meets with native Chiefs who desire to purchase his Guns, and Dr Kendall more and more gives in to drinking, for which accommodation he finds no end of Taverns in this unfortunate town. Sometimes he disappears for the Entire day. I fear I will not learn much of the doctoring trade from him . . .

There were several passages of Emmanuel Dart's description of Kororareka; of drunken brawls by riotous sailers; of deserters from whaling ship crews who, when caught, were lashed with whips or shot on sight; of the prostitutes, the thieves, and the charletons who sold quack remedies for every malady known to man—all working the crowded, muddy street, oblivious to the relentless rain and relentless missionaries. Then she caught sight of something and a prickle of excitement ran through her. She read slowly, biting her lip in concentration.

Most amazing are the Natives. The men walk about with great ferocity and tho' they are very Wild and stern of countenance, they are possessed of a most natural Courtesy. Dr Kendall told me these natives are call'd Mowree and they are fond of War and heathen Ceremony, and they take Slaves and the severed heads of their Foes. Daily I see their great carved Canoes, paddled by a dozen men, slipping past our anchored ship. The warriors have dark lines tattooed across their entire face, most horrible and wondrous to see. They show Willie how they open their eyes wide and stick out their tongues to cause Mortal Fright in their enemies. They are attired in the most outlandish manner, mixing hats and trousers of Whalers with the scraps of their own heathen dress woven of matted grass and feathers, and they hang heavy carved Pendants upon their naked chests which they call Greenstone. This all most fascinates Willie, and the Natives have made a Pet of him.

She turned the page. More of Emmanuel Dart's appalled description of the port of Kororareka. She skimmed impatiently now, turned another page.

. . . and certainly above all, this town fosters Sin of every kind and magnitude, so the missionaries find no lack of occupation. The Native women sell whatever they can to the sailors, including the Services of themselves and each other, and are most wanton and Shameless in their approach. But with Willie these women are always kind and motherly, as they are to all the brown children who run naked everywhere. They delight in making him laugh and clap his hands, and so we are entertained every day. There is in particular one Native woman who sells the woven bags of flax they call kitees. *She is ancient and toothless, with tattooes around her mouth and chin, and given easily to loud and intemperate laughter. She sits with the other women on the Wharf where the sailors come and go, but she appears to command much respect among these women and has several female Slaves whose services she sells and who do her*

bidding. There is one such girl, very pretty, and young, in years looking no older than myself, but the Sadness on her face suggests a hard and difficult Life. She is quiet and marvelously obedient of manner. She seems esp. fond of Willie, and when she is not being bid to carry her Mistress's load of flax, she plays with him patiently, tho' without speaking. Willie tells me her name is Teeanniwa.

She stopped reading, shaken. Teeanniwa. *Te Aniwa.* It had to be the same name! Was this David and Tangi's lost ancestor? She took a deep breath and continued.

It is late March, and winter is closing in, and I have heard the Captain talk of setting sail to leave. The Agatha Ann *is taking on timber and flax and skins from the seal hunters in the Southern islands. I am Willie's constant Companion, as Capt'n Thorpe has little time for his son. When the Captain is not trading with the Mowree he is oft in serious conversation with his friend Dr Kendall. Also I have noticed the Captain many times talking with the toothless old woman on the wharf and pretending interest in buying her flax bags. However, it is not bags he looks at, but the girl Teeanniwa, toward whom he directs a most unseemly attention. This poor girl reveals no Feeling of any kind, but does as she is bid without argument or Struggle. It troubles my heart to see her. Oh, I wish our return voyage will soon be underway, for I do not feel easy here at all.*

Wim heard a door slam in the house and looked up with a start. It was after four, and her mother was home. She listened tensely for a moment, clutching the remaining two pages, then read as quickly as she could.

I have made acquaintance with the Rev John Garret, whose

Mission is established here. He is staunch Methodist, with little humor, but he is fond of Willie and gives him Simple tasks to perform such as delivering Tracts to our crew. He metes out generous praise along with little sweet cakes baked by his Wife. Mrs Garret is much concerned by the Native traffic in women, which is a prolific business, for Kororareka is over-run with sailors of every disreputable breed. The Rev Garret tells me that the girl Teeanniwa was captured only shortly ago in a tribal raid, where her husband was killed, and that now she is a Slave. He says her babe was taken from her and given to his Mission by her captors, as this is the way the Mowree try to curry favor with the Americans and British. But Mrs Garret says bitterly that Teeanniwa is worth more to her Mowree captors as a slave whose services they can sell or barter, and no amount of begging on her part will induce them to release the girl to the Mission. Can nothing at all be done? I ask her. Is it not the highest cruelty that a mother's babe be taken from her and the mother left to suffer in slavery? But Rev Garret sighs and says, At least her child will receive the Grace of God and be saved and raised as a civilised Christian soul. But he fears, he tells me, that a girl as comely as Teeanniwa will soon be sold to any man willing to pay the price.

"Wim!" The door of the cottage was pushed open and her mother looked in. Wim hurriedly slipped the pages into the pile on the desk. Carol frowned. "Wim, didn't you hear me calling? What on earth are you doing in here?" she demanded.

"I was just reading—"

"You can't just come in here when you want, Wim. Your father is renting the cottage out," Carol snapped.

"David doesn't mind—"

Again her mother interrupted. "Oh, I'm sure he doesn't mind," she said dryly. "David is very charming, Wim. He has a bit too much charm, as far as I'm concerned. Believe me, I can see how easy it would be to get attached to him." She ignored Wim's furious glare and started out the door just as Tangi, dripping from her swim, came in. Carol did not acknowledge her but added to Wim, "I hope you're ready to go. There are a few things I'd like to talk about before we go to Ginny's."

She left, and Tangi commented, "Whew, she's having kittens. What's her problem? I suppose she doesn't want you hanging around with *me,* eh."

Wim gave her an embarrassed smile. "Actually, it's your uncle she's worried about."

"Oh. Well, yeah. She may have a point, then," said Tangi with a knowing grin, and snapped her towel playfully at Wim.

And they were laughing again. Carol called from the house. Wim sighed. "I have to go," she said. At the door, she turned. "David didn't find my father by chance, did he?" she asked softly. "He came here especially to find him, didn't he?"

Tangi gave a barely discernible nod.

"Can't you tell me why?"

Tangi's eyes were unreadable. "He wants to tell you," she said. "But he's not ready yet."

"Wim!" Carol yelled. Wim jumped.

"Wait, wait," the girl said urgently. She took a step toward Wim, wary suddenly, hungry. "In hospital, when you were talking to your auntie, you told her I was your friend. Did you mean that?"

Wim smiled. "Of course," she said. The girl smiled back. "What does *aroha* mean?" asked Wim.

"*Aroha?* It means 'love.'"

And then it seemed there was nothing more left unsaid.

Eleven ꙮ

Wim sat at the table, too tired to respond to her mother's angry tirade. She felt as scrubbed bare as the pans Carol was scouring in the sink. Strangely fascinated, she watched Carol and wondered why her mother always went into a frenzy of cleaning when she lost her temper. Her mother's words battered at her until she wanted to curl up and close her eyes.

"And I'm tired it. I'm tired of being so *left out* of your life, Wim. I've tried to be patient. I've tried to understand. I know what Jilly meant to you. But we're your *family* and you treat us like we're *nobody*. Me, your sisters, even your father—and then along comes this perfect *stranger*, this *David*—" She spoke the name with vehemence. "There's such a thing as alienation of affection, you know," she continued. "You're so focused on him it's as if we don't even exist. I'm not suggesting this is your fault—I know you're emotionally vulnerable. But he's taking advantage of it. He—"

Wim was adrift in heavy seas. Wave after wave battered over

her and she clutched desperately for something to keep her from drowning. *Jilly. Jilly.* But Jilly had become too insubstantial a twig of memory now to support her, and she felt herself going under in the tide of her mother's words. *David . . . ?* But no. He was too elusive, spinning and rolling in her thoughts; trying to get a hold on David was like trying to hold onto a slippery log in the marsh. *Aunt Kia? The Kid?* But all she could see was an angry, solitary horse pacing back and forth along a fence and an old woman tottering down a dark road.

"You have to start dealing with your life, Wim. You can't hide away forever. You're almost eighteen. You've got a *future* to think about. Jilly's been gone a year. I know it hurts to hear this, but nothing can bring her back," her mother was saying, and the sea whirled Wim with dizzying speed and dropped her into a deep trough. "Wim! Will you at least look at me! Stop staring out at that damned cottage! David's not going to fly out and take you away from all this. You have to deal with it yourself."

Fly. Fly away. The great white heron rose before her, lifted her from the turbulence, and swept her up, up, wings beating as steadily as a heart. She was sailing over golden grasses undulating in the wind, over silvery ribbons of creeks and dunes white and polished as sculpted marble. There was no sound but the soft breathing of air through feathers. She closed her eyes. The white heron brought her to the center of her own solitude and set her gently down. The breathing became her own, the rhythmic wingbeats became the beating of her own heart, and there was solid ground beneath her feet.

"But she's refusing to *go* to Boston," she heard her mother say, and she realized without interest that her father had come into the room. "I can't just drag her there bodily, Sam. Look at her. Don't you see what I mean? I don't think she's even *listening*. She went to see Kia when we asked her not to, she's over in the cottage every time I turn around. She's totally disconnected from us. It was bad enough when she was at the barn all the time. Now—"

"I'm going to bed," said Wim. She got up, walked through her parents' silence, and went up to her room. A strange happiness drifted through her as she lay in the dark warmth, and she fell asleep.

She woke late the next day. The house was quiet. The July sun danced in shimmery heat over the still water of the harbor, and in the yard, the dogs barely stirred from under the bushes to greet her. She filled their water bucket and went to the cottage. She felt no surprise to find the door closed. There was a note tacked on it:

Kia ora, Wim. We have gone to Connecticut for a few days. See you when we get back.

Aroha nui, David and Tangi

She folded the note carefully and put it in her pocket. Then she pushed open the cottage door and went inside. It was stifling hot with the windows closed and the shades drawn. It seemed an unreal memory, as from a dream recalled in fragments, that she'd laughed in this room with Tangi the day before. She looked around. The desk was cleared, the laptop gone, the printer empty of paper. On the floor near the desk were several boxes taped shut. In the dim light she had to squat to read the labels and found herself whispering, claiming a momentary intimacy by speaking the unfamiliar place names aloud. "David Te Makara," she said slowly. "Paturoa Bay. Titirangi. Auckland. New Zealand." She shifted the boxes. "David Te Makara. Private Bag. Department of History. University of Auckland." The boxes had the solid heaviness of books. Suddenly she stood up. The journal . . . where was the journal?

The cot was neatly made. There was no clutter of books and papers on it or on the floor, no clothing draped over the chair, no litter of donut and pizza boxes. She glanced into the back room. Shades drawn. Cot made. Clothing gone. The only thing left on the walls were a few scraps of tape. She turned to go, her breath quickening. But her eye was caught by a gleam and she stopped. Looked back. The white heron seemed to float out of the darkness.

Slivers of green light coming in at the edges of the window shade gave the bird an ethereal look, as if it might dissolve in midflight. Tangi's painting was propped against the wall on top of the dresser. Scattered around it were rolls of packing tape, a pair of scissors, labels, and the marker they'd used to address the boxes in the other room. She stepped closer and stubbed her toe against something. On the floor by the dresser was another cardboard box, closed and addressed but not taped shut. Wim turned on the light and sat on the floor, pulling the box toward her. She knew before she opened it what was inside.

The sheaf of papers was thicker, so she knew Tangi must have printed more of the transcribed journal since yesterday afternoon. She searched through the pages until she found the final entry she'd read the day before. There was a break, and the journal continued.

April 15. Kororareka, Bay of Islands. Willie is very taken with the girl Teeanniwa. He directs me every day to take him to the wharf in the hopes of seeing her. The Captain has forbid me to let Willie go about this rough town alone, so I must give in to all his wishes else he will slip away from my sight. Willie and the girl play as children, altho' it is only Willie who laughs, for the girl never even smiles. Dr Kendall says Teeanniwa must remind Willie of his older sister, who died of the same Smallpox that rendered him simple.

I am more and more troubled by Capt'n Thorpe. He conversed again today with the toothless old woman who is Teeanniwa's mistress, and who I know to be greatly opportunistic of nature and devious of motive. They appear to be haggling, as if over the trade of Goods. Once, she took the girl by the arm and forced her to stand before the Captain, and the Captain looked her over, and all the women on the Wharf laughed uproariously. When he saw that I was nearby, Capt'n Thorpe commenced to strike a bargain with the old woman over the price of her flax bags and went away with five or six. But I know it was a Pretext, for later I observed him toss those bags into the harbor, as tho' they were of no account and he had no interest in them. I am uneasy in my mind, yet there is not a soul I can question about this.

Wim frowned and read the entry over again. Emmanuel Dart's apprehension had affected her now, too. She could feel the questions that had troubled him tossing and turning in her own mind, although she could not quite put them into words. She turned slowly to the next page.

April 24. We have been blessed with good weather for several days, and the crew is busy setting the ship to rights for our departure. The decks are crowded with men loading Goods, mending sails, and tarring the deck. Day and night these men must row continuously from shore to ship with boxes and barrels laden with supplies. The Captain works his men meanly, and they mutter with the weariness of their toil, but they stay clear of his temper, which grows fouler by the day. Yesterday he caused a man to be whipped for complaining of fatigue. Last night from my bunk I overheard the Captain in terrible arguement with Dr Kendall. I could not hear all amidst the constant noise of toil around us, but Dr Kendall raised his voice first and said, It will never work, man! She is sullen, and not Christian. And Capt'n Thorpe rebutted, That is a small matter. She will convert. Then I could hear only unclear voices until the Captain shouted, Why do you always talk of Willie? I will get nothing from Willie! Nothing! Do you not understand? Am I not a man, with a man's Natural needs? What else can I do? You know my wife is barren and keeps me from her bed. How else can I have this girl? It will not harm Willie. And what Christian woman would marry with Willie, I ask you? I will get no other heir otherwise, and everything I have worked for will be lost. Then Dr Kendall replied with great heat, You must accept the will of God, Charles. What you contemplate is a most grievous Sin. But the Captain roared at him, The will of God be damned! I'll sin, then! And if you desire that my Patronage of you continue, you'll say no more! A door slammed and that was all I heard.

Wim had come to the last page. She could hardly focus in the hot room. Perspiration trickled down her face and into her eyes, and she rubbed them impatiently.

April 29. We bid Kororareka farewell. I silently thank God, and the sailors toss their white clay pipes overboard into the harbor for good luck. I wonder at these small tokens, made of good clean Cape Cod clay, left behind forever to roll under the sea a world away from home. My heart was always gladdened when Willie and I found broken bits of the pipes of earlier sailors, washed up on the beach at Kororareka by the tide.

She saw David's hand as he held out to her the fragments of pipe stems and heard his voice as he told her, "*I don't think I knew it then, but I had claimed my* turangawaewae." She felt his hand around her own again, and the sudden heat in her face was more than the hot room had caused. She bent her head and read more.

April 30. We cleared the entrance to the harbor on the night tide and morning reveals the open sea. The men are jolly and they call out with much laughter to the Mowree who race us in their high prowed canoes. But I have just come up from below and am sitting in the lee of the wind under a dory. I can hardly bring myself to keep this record, for shock and sorrow over the travesty I have been forc'd to Witness. Oh, these ignorant, merry sailors! What luck will their pipes bring, now that God will surely turn His face from us? For they do not know, as I do, the awful shame and sorrow this vessel carries. Oh why have I been chosen to bear such a terrible secret! But Dr Kendall has made certain that I will carry it to my grave, for he warned me that he will continue to sponsor my education only if I do not divulge anything of what I know. And without a trade, how will I provide for my good Mother and two young sisters, who since my poor Father's death have only me to depend upon in this world?

If God in His infinite forgiveness allows this ship of shame to reach the belov'd shores of Cape Cod, I make this sacred vow: Altho' I have been forced to take part in this blasphemous Deed, and must keep this secret all my Life, I will leave directions for my journal to be transcribed from its code after my death. I never intended that my words be read, but Capt'n Thorpe's descendants must know their true story.

The entry ended abruptly. There were no further pages. She searched frantically through the box. Nothing. She turned the sheaf over. Nothing. This was the last page Tangi had transcribed. She got up and went into the other room, looked everywhere for the box that had contained all her father's material, all the letters, deeds, logs, and Emmanuel Dart's leatherbound journal. But she could not find it. She was at a loss, hearing the flies buzzing against the windowpanes, hearing far out in the harbor the sound of a fishing boat's horn. After a moment she knelt by David's cot and held his pillow against her as before. But it smelled only of musty heat and age. Faintly, from the house, came the sound of the phone ringing, and she realized that it had been ringing at intervals for some time. She waited for it to stop, then put the pillow back on the cot, smoothed it, and left the cottage.

The panting dogs followed her to the house. The kitchen had been left immaculate by her mother's rage the night before. When she looked into Kia's room, she saw that it, too, had been cleaned. She went in, apprehension pricking at her. The bed was stripped and the old woman's possessions had been packed into boxes and suitcases, each one marked in her mother's neat handwriting, ROSE POINT NURSING HOME.

Wim gazed around. The light coming in the window illuminated the far wall, reflected off the mirror, and glinted faintly on the dusty glass that covered Sam Thorpe's genealogy chart. She went to it and ran her finger down the generations, marking a line through the dust. Again she found herself whispering. "Captain Charles Williamson Thorpe," she read. Then, "Williamson Alexander Thorpe." Poor, simple Willie, the captain's only child, who he feared would leave him with no heir. She frowned. Of course there *had* been an heir, or else she wouldn't be here. She leaned closer and rubbed the dust. There: "Thomas Alexander Thorpe," she whispered. Willie's son. Aunt Kia's great-grandfather, whom she called Grampy. But there was no other name. Grampy had no brother . . .

She traced along the chart again, this time reading the names of all the wives next to their respective husbands. "Agatha Alexander; Anne; Emily Phelps; Sarah Butts; Mary Wil . . . ." She caught her breath. Went back. *Anne. Anne* what? Just that: Anne, b. date unknown; d. 1843. Willie's *wife!* Wim did the math in her head, chewing her lip in concentration. Grampy had been born in 1835 — so his mother, Anne, had died when he was only eight years old. His mother, who had given him a necklace . . .

She traced a spiral round and round the date of Grampy's birth, pondering. The last entry she'd read in Emmanuel Dart's journal had been dated April 30, 1835, when Captain Thorpe had sailed from New Zealand toward home. And some time that very same year, his son Willie — poor, simple Willie, whom no woman would ever want — had married a woman named *just Anne* and produced a son and heir! The heir the captain had believed he would never have, but who had passed on the Thorpe name all the way to Wim.

The dusty glass was now a maze of lines. Once more she traced her finger down through the generations to the bottom of the chart. Lightly, she wrote her name in the dust. Charlotte Williamson Thorpe, b. 1981. The sun hit the glass at an angle and for a moment her name shone, dark and clear. Then the sun went under the clouds, the light dimmed, and the glass became opaque. She blew on it, drew her forearm across it, and wiped it clean.

Suddenly she could not bear to be in the house another minute. She rushed out, called the dogs, and went automatically to the barn, but she did not want to see anyone, especially not the Kid. In the office she sat at the desk and tried to concentrate on several days' worth of untended business. But she could not work. She was jumpy and distracted and nothing she did could drive away the unease clamped in her stomach.

Evelyn found her half an hour later, stood in the doorway, and gave her a long look. "Where the heck've you been, Wim?" she barked. "You've been gone days. I've been calling you all afternoon." When Wim did not answer, she asked more kindly, "So how's the old aunt?"

"She has pneumonia. She almost died," Wim answered curtly.

Evelyn narrowed her eyes. "Don't you do this, kiddo. It wasn't your fault and I don't want to see you beatin' yourself up over it. Kia's your dad's responsibility and he has to—"

"It's all right. They're taking her to Rose Point as soon as she's better anyway. It doesn't matter." She didn't look at

Evelyn but shuffled through the papers on the desk and pretended to work.

Evelyn watched her a few minutes in silence. She turned to go, but then she stopped and said abruptly, "I gotta tell you this, Wimmie: Tam's decided to clear out Jilly's room."

The tears came to her eyes so quickly she couldn't hide them, and she spun violently on the desk chair away from Evelyn. The woman said gently, "Geez, Wim. I know. I'm sorry. But we need the space, and we can't . . . Tam doesn't want to just keep the room like that forever." She hesitated. "She thought you might want to help. Might not be such a bad idea, you know. Closure and all that."

Wim stared stonily at the desk, afraid to move. Her tears dropped onto the calendar and smudged the ink. Evelyn came back and put her hands on Wim's shoulders. Wim jerked away. "Leave me *alone!*" she hissed.

Evelyn turned her around in the chair to face her. "Goddam it, Wim. I'm *not* going to leave you alone. That's how you want to deal with everything. But it just can't always work out that way. I know you want— "

"I want Jilly back!" Wim cried furiously. "That's all. I don't want anything else! Just Jilly. I just want everything to be the way it was!"

Evelyn squatted and took her hands, looking up at her. "Wimmie. It was never right, the way it was. You were a good friend to Jilly. But she wasn't a good friend to you. She was too screwed up. You know that . . . you knew it then. The friendship was more in your head than anything. You gotta stop hanging on to something that wasn't even . . . even *real.*"

"It was real," Wim whispered, desperate.

"What was real was that Jilly *needed* you, Wim," said Evelyn firmly. "She needed you like Angelo needs you. Like the Kid. That's not a friendship. A friendship is where you stand on equal ground with someone."

If she had the courage of the Kid, she would rage and lash at her tormenter, kick and kick until she kicked the hurt out. But she could only spit out words. "I'm sick of everyone telling me what kind of friends I should have!" she said in a bitter voice. "What is everyone so worried about? The kind of friends I find end up going away anyway. Aunt Kia's senile and going to die soon. Tangi's just a pissed-off kid, and she's leaving, so what does it matter? And David is . . . Mom thinks David's some kind of sex offender, but that doesn't matter either. He's leaving, too."

Evelyn said nothing for a moment. Then she dropped Wim's hands and stood up. "You're right," she said at last. "It's nobody's business who you have for friends." She went to the doorway again. "But if they *are* your friends, it's *your* business not to lose them. You can't do much about death. But leaving— hell! The world isn't big enough to keep real friends apart." And she left the barn.

In the end, she had nowhere else to go but the corral. The Kid greeted Wim with a low nicker from the far end. She leaned on the fence and watched him. The sun was blinding her. A shadow on the ground a few feet from the horse looked like the huddled form of a person. She blinked and moved quickly away, into the shade of the barn. The Kid followed. There was a pile of loose boards next to the fence where she stood, so she moved a little farther on. The Kid ambled after her. She was by the gate now and without thinking, without any conscious intention, she opened it. The Kid did not hesitate.

He followed her, blowing softly through his nostrils, down the sandy trail through the pines. Sometimes he was so close behind her she could feel his hot breath on her shoulder. Sometimes he lagged back. But she did not call him or look around. Angelo trotted at her heel. She walked for a long time with no destination in mind, knowing only that she needed these two beings who needed her.

When the trail curved out across an open space, she smelled the sea, and with it came purpose, and direction. The animals felt it, too, Angelo wagging his tail as he loped beside her, the Kid kicking joyfully in midstride as he trotted in a wide arc around them. The sun danced over the white sand. All at once the Kid skittered up close beside her; she reached out, put her hand on his neck, and they walked together for a long time.

When they climbed the ridge of the last dune she saw, far from the public beaches, the shoreline curving away in either direction into a haze of light and spray. Throwing up his head, his white mane streaming, the Kid plunged down the steep dune and galloped out onto the beach. Wim followed; Angelo barked excitedly. The tide was out, the high-water line a dark rope of seaweed and debris. She walked along it slowly, wind-driven sand peppering her hot face, and idly searched through the tangled skein of driftwood, seaweed, shells, Styrofoam buoys, feathers, scraps of trash and net. She stopped. Bent, reached for a glimmer of translucent green. A shard of bottle glass, worn smooth by the sea. She held it tightly in her hand as she walked. It was warm as her own body.

The sun beat down on her. She lifted her face to the cool spray, took off her shoes, and rolled her jeans up to kick through the foam. Time had grown as hazy as the distance. The light broke milky green through the waves, white crests whipping like the Kid's mane, and she wandered along lazily, watching strands of kelp drifting in the current and schools of tiny fish dimpling the sandy bottom with shadows. Ahead of her the horse spun and leaped and kicked in the water, dizzy with freedom. Wim smiled and followed.

With each wave, the sand gave way imperceptibly beneath her feet, so without realizing it she had gone in deeper. There was something wonderful about this gradual release, something mesmerizing about this slow giving in to weightlessness. Now her feet sank into the shifting sand, now she was lifted effortlessly in the cool, swaying depths, now again the brush of sand. Rhythmic as breathing. She spread her arms and floated, and as gradual as her release from the earth came her awareness that *he* was floating beside her . . .

The sun played over his brown face, water shining on the dark, familiar lines etched into his skin, his long black hair floating around him like a cloud of seaweed. He drifted beside her, rising and falling with the waves, and it seemed to her that he was holding out his hand for her to take. She reached for him, touched, and drifted with him beyond the pull of all that was known to her. She sank into the fathomless depths of his eyes and he held her and she wanted to give him everything.

Something solid bumped against her. She floated away. Again she was bumped, more insistently, and she felt within herself the faint, troubled stirring of demand. But the man with the tattooed face held her hands with his own and looked into her eyes as they swirled slowly around and around, and she wanted nothing more. When the bump came again, it hurt. Something sharp and hard knocked against her leg. She gasped, swallowed a mouthful of water, thrashed wildly. She could no longer see anything but churning water and dark, unidentifiable shadows. Panic filled her. He had gone. He had left her. The solid thing rose again beneath her; in sudden fury, she kicked and fought and finally, she felt his floating hair brush over her hand. She grabbed and held on desperately, felt herself immediately dragged, half supported, half holding on, through the suffocating water. Instinctively she clutched tighter to what she had grabbed; she wrapped her arms and legs around the solidness beneath her. Only when she felt air against her skin, felt herself lifted above the waves, did she realize she was on the Kid.

She clasped her legs tightly around his slippery sides and he staggered up to stand, splay-legged and breathing heavily, on the packed sand. He snorted noisily. A dog was barking and barking, and eventually Wim's mind cleared and she looked around.

"Hey, Angelo," she whispered. "Hey, Kid."

The dog sat looking up at her astride the horse, whimpering, and she spoke to him again. A fierce, triumphant exhilaration filled her. The horse shook his head energetically and a sunlit spray of waterdrops enveloped them for a moment in a rainbow. She wanted so much to laugh with pure joy, and then suddenly she did laugh, and the sound seemed to break from her in the same glittering droplets. She took the horse's mane in one hand and rode him at a walk along the edge of the sea. Just beyond the break of the waves, a golden-brown shadow drifting with the current seemed to follow them.

Her strength returned in a rush and she called out to the horse with wild exuberance. He stretched into a gallop along the flat sand. She nudged with one leg and he turned, and again, and he circled back to meet up with the old dog, and she slowed him with her voice to a trot. His gait was smooth, floating; he responded to her voice, to the slightest shift in her balance, to every momentary pressure of her legs. She let him walk then, and shortly after, an urgency to get back came over her so strongly the horse sensed her intent and turned toward the dunes before she even signaled to him. Without hesitation he took her over the dunes to the trail, and up the trail to the gate at the corral. She slid from his back, and the Kid walked in the gate to his feed bucket and nickered. *It's all so simple,* she thought. Why had everything seemed so difficult?

She fed and watered the horse, changed her clothes in the office, and went across the yard to the house. The ground felt strangely solid beneath her feet, as if she was suddenly aware of what, she realized, must have always been. Such a simple thing: *The ground is solid,* she thought, and smiled to herself.

From an open window on the second floor of the house, Tammy was leaning out, shaking a rug. Jilly's rug. Wim remembered when they'd bought the brightly braided thing at a garage sale soon after Jilly had moved in. Tammy disappeared, then reappeared a second later with a full trash bag that she dropped out the window. On the ground was a heap of bags, draped with curtains and blankets and clothing. Wim watched, Angelo leaning against her leg. She recognized every single thing, remembered Jilly using each one, remembered its place in her room. But there was no sadness. She did not go over to the pile. She did not want any of it.

Tammy waved to her from the window and Wim waved back. Evelyn called out from the riding ring where she was giving a group lesson, "Hey, Wim. How you doing?"

Wim called, "I'm fine," and turned to go back to the barn. The urgency had become, all at once, a conscious purpose. She closed the office door and picked up the phone, pushed the buttons, waited. "ICU," she said, and waited again. When a nurse answered, she said, "Katherine Thorpe, please."

There was a click and then Kia said, "Charlotte. Where have you been? Why didn't you come to see me today?"

Wim grinned. "How'd you know it was me, Aunt Kia?"

The old woman snorted into the phone. "I don't need to be told it's you to know it's you," she said. "I've been waiting for you all day."

An overwhelming sadness surprised her and she swallowed. "I miss you, Aunt Kia."

"Charlotte," snapped Kia. "Don't waste time. Your father's coming to visit any minute. Why did you call me?"

She was jolted out of her sorrow, and she smiled. "I *did* have a reason," she said softly and then stopped, suddenly tongue-tied. In the background she heard low voices, the sound of a curtain being pulled, the *beep-beep* of the monitor.

"Hurry, Charlotte," whispered Kia, and the urgency in the old woman's voice stirred the urgency in Wim.

"I saw him," she cried in a low voice. "Aunt Kia! I saw

him . . . in the sea. I mean—I mean, I was *with* him in the sea. He let me *touch* him, Aunt Kia!"

"How did you get away?" the old woman demanded. "Charlotte! Did he want to take you with him? Did he ask you for anything? Listen to me. *Did you give him the necklace?*"

Startled, Wim said, "No—no. I didn't have the necklace. I didn't see it . . . I only found a piece of green glass." She hesitated. "Oh, Aunt Kia! Why won't you tell me more? *Why* does he want it? Who *is* he?"

She heard the old woman groan. "Sam's here, Charlotte," she whispered hoarsely. "Listen. I've told you before. *He* wants the necklace because his mother had given him one just like it, when he was a baby. It was all he had of hers. *She* kept the other one. Do you see? He was looking for his mother, and he couldn't find her, and he didn't know she'd died. But he found Grampy with the same necklace, so he knew they were brothers." Her voice trailed off.

"Aunt Kia!" cried Wim. She could hear her father's voice in the background. "Aunt Kia—what was her name? Their mother? Grampy's and . . . the man with the tattooed face?"

"I told you before . . . I told you."

Sam's voice said, "Who is that on the phone, Kia?"

Wim whispered, "Her name was *Annie*, right? Or was it—"

"Yes, Annie—" began Kia.

"Who is Annie?" Sam asked.

"Aunt Kia! Tell me! Was it Annie, or was it *Te Aniwa?*" She willed the old woman to answer, the purpose that had driven her back from the sea driving her still. "Can you remember? Was it *Annie* or was it *Te Aniwa?*"

"Charlotte—"

"Is that Wim?" asked Sam sharply. "Let me talk to her. Carol's been trying to reach her all day long."

"Annie or Te Aniwa? Aunt Kia!"

"It was both! It's the same name!" Kia gasped. "Sam, stop! It's the same name, Charlotte! That's what they called her, after they bought her—"

Sam came on the phone. "Wim, what on earth are you two talking about!" he said. "Look how riled up you've got her! Where are you, anyway? Are you at the barn? You need to get home. Your mother's been looking for you."

All the strength and urgency left her, as if she'd been punched and had the wind knocked out of her. "Okay," she whispered and hung up, letting the phone slip from her fingers. After several minutes Angelo whined and pawed at her leg, and she got up numbly and went out.

She found her mother in the kitchen making lemonade, still in her uniform. "I made it with real lemons. The way you like it," Carol said, dumping a tray of ice cubes in the pitcher.

They both sat, and Carol poured them glasses full to the top. Suddenly aware of how thirsty she was, how dry her mouth was from the wind and salt, Wim gulped half the contents before the bitterness registered. Carol looked like she might cry. "I forgot the sugar!" she said, jumping up.

"Mom—it's okay. I like it this way," Wim mumbled.

They both sat silent a moment. Then her mother whispered, "I thought you wouldn't come back at all. I thought you might move in with Evelyn and Tammy. I thought . . . I was afraid I'd lost you."

"Oh, Mom. Here I am. I'm not lost."

"All those things I said . . . I'm sorry."

Here I am. I'm not lost. She felt the solid floor beneath her feet, and under that, the foundation of the house that had held solid for more than a hundred and fifty years, and beneath it all the earth itself and her steady upon it, and when she spoke, she spoke from that place. "It's all right, Mom," Wim said softly. "I understand. But don't worry about me. I know where I'm going."

Twelve ෩෨

The next day, Wim went home for supper immediately after evening chores at the barn. She sat with her mother and father at the table wondering if the three of them would ever feel they were a family, no matter how hard they tried. Sam was telling them, "She really looked so much better. I told you she was a tough old bird. I think they'll discharge her before the end of the week."

"Did you remember to arrange for the ambulance?" Carol asked.

"All set," said Sam. To Wim, he added, "She'll be going straight from the hospital to Rose Point—much less confusing for her that way."

She nodded but could think of nothing to say. Later, as she helped her father sort through the boxes packed with Kia's things, Sam told her enthusiastically of all the activities and programs Rose Point offered for its residents. Once he interrupted himself to comment, vaguely perplexed, "You seem sad tonight, Wimmie."

Sad? She realized his puzzlement was genuine and could find nothing to say in reply. Nothing they were doing now, nothing her parents had been speaking of, had the remotest relationship to the story that she and Kia shared. It was impossible to reconcile the Kia her father was preparing to bring to a nursing home with the Kia of the green stone necklace, the Kia who could see the man with the tattooed face. Involuntarily, Wim glanced at the genealogy chart.

She looked away quickly, but Sam had caught her glance and smiled, reflective. "I had that made when we decided to move to Provincetown and fix up Thorpe House. It was the year before you were born . . . just before Kia started getting . . . well, strange."

"What do you mean?"

Sam sighed, studying the chart. "You see how she is now . . . well, that didn't just happen overnight. It's been coming on for years. The year before we left, she started getting confused. Muddled. Just little things at first—how old she was, where she was." He glanced almost apologetically at Wim. "But it got worse. It seemed like she was *seeing* things—I don't know. Hallucinating. Alex agreed. We took her to doctors, specialists, everything. No one was much help." He stopped. For several seconds he said nothing. Wim watched the struggle on her father's face. Finally he admitted in a low voice, "I guess I've always wondered if Kia's problems happened because we weren't taking her with us. Kia wanted to come back to Provincetown. She was born here, and she spent her first ten years in this house—"

"Why didn't she come with you, then?"

Sam didn't look at her. "At the time, it just felt like the right decision. After all, Kia had lived in Florida most of her life. And I wasn't sure what shape this old house was in, how much work I'd need to put into it to make it livable. Kia was comfortably settled at my brother's . . ." He gave her a tentative smile. "Besides, by the time we began getting ready to move, you were on the way. We were going to have our hands full."

She stared at the chart. After a long moment she said, incredulous, "You mean, you didn't want Aunt Kia to move to Provincetown with you because *I* was going to be born? And she started getting strange after that?"

Her father had picked up a box; now he paused in the doorway of the room, troubled. "Well, I don't really think it was all *connected* like that exactly."

They were both silent as they drove to Rose Point Nursing Home. Wim stared out the van window at the warm summer night, lit by evening barbecues and shops open for the late-strolling crowds, and wondered at what a simple, well-defined world it seemed, familiar from her childhood but somehow inaccessible to her now. Sam took the shore route from Provincetown toward Truro. She remembered how, as a child, she had loved coming home on this road where, from a certain hill, she could see the end of the peninsula set like a delicate hook in the hazy sea, their tiny gray-shingled town clinging to its inner curve. The sight had always filled her then with an immense, satisfied comfort. Now it seemed merely a moment of earth, a mere pause in a story stretching infinitely before and beyond it. Kia, too, must have seen this sight as a young girl, and now she had returned to die, but those boundaries of her life seemed to Wim no more substantial than the haze at the horizon where sea and sky meet.

An attendant met them at the door of the nursing home, and Sam said, "We're setting up Katherine Thorpe's room—room 32? She'll be moving in soon."

They unpacked Kia's clothing and hung it in the freshly painted closets. Sam fussed over where to put things, moving furniture back and forth, arranging and rearranging photos and knickknacks on the dresser and bedside tables. In the last box, Wim found the photo album containing pictures of the family when they'd lived in Florida. She held the thick book on her lap and sat on the bed while Sam moved things around her. Finally he sat beside her.

"It sure is a nice room," he said, with hearty cheerfulness.

"Yes," Wim answered. It was a conscientiously pleasant room, with cool, peach-colored walls, airy curtains, and new furniture so polished she could see her reflection in the wood. No shadows here, nothing hidden.

"She'll be happy here. It's safe and quiet, the way she likes it," Sam said, almost defiant.

The photo album slipped off Wim's lap and fell open on the floor. Kia, astride the tall black horse, faced them with her dark, vivid eyes. Sam made a small sound and whispered, "Oh, God. She'll die in here."

Wim bit her lip. So he did know. That made it worse. She reached for the album, closed it, and put it in one of the dresser drawers. They didn't look at each other as she helped her father straighten everything and clear away the boxes. It felt like they were both doing something shameful.

The next morning at dawn, a cool, wet sea mist hung over the town. The dogs jumped eagerly from the truck when Wim got to the barn. She let the horses out, checked on the Kid, fed the barn cats. The routine acted as a balm. Everything was so ordinary, so predictable. As though life was going the way she'd planned it, back when school had let out. When her heart contained only the Kid, the other animals, and the absence of Jilly, and that had been enough. And now, on this foggy, quiet morning, she could almost believe it was still that way. If she just stayed here at the barn, worked hard at the things that needed to be done, it *would* be that way.

So she graded the large riding ring, going over it with the tractor until it was smooth as a dance floor. She repaired fences, fixed the hinges on a stall door, and picked up the grain order in Orleans. In the evening she mended and oiled tack. She went about the familiar routines alone, Angelo trailing wherever she went, and was content. The summer bustle around the barn, often such an intrusion in the past, struck her now as pleasant, even welcome. The days ran into each other, three or four or five; she lost count. She fell asleep each night on the office sofa, lulled by the rustle of horses and the purring of cats, the call of an owl in the pines, the yip of a fox. In the stillest hours before dawn, she could sometimes hear the indistinct boom of the sea beyond the dunes.

Sometime during those days, Kia was moved to Rose Point. Carol stopped at the barn on her way to work one day to tell Wim. Didn't say much else, didn't ask her when she was coming home. Another day, when Wim went home to get some clothes, she met her father in the kitchen making lunch.

"Kia's settled in fine," he told her, and she nodded absently. It was abstract information, fitting no place in the concrete, self-contained world of the barn. At the barn, there was nothing but the simple present, and she busied herself with the horses and the office and the myriad tasks that came up every day. Once, Evelyn remarked with a dry smile, "Well, now I remember why I hired you. Place looks better than it's looked all summer. No wonder we miss you when you aren't here."

Wim said fervently, "I'm always going to be here."

Evelyn gave her a quizzical look but said only, "Glad to hear it."

Wim spent every evening with the Kid, brushing him, combing the mats from his mane and tail, trimming his hooves. She moved slowly in the small corral, talked to him, fed him his grain handful by handful, and he followed her like Angelo did. A profound peace grew in her. Everything felt *right*. The solid ground was holding. She needed nothing else.

Evelyn came to the corral one evening just as she was shutting the gate, and they talked together by the fence. The warm, sweet air washed over them, filled with cricket song and stars and the whisper of the pines. The Kid dozed. All three dogs had collapsed peacefully on the cool sand. Wim leaned against Evelyn's shoulder the way she had when she was younger, and Evelyn leaned back. They stood awhile in companionable silence until the Kid ambled over and blew against their faces. "Get away, you brute!" Evelyn laughed. "I'm going on a date with my sweetheart and you're slobbering all over my best shirt."

"You and Tammy going out?" asked Wim.

"Do you see any other sweethearts around?"

Wim grinned and turned around to lean her back against the fence. She asked thoughtfully, "Did you really know Tammy ten whole years before you got together?"

"Yep," nodded Evelyn. "Ridiculous, huh? All because I was frightened to death."

Wim stared off into the darkness of the trees, her heartbeat suddenly quickening. All at once she knew that something had been gathering within her under the peaceful surface of these last days. She caught her breath, fighting it off. Unexpectedly, Evelyn said, "You've been hiding out here again, haven't you, Wimmie?"

The Kid slipped his head between them, and Wim pressed her face against his warm cheek. "Yes," she muttered finally. "And I don't want to talk about it. I don't want to think about anything."

She heard Evelyn sigh. "Oh, Wim. You sure as hell make it tough on yourself."

Wim didn't answer. She closed her eyes. The darkness cradled her silence as gently as she was cradled against the horse, and her words when she did speak were held by the same enveloping night. "Does being in love always feel like this?" she whispered.

Evelyn chuckled. "Oh, yes."

Barely audible, Wim said, "I hate it."

"You're just afraid of feeling it, that's all," Evelyn said bluntly. "Like you're afraid of what you'll feel if you go see your Aunt Kia."

An angry flush came over her. "What's wrong with being afraid of something that *hurts!*" she cried.

"Nothing," Evelyn answered, complacent. "If you're a mouse."

The Kid butted Wim on the shoulder so hard she almost lost her balance. Evelyn chuckled again. "There," she said. "He said it better than I can. You oughta listen to him."

Despite herself, Wim muttered, "What do you mean?"

"Well, the Kid was afraid of being hurt, wasn't he? And he sure had good reason to be. It had happened to him before, right? Would it have been better if we'd just left him alone— if we hadn't tried to change his mind?" Evelyn slapped the horse affectionately on the shoulder. "Tammy's going to think I stood her up. I gotta go."

Later, Wim sat in the doorway of the barn watching the stars arc over her in the night sky. The air had grown sharp and clear, and she, too, was filled with an overwhelming clarity. It was, after all, very simple: She could not let David disappear from her life. She could not allow Kia to die at Rose Point. And somehow, she had to answer the man with the tattooed face. Whatever Emmanuel Dart's "terrible secret" was, it bound them all together.

The next day, Wim drove up the wide driveway through landscaped grounds and parked the battered Dune Forest pickup in the shade near the entrance to Rose Point. The brick building was surrounded by gardens with paths and benches, so perfect looking it didn't feel real. Wim jabbed her fingers through her tangled hair, brushed off her jeans, and went inside.

Everything gleamed in the morning sun. The tile floor, the sparkling fish tank in the front lobby, the chrome on the wheelchairs lined up near the doorway. Even the nursing attendant's smile had a shine to it. "Let me check to see if Miss Thorpe is ready for a visitor," said the attendant, flipping through a chart. "You're her niece? Yes, I see your name right here."

Wim sat awkwardly on a chair to wait while the attendant disappeared down a bright hallway. She took a deep breath and looked around. The surroundings seemed to have polished the vitality out of the elderly people sitting in the open rooms off the lobby. A group was huddled in front of a television, and a few others were playing cards at a table. Most were dozing in recliners or staring into space. She could hear the cheery bubbling of the aquarium. From time to time a wheelchair drifted past, aimless as the fish.

The attendant, a young woman with a placid manner, returned to take Wim to Kia's room. "She's a little disoriented," she explained as they walked down the corridor. "It often happens, when they first arrive. Just give her time."

But even the word "disoriented" could not adequately describe the old woman who sat motionless in a chair turned toward a window. Nothing was left in that passive form of the fierce, wonderful, sublimely confused Katherine Irene Thorpe. Wim sat on the stool the attendant pulled up for her and took the old woman's flaccid hand in her own. "It's me, Aunt Kia," she whispered. "It's me, Charlotte."

A thin line of spittle ran down the crease at the side of the old woman's mouth and Wim wiped it with a tissue. "She was asleep—" began the attendant, but Wim gestured her away, her eyes burning with tears. She leaned her head against the old woman's, pressed her cheek against the thick hair that was so like her own. Suddenly she felt a quavering touch on her face. "Charlotte?" The voice was a dry rasp. "Charlotte. I've been waiting for you. I want you to take me home."

She was overcome by helplessness. Kia's eyes were open now, and she was looking around with growing comprehension. "This is not where I belong," the old woman said, her voice sharper. "Sam should know better. Charlotte, help me get my things." She pushed herself up from the chair with alarming energy. The attendant passed by in the hall, glanced in, and Wim caught her eye. She felt immediately like a traitor.

"Miss Thorpe?" said the attendant, coming into the room. "How are you feeling? You had such a long nap. And I don't believe you've taken your morning meds. Here, let me pour you some water." She was already holding out the paper cup containing pills that had been left on the bedside table with a pitcher of water.

Finding her voice, Wim gasped, "Oh, please . . . please wait! Let her . . . don't make her take anything yet. Can't you—"

The attendant looked at her watch and frowned. "It's already late. It's just to calm her."

"I'm calm," said Kia suddenly, craftily.

The attendant hesitated. A buzzer sounded from farther down the corridor. "I'll be back," she said and went out.

Kia said, "She will, you know. They'll get me in the end, Charlotte. They put it in your food if you don't take it yourself." She turned abruptly to face Wim. "Charlotte! Are you listening to me? Pay attention then! You have to take me home. I have to get to the sea. You promised."

Wim struggled to keep her voice calm. She felt as though

she were mired in sand and that with any movement, any word, a dry avalanche would smother her. She licked her lips. "I can't take you today, Aunt Kia. But I'll—"

Kia whacked the bed viciously with her cane. Wim stared at her, shocked. Kia came close. "You're a coward, Charlotte," she hissed. "I thought you'd be different. I thought . . ." The old woman fell back in her chair, silent a moment. Then she said sadly, "I didn't think you'd be like me. But you are a coward, just like I am."

"You're not!"

Kia laughed. "Don't be fooled, Charlotte. Real fear is like real courage: it's not always obvious. Oh, yes. I'm a coward. It doesn't matter that I'm the only one who knows it, and it doesn't matter that everyone benefited from my cowardice. That doesn't make it any better."

Wim sat on the bed, too stunned to respond. Kia gave her a grim smile and again showed a startling strength, yanking the chair around to sit facing her. "I didn't raise Sam and Alex when their mother died out of the goodness of my heart, Charlotte. I moved in with my brother because it was easier. Safer. Because I was afraid."

"Of what?"

Kia said fiercely, "I loved someone."

Her black eyes glittered. Wim could only stare in astonishment. The old woman tossed her head defiantly. "Oh, you can look amazed. But I did."

"What happened?" She and Kia were leaning toward one another, intense and somehow wary, as if engaged in a match of wills.

"He married someone else," Kia said abruptly. "He loved me, but he didn't have the guts to know it, and I let him walk away. I was too proud to confront him, and too afraid he'd reject me, and I convinced myself that life with him would be too unpredictable anyway. It was easier to stay where I knew I was needed." She sat back in her chair and surveyed Wim with narrowed eyes. "Just like it would be easier to stay here and drift away," she said, her voice deceptively serene.

There was a movement in the doorway and they both jumped. But it was only an assistant rolling a rack of freshly laundered clothing into the room to get it out of the way while she paused to talk with someone in the hall. Across the hall a window was open and a breeze that smelled of the sea stirred the clothes on the hangers, casting mottled shadows over the freshly painted wall of Kia's room.

They both saw him at the same instant. Kia said with triumphant satisfaction, "There he is, Charlotte." Neither of them moved. The man with the tattooed face watched as he had always watched, his proud, fierce eyes infused with longing. "*He* brought me all the magic in my life. He brought me to the man I loved," Kia continued softly. She reached out her hand and addressed the image in the shadows. "But don't you understand? Don't you? I was as frightened as your brother was of going somewhere I'd never been—" The pale shadows quivered. Wim caught her breath. For a moment she thought Kia would get up and move closer to the man with the tattooed face. His eyes glittered more hungrily than she could ever remember. Kia leaned toward him. "Rereahu," she said clearly. "Rereahu. Why did you come? I do not have the necklace. I have nothing to give you."

The assistant pulled the rack of clothing from the room, the shadows dissolved, and Kia sank back in the chair. A nurse came into the room. "Good morning, Miss Thorpe," she said kindly, pouring a glass of water and handing it to Kia. "I hear you haven't taken your meds yet. How about it?" Kia did not open her eyes but swallowed the pills she was given. When the nurse left, Wim sat in silence for a long time. Kia did not seem to be asleep, but she sat motionless and unresponsive. At last Wim got up.

"I will take you to the sea, Aunt Kia," she said quietly. "I will come back, and I'll take you to the sea."

All through the rest of the day, through the busy afternoon at the barn and the evening chores, the name resonated through her thoughts. "Rereahu," she whispered as she raked the stalls. "Rereahu," she repeated under her breath as she filled the water buckets. And though she curled up in restless exhaustion on the office sofa later that night, she could not sleep. For hours she lay staring into the darkness. After a long time she whispered aloud again, "Rereahu," and sat up abruptly. She pulled on her jeans and tee shirt, got in the truck, and drove home. She was not surprised to see David's rental car parked beside the cottage.

She sat for a while on the back steps. It was very late; no moon shone through the low haze obscuring the stars that had been so brilliant the night before. She could hear the muted lapping of water along the harbor beach, a lonely, uneven sound that brought her no peace. Her thoughts were as obscured now as the stars, and it was not thought that urged her to get up and walk across to the cottage, but the tenacious ember of a name burning through the darkness. *Rereahu. Rereahu. David.*

She did not hesitate but pushed open the door and shut it

noiselessly behind her. Her eyes, long adjusted to the dark, made out David's sleeping form on the narrow cot. She went quickly across the room and knelt beside him. She lay her head on the pillow next to his and stayed there motionless, hardly breathing.

After a long time her knees began to ache, and then her back, from the strain of not moving. And unexpectedly, she was angry. There was no comfort here, either. She felt absurd, foolish, and made the first cautious stir toward leaving. Immediately, David's hand stroked her hair. The blood rushed to her face.

"I heard your truck," he whispered. "Noisy."

"It needs a new muffler," she mumbled.

His hand was smoothing her hair, his fingers caressing her face. She was still afraid to move. Her left arm had fallen asleep and to her horror, she realized she was trembling. David rolled onto his side, slipping his arm around her, and pulled her closer. She felt his lips briefly on her cheek, felt him smile. "You can't possibly be comfortable," he said.

"I'm okay," she said, her voice muffled against his neck, and waited for him to ask her to get into the bed with him.

He laughed, very softly. "You are not okay, *hine*," he said. "You're going to suffocate." He swung his legs over the side of the cot and slid down beside her on the floor. She did move then, and he gathered her against him with both arms, and held her firmly. She lifted her face to his, but he only gazed at her with serious eyes. She looked away, confused, but after a few minutes her heart stopped pounding and she relaxed. "Better?" he asked, his mouth soft against her hair. She nodded.

He held her a long time. As he laid his head against hers and rocked her a little, an inexplicable sorrow pushed against her throat. He took her hands and placed them on his chest, and while she was looking into his eyes she felt as if she was drinking in his heartbeat through her fingers. Gently, so she would not startle him, she asked, "Are we related?"

He smiled at her. *"Ki'ora,* cousin," he whispered.

She touched his face, traced over his cheeks and forehead and chin the spiraling lines she had known forever. He closed his eyes. She traced around his mouth, brushing her fingers lightly over his lips. He sighed deeply, bowed his head, and took her hands between his own. "You need to go home," he whispered.

"No."

"Yes," he said. He stood up and pulled her up with him. "Come on." He led her by the hand outside into the dew-cool night.

"But why! Why!" She wanted to shake him, but in the faint aura of the streetlight through the leaves of the oak tree, she saw suddenly the conflict on his face, did not understand, knew only that he was frightened. She threw her arms around him. He held her as tightly as she held him. In the end, she let him go and turned to go to the house.

Thirteen ⊚⊚

From the corral came a high, demanding whinny. "He's calling for you again, Wim. Didn't you go see him when you got here this morning?" Evelyn grinned with mock exasperation. "You know he won't shut up all day if you don't. You've got a one-person horse there. I've seen it before. No one else can ride them."

"Good asset in a riding stable," commented Tammy acerbically, without turning around from making breakfast.

Evelyn asked, between bites of her bagel, "Hey, Wim. You going to call the vet today for Muenster? That bruise should have healed by now."

Wim was absently twirling her uneaten bagel on the plate and gazing at nothing.

Tammy said, "I can call—"

"Wim!" Evelyn prodded her. *"Wim!"*

"What?"

Evelyn snapped, "What the hell's with you? You act like you've had a lobotomy."

Tammy slammed the oven door shut and muttered sarcastically, "Well, that ought to get her to open up to you."

"I'm all right," Wim said, struggling to keep her tone casual. She knew they wouldn't accept that, so she added with a shrug, "I went to see Aunt Kia at Rose Point yesterday, that's all." She got up to take her plate to the sink.

"Oh, yeah, that's all," said Evelyn, leaning back in her chair. "Well, far be it from me to pry . . . By the way, your David called and left a message on the machine earlier."

Her heart raced. "He's not my David," Wim muttered. But her voice stuck in her throat. She swallowed and asked, without looking around, "What did he want?"

Evelyn shrugged. "You, I presume. I don't know. He said something about going to New Bedford and wanting to drop his niece off with you."

The disappointment seared her. *He thinks I'm a child. That's why . . . last night . . . that's why he doesn't want—* She gulped the coffee Tammy had left for her on the counter; it burned the way the rage was burning through her, and she choked.

"Cripes, Wimmie," said Tammy, and Evelyn growled, "He better not be jerking you around, damn him."

She felt like the rat that Bart had brought to bay in a corner of the grain room. She could almost feel the snarl baring her teeth. She looked coldly at Evelyn. "You told me to have courage."

Evelyn met her eyes squarely, but for several moments she said nothing. Then she put both hands on the table and leaned intently toward Wim. "And I'm still telling you that, kiddo," she said. "I'm talking about *heart*, Wim. You know how we say that a horse has *heart?* Same thing. Your heart's the only thing you can rely on. It's the only solid ground you have. Sometimes it's the only place left to stand on."

Turangawaewae. The word came to her unbidden. *Turangawaewae*—standing place. But that was David's word, not hers. She averted her eyes from the two women who gazed at her with concern. "I don't think there's much left of my heart," she said, her voice flat. She went to the doorway. "There's no point going to see Aunt Kia. She's just wasting away. I can't do anything for her. And David isn't jerking me around. He's just going away, that's all. I can't do anything about that, either. It's stupid of me to feel anything for him." And she left the room.

But she didn't want to leave the house. She wandered into the living room, which was virtually unvisited during the day, and looked around at the clutter that in the evening seemed so homey and comfortable. Now it appeared simply a mess. She shoved a pile of magazines off the sagging couch and curled up, edgy and irritated, listening to the low voices of the two women in the kitchen. A cat came in, mewed, rubbed against her; she ignored it. Presently she heard the screen door slam and the sound of Evelyn's boots on the steps, and she was overwhelmed by a sickening loneliness. She reached for the cat and clasped it against her chest, burying her face in the dusty fur. When she looked up, Tammy was standing in the doorway.

"Thought I heard you come in here," she said softly. "You want me to save your bagel?"

Wim shook her head numbly.

Tammy smiled a little. "That's good—I think I hear Bart

eating it right now." Her words were punctuated by the sound of a plate clattering to the floor. "Beast." She came in, took a small package wrapped in brown paper from a bookshelf, and sat next to Wim. "I did save this for you, though. I didn't know if you'd want it, but . . . well, here." She thrust the package at Wim.

She unwrapped it slowly, knowing instinctively before she opened it what was inside. She remembered so clearly when the photograph had been taken. Five years ago—the summer she and Jilly had been twelve. They had posed, arms tight around each other, in front of the barn. Jilly, her blond hair drawn sleekly back in a long braid, had been dressed for a recital, her willowy body almost ethereal in the pale pink dancing tights. Wim pressed beside her in dark contrast, her black hair unruly as always, dressed in her scruffy barn clothes. They were both laughing straight into the camera lens, full of delight. Wim traced a finger over the tarnished silver-plated frame Jilly had bought at an antique shop. She'd kept the photo on her bedside table, turned toward her, she'd told Wim, so it would be the first thing she saw every morning when she woke up.

Tammy took the photo for a moment, gently wiped the glass with the hem of her tee shirt. "She was so lovely," she murmured. "But she was hardly here, was she? Hardly on this earth. Even when she was really little, Jilly just seemed to float around half off the ground. Like she couldn't decide whether to stay here or not."

"That's why she was a dancer," Wim whispered.

Tammy gave her back the photo. "You were a good friend, Wim. She knew how much you loved her."

Wim nodded. "You were, too," she said softly. "You gave her a good home."

They looked at each other, silent a moment. "Guess that's the best you can ever do for anyone," Tammy said finally. "Just love them."

It had been more than a year , and she hadn't thought she could ever go up to Jilly's room again, but she found herself standing in the doorway clutching the photograph tightly against her. Faintly, so faintly she thought it must be her imagination, she caught Jilly's scent, as elusive as the girl herself. Tammy had washed and rehung the curtains, which stirred slightly now at the open window. The braided rug had been cleaned and put back on the floor by the bed. The rose-patterned quilt was folded at the end of the mattress. Other than these, and the darker squares on the delicate yellow wallpaper where Jilly's dance posters had once hung, there was nothing left.

Wim sat on the bed. She placed the photo on the bedside table and turned it toward the pillows. "I miss you. I miss you," she whispered, and the words seemed to float with the faint scent out the open window. The room felt airy and bright and open. She drew her knees up and wrapped her arms around them and stared at the photograph. She gazed so long she thought she heard Jilly's voice down in the kitchen, and she caught her breath; at any moment, she'd hear the quick, light sound of her running upstairs, down the hall, into the room . . .

She jerked her head up. Tangi burst through the door, crying, "Oh, good! *Ki'ora!* Crikey! Haven't seen you for *ages*, eh! Uncle David dropped me off. We phoned, but we only got the machine. Hope it's okay. I can't bear spending another *minute* with him in one of his grotty old museums. He's been dragging me around for a week." She cocked her head and grinned. "Hey. I missed you. And I'm not the only one—Uncle David's totally *rapt* about you, eh. Couldn't stop talking about you all week. True! I got quite sick of hearing it. He's off in the never-never. Hope he manages to remember me in time for tea."

The girl paused for breath and Wim, dumbfounded, managed in desperation, "Be quiet. Just be quiet. Can't you stop talking for a *minute?*"

Tangi bounced as she sat on the bed next to Wim. She reached across and picked up the photograph, gazed at it somberly. "This your friend? The one who died?" she asked.

"Jilly," Wim answered stiffly. "Her name was Jilly."

Tangi studied the photo for a long time. Wim ached to take it from her. Tangi said suddenly, "I had a friend who died. Car smash. Her dad was drinking." She put the photo back on the table, gently, turning it to face the bed as it had been. "Makes you mad, eh."

"Yes," whispered Wim. She couldn't move, even to hide the tears running down her face.

Tangi sighed. "You two look real close. Real mates." She hesitated, then, startling Wim, she slipped one thin arm around her waist, saying softly, "Just want to see what it feels like—"

"It's not the same. It could never be the same." But as roughly as she spoke, still she could not move away from the girl, and Tangi did not take her arm away. Her narrow shoulder pressed sharply against Wim's. The morning sun drifted in the window with the breeze, turning Tangi's skin golden brown, turning the skin on her own arm the same color. Her face, cool where the tears had wet it, warmed in the light. Wim said, hardly hearing her own voice, "I think we are related."

"*E te tuakana,*" answered Tangi. "Sisters."

Wim's arm went around Tangi's waist. She stared into her lap. She could not look at the photograph. They sat for a long time, silent, until Wim whispered, "Why does your uncle keep everything such a secret from me?"

The girl stirred beside her. "He's not keeping secrets," Tangi said at last. "He wants to let the story live itself out in its own way. He came here so the missing pieces of the story could speak in their own voices."

"It's because he thinks I'm just a child," Wim contradicted bitterly.

Tangi looked at her in amazement. "He doesn't think that," she said.

Wim didn't answer. The girl moved away and sat cross-legged on the bed to face her. Her eyes were thoughtful. "I don't know much about blokes really," she said. "Especially old blokes, like Uncle David." She grinned in mock innocence. "After all, I'm only fifteen . . ."

"I'm sure you know plenty," muttered Wim.

Tangi laughed aloud. "Yeah. Well, at least I know when someone's head over heels, anyway . . . and that's more'n you seem to know. You want to hear what he told me?"

Wim blushed furiously, looked away and didn't answer. Tangi continued blithely, "He told me you were the missing piece of *his* story."

"Oh." Disappointment again, and her stomach flopped. "His work."

Tangi frowned in disgust. "You're thick, aren't you. Not his work, idiot. His *story*—his *life*. You're the missing piece of his *life*."

The whole world seemed to compress around her into that one single moment. The mockingbird's song outside the window, the warm breeze, the high, eager whinny of a horse all concentrated, all intensified within the pounding of her heart. "I love him," she whispered.

"I know," said Tangi.

They smiled at each other. Wim stood up. "I need you to help me," she said. "I'm going to get Aunt Kia."

Tangi stayed oddly quiet all the way to Rose Point and stood silently behind Wim when she told the nurse at the main desk, "I've come to take my aunt, Katherine Thorpe, out for a drive."

The nurse looked doubtfully from Wim to Tangi and down at her chart. "She hasn't been out with you before. It's always your father who takes her out. Are you sure you can handle it? She's—"

"I took care of her for weeks before she came here," said Wim, firm.

The nurse hesitated, then she put the chart down. "Well, I'm sure she'll enjoy an outing. Let's see how she's feeling this morning."

Tangi trailed behind unobtrusively as Wim walked with the nurse to Kia's room. The old woman was in the chair facing the window as before, but she turned when they came in. To Wim's intense relief, her eyes were clear and focused. She sent Wim a penetrating look, started to speak, looked beyond her to the nurse, and stopped. "Hi, Aunt Kia," said Wim softly. The old woman, watchful, said just as softly back, "Hello, Charlotte."

The nurse had poured a cup of water and came toward Kia smiling. "Your niece would like to take you out for a little, Miss Thorpe. Do you feel up to it?"

This time Kia glanced at Tangi, then looked shrewdly back at Wim. Their eyes held a fraction of a second. "Certainly," said Kia. "I am ready to go."

The nurse leaned over her, handing her the cup. "Let's take these before you go," she said. "I'm sure you'll be back in time for your afternoon meds." And she tapped out some pills into the old woman's hand. Kia raised her hand to her mouth.

Suddenly Tangi stepped forward, bumping awkwardly against the nurse and grabbing her arm to steady herself. "Oh! Excuse me!" she exclaimed.

Kia drank the water in one gulp.

The nurse straightened the sleeve of her uniform. "I'm really sorry," Tangi said. The nurse brushed away the apology, masking her irritation by saying brightly to Kia, "Swallowed those down? Good. Don't forget to sign out before you go." And she left the room.

There was a little silence. Then Kia smiled. "Thank you, Te Aniwa," she murmured. Wim looked from one to the other, puzzled. Kia chuckled, opened her hand. Two white pills lay on her palm. "Flush them down the toilet," she commanded, and Wim did it without a word.

In the truck, with Kia sitting between her and Tangi, Wim

tried to concentrate. She had no plan, no clear idea even of her intention. *The sea,* she thought. *She wants to go to the sea.* She went over the ocean beaches in her mind. There was Head of the Meadow, Race Point, Herring Cove, the National Seashore in Eastham . . . but they would all be crammed with summer crowds. She glanced quickly at Kia. It was hot; the old woman would not be able to withstand the sun for long, even dressed as she was in cool white linen slacks and a loose shirt. New clothes, Wim thought distractedly. Dad must have bought them for her. Her heart constricted. Sam was in Hyannis. On his way home, as always, he would stop at Rose Point. She fought down an unidentifiable panic.

"We're going to the barn," Wim said, speaking before she was consciously aware she'd decided.

Kia glared at her. "The sea," she demanded. "You promised, Charlotte."

Wim faltered. "I know."

Without warning, the old woman slumped back in the seat and began to cry. She made no sound, but the tears ran down the deep creases in her face. A roaring grew in Wim's ears and she clamped her hands around the steering wheel. Suddenly Tangi began to sing. As before, it was the haunting, undulating song she'd learned from her grandmother. To Wim it sounded part lullaby, part prayer. A strange peace filled her. Kia closed her eyes. "Grampy!" she cried softly, her voice trembling. "Grampy, Grampy."

With hardly a change in her voice, Tangi crooned, "Grampy sang you this song, didn't he, *e kui*?"

"Yes," whispered the old woman.

Tangi bowed her head. "Oh, *e kui*," breathed the girl. "Who taught your Grampy that song?"

Kia put both hands to her face and rocked a little on the seat. "He only sang it for me," she said in a low voice. "He sang it to me because he loved me. He loved me more than anyone in the world. That's why he sang me his mother's song. Annie. She always sang it to him. She died when he was a little boy, and he wasn't allowed to sing it, but he remembered the song, and he told me not to forget . . ."

"You've remembered well, *e kui*," said Tangi soothingly.

The old woman sat up and looked squarely at Tangi. "Yes, I have remembered," she said, her voice suddenly strong. "*He* sings it to me, you know. In my dreams. *He* comes to my dreams now, you know."

"Who comes, *e kui*?"

Wim said, "Rereahu," and turned up the drive toward the barn.

She heard the soft intake of breath from the girl and felt the silence fall around them. She parked the truck. "I've seen him all my life," she told Tangi quietly. "A man with a tattooed face. So has Aunt Kia. David knows who he is. But he won't tell me."

Kia broke in. "Of course we know who he is, Charlotte. What are you talking about? Rereahu is Grampy's brother. I told you. He came looking for his mother."

The door of the house slammed and Tammy came out on the porch. "Hey, Wim! Phone call for you. You going to sit in the truck all day?"

Wim got out, saying, "I'll be right back. Take Aunt Kia into the office—it's lots cooler in there with the fan." She ran across to the house to get the phone in the kitchen.

"Hi," said David. "*Ki'ora.* I'm glad I finally got you. You're hard to reach."

Flustered, Wim stammered, "Oh! Well . . . you want Tangi? She's right here. I mean, I'll just go get her—"

David laughed. "Slow down, *hine.* I wanted to talk to you." He paused, and she sensed his uncertainty. He continued in a rush, "I just wanted to see how you were doing, after . . . after last night. I tried phoning this morning—"

"I know. I guess I wasn't around. I get here pretty early." She was babbling and she forced herself to stop, to take a deep breath. "I'm okay," she said.

He laughed again. "Oh, yes. I know. You're always okay." They both paused. Her mind was blank. David said softly, "Oh, *hine . . .*"

She wanted frantically to say everything. To spill her heart. To ask for all she wanted so much, to plead . . . but she could not. She was mute, the phone pressed to her ear. She heard David sigh. "Well, I just wanted to make sure you were there," he said at last. "I'm in Wellfleet now, at the library. I'll be along soon to collect Tangi. Okay?"

"Okay," she choked out.

She put the receiver back and stood still, gazing at nothing, her thoughts hidden under the feelings his voice had left in her. She closed her eyes; his presence flooded through her like a warm current, and for a moment she lost herself within it. Then she opened her eyes. *David is leaving,* she told herself. It was one thing for Evelyn to tell her she didn't have to lose him.

But what could she do? Dreaming wouldn't help. He lived on the other side of the world. She almost shook herself, the way a horse shakes to get rid of flies. At that moment, a horrified shout came from the direction of the riding ring.

Wim ran out onto the porch in time to see Evelyn vault the fence and race toward the back of the barn, bellowing over her shoulder, "Wim! *Wim!* Get over here!"

But she had no time to move. From behind the barn, his dappled gray coat gleaming like burnished pewter in the sun, trotted the Kid. Free of saddle or bridle, his white mane and tail billowing around him, he swept past with Katherine Irene Thorpe astride him like the captain at the prow of a ship. Wim stood motionless, awestruck. Evelyn, too, seemed caught in a spell. But Tangi stepped from the shadow of the barn, stood with her head high, her arms at her sides, and called out in a strong, eerie chant, *"Haere ra. Haere ra, e kui."* The words rang like a tribute. *"Haere rangimarie. Haere, haere."* Over and over she called the words as the horse trotted along the fence line and headed down the sandy trail into the pines. Then Tangi stopped. She bowed her head. *"Tena ra koe, e kui,"* she said. "Thank you. *Kia kaha. Kia tau te rangimarie."*

Her voice broke Wim from the spell and she ran down the steps to confront Tangi, her heart pounding. "What happened!" she demanded.

Startled, the girl protested, "I didn't—" Then she shrugged, her old defiant manner returning. "We were in the office. She asked me to get something she'd forgotten in the truck. So I went."

Wim grabbed her arm, incensed. "But you weren't supposed

to *leave* her! You know that! How could you let her trick you like that!"

The girl turned to face her for a moment, her dark eyes unreadable. "I didn't let her trick me," she said, level-voiced. "She needed to go. I knew she was going to. I just let her go." She paused, then added, "You asked me to help you. You would have taken her back to that place."

They stared at each other. But before Wim could collect her thoughts, Evelyn rushed from the barn leading a horse. "Wim!" she yelled. "What the hell is the matter with you! Go after her!" She grabbed Wim by the shoulders and shoved her toward the horse. "Get going! Macho's fast enough to catch up. Just stop her before she kills herself. I've already called the park rangers."

In a daze, Wim mounted the jittery horse, but Evelyn still held the reins. "Do you have any idea where she might go?" she demanded. "I've got to give them some idea where to look."

Wim's eyes met Tangi's. The girl's expression was still inscrutable. Evelyn gave Wim's leg a stinging slap. "Wim, for God's sake!" she cried. Wim dropped her eyes and muttered, "She's going to the sea. The Kid's taking her. That beach across the dunes from the visitor's center—just south of there."

She wondered how she could say this with such certainty, but Evelyn did not question her. She just gave the horse's rump a sharp slap and cried, "Get going!" Macho sprang off and Wim guided him down the trail at a full gallop.

She lay against his neck to avoid low branches until they burst from the trees, then urged him even faster across the open meadow toward the wooded uplands. Within minutes, the horse's lather soaked her and she was breathing as heavily as he was. She was beyond thought; the instinct that had made her so certain where the Kid would go guided her off the trail and across the dunes. The horse labored more slowly in the hot sand, and it seemed forever before they crested a ridge and she caught her first glimpse of the Kid below her. The gray horse was plunging on his haunches down the steep slope, sand frothing on either side of him like the wake of a ship. At the bottom he gathered himself up and raced on, lighter on the sand than Macho was. He appeared almost to skim across the surface, his mane and tail billowing white sails, with Kia no more than a dark blur on his back. It was the most magnificent, wild sight Wim had ever seen.

At that moment, she stopped chasing. She knew suddenly, with a knowledge clear and sharp as the shadow of the Kid against the blinding sand, that she was there to *witness*. To watch. That this was her part in Kia's story, until Kia passed the story on to her. She followed the Kid's churned-up track through the sand and did not attempt to close the distance between them.

The horse and the old woman had already descended out of sight ahead of her over the last dune before Wim saw the ocean. She allowed Macho to walk up the slope to get his wind back, and at the top she pulled him in and gazed around her with wonder. Never had she seen the ocean such a pure, jewel-clear blue. The water was a deeper, more concentrated color than the cloudless sky, as though the sky had risen from the ocean's depths and mixed to a paler shade with the light of the sun. The white beach curved off in either direction into shimmering haze. The only break in its emptiness was the shadow of the horse racing far off to her right.

Macho slid down the final slope and trotted out onto the hard-packed sand along the water's edge. Wim felt a twinge of apprehension. Far down the beach, the Kid and Kia were only a dark speck. The sun was blinding her. She was losing them. But the Kid seemed to sense her doubt and veered suddenly in a wide circle and headed back toward her. She pulled Macho up and waited. The gray horse slowed to a walk when he came near, snorting and tossing his head in greeting, his rider gripping firmly to his back.

Kia's thick hair was loose from its braid and hung tangled down her back. The black eyes gleamed and snapped with life. The face that had been so slack in the nursing home now glowed, and even the old skin was smoothed somehow by the sun and wind. "Charlotte!" she cried, her voice strong and joyful. "Thank you! Thank you!"

She remembered Tangi's last words to her and could not reply. The Kid danced closer and rubbed his head against her leg. She reached to stroke him, and for the first time it registered on her that Evelyn had attached a coiled lead rope to Macho's saddle. All she had to do was slip it quietly around the Kid's neck. It seemed at the moment, as he nuzzled her, that he was giving her the choice.

She looked at Kia. The old woman was sitting up straight, facing the sea, the wind whipping her hair. Wim dropped her hand from the Kid's neck and immediately he stepped away and began to walk along the line of froth where the waves subsided into the sand. Wim followed. Kia rode with a steadiness that belied no fatigue from her journey across the dunes. They did not speak but rode side by side until the thunder of the waves had become the beat of life within them both.

And then the Kid stopped. He faced the sea and tossed his head. The sun, low against the water, flooded each rising wave with blue-green light. Strands of kelp etched dark lines across the translucent blue, and, in the depths beyond the breaking waves, a dark patch pulsed with the current like a heart at the center of a mystery. Wim was not aware she'd dismounted until she felt the cold bite of water around her knees and the spray cooling her face. But Kia rode farther out beyond her on the Kid, out into the sea. The waves lifted the horse gently, carried him farther still, until she had to squint to see him at all.

The water swirled around her and she was filled with a dreamy sense of timelessness; there had never been any other moment than this one and there never would be. Then a huge wave crashed into her, and with it fear, and she stumbled back in the flowing sand and screamed, "Aunt Kia! Aunt Kia!" The wind tore her voice to shreds. She ran after the receding figure of the horse, thrashing through the surging waves, plunging deeper, gulping water and air, crying, "Aunt Kia! Come back!" She lost her footing, fell to her knees, slipped in a tangled skein of brown kelp and was swept deeper out. She fought to swim back. Beyond her she caught sight of the horse, the silvery sheen of his coat and his white mane mingling with the white froth of the waves. "Kid! Kid!" she screamed. Her mouth filled with water and she sank below the surface.

At once something solid bumped against her. The Kid! Relief shot strength through her and she flailed around until she grasped the flowing mane of the horse. A warm, powerful body held her up. She could breathe. She struggled to see. But the Kid was still out beyond her! The wind carried the sound of Kia's laughter and she caught a glimpse of the old woman playing as joyously as a child, rising and falling in the waves, whirling something around her head that flashed and glittered with green fire. And then she let it go. It flew like a comet, burning through the sunlight, arcing high into the sky. Green fire, green stone, flying with Kia's laughter out over the water.

It flashed so close she flinched. The brown arm that held her reached out and caught it between sky and sea. Wim gasped in terror, swallowed bitter water, choked. She struggled against him violently. But she was held firm, clasped tightly against his body in the rocking darkness, taken deeper in until her lungs burned and her eyes were scalded with salt, until her ears filled with roaring and her whole body was torn from her. "Let go! Let go!" She thought it was her own voice, but she could not speak; she was choking. "Let go! Stop! Wim— Open your eyes."

Over and over, relentlessly, the voice pounded her. She struggled weakly. "Open your eyes, Wim." The light seared her salt-swollen eyes. She blinked painfully. Moved her legs. There was solid ground beneath her.

And the man with the tattooed face had not disappeared. He was still holding her, looking at her with smiling eyes. She reached up, traced the dark lines spiraling over his face, touched the glistening green stone that hung around his neck. She whispered, but she did not know what she said. "Yes," he answered. "Yes." She relaxed. He kissed her.

Fourteen ⟲

Neither Kia nor the Kid was ever found. No bodies washed to shore, even though a stiff onshore wind picked up and blew for several days. After a week, the Coast Guard and various Province Lands officials could no longer consider the search for the body of Katherine Irene Thorpe a priority. Sam Thorpe had to accept, finally, that Kia had been swept far out into the Atlantic. Wim understood these things vaguely, from the bits of conversation she heard during the groggy days that followed. She lay on the bed or sat in the chair in her room, not sick or well, not asleep or awake. She asked nothing and thought nothing. She was motionless much of the time. Within herself she would drift down, down into a swaying darkness where she was solitary and safe. But whenever her parents came she would be forced to struggle reluctantly back, rising through realms of formless shadows, through flowing kelp, through silent, diffused light that fragmented the solid world of people and words. "It's shock," she heard her mother say. "She almost drowned. And she watched Kia die." But the explanation meant nothing to her. She had no questions, no thoughts, no feelings about anything.

She didn't mind when her father sat with her. If she was in bed, he would smooth the hair from her forehead as he had when she was a little girl and murmur things that needed no answer. If she was in the chair, he would sit on her bed and read the newspaper in companionable silence. But her mother came and went busily, bringing food, making the bed, urging her to eat or walk or drink. And talking, always talking. Her mother's words washed in and out through Wim like the tide, inexorable, inescapable. So she slept more and more.

Once, she drifted awake and saw the white heron flying over her. She stared at it for hours. Her mother came in and said, "Tangi brought that for you. Do you want me to leave it, or take it away?"

Wim had no response. Carol put the tray of food down on the table by the bed, hesitated, then went to the painting and took it down. Wim caught her breath, almost inaudibly, but her mother turned to look at her. "You need to speak, Wimmie," she said softly. She was holding the painting so Wim could not see it. "Do you want me to leave it?"

Wim turned her face to the wall. After a moment, she heard her mother sigh and leave the room. When she opened her eyes, the painting was back where it had been on the dresser. The white heron flew on wings of light across a storm-dark sea, traversing two worlds. She sat up slowly and gazed at it. Beside her on the table the food her mother had brought grew cold as usual. She was never hungry. The house was still; the air stagnant and warm. She looked around at her room, felt a momentary stir of familiarity. It frightened her. She curled up on the bed, squeezed her eyes shut, tried to drift away again. But the image of the white heron was emblazoned in her mind's eye. Each time she began to sink into the swaying depths, its white wings would cut across the darkness, and her eyes would open of their own accord.

She fought against it until she was exhausted. Carol came back in, gathered up the untouched food tray; she could feel her mother watching her. After a moment Carol sat on the bed, and gradually Wim became aware that her mother was crying. Carol whispered, "Oh, Wim, come back. I don't understand what's happened to you. I don't know what to do. I don't know what to do without you."

Wim opened her eyes. The white heron lifted her effortlessly on its great wings. "Why?" Wim asked.

Carol gasped softly. "Because I love you," she cried in a low voice. "Because you are my miracle. You are the miracle of my life." She reached for Wim's hands and held them tightly, an expression of frightened intensity in her eyes. "Oh, God . . . if you had drowned . . . oh, thank God David found you in time."

The faintest tingle of something shot through her, like sensation returning to a limb that had been asleep. She faltered. "David?"

"David saved you, Wimmie," Carol said. Her voice broke a little, and she spoke quickly, nervously, like she was afraid Wim would disappear before she finished. "You got caught in an undertow. The rangers were looking, the Coast Guard, everyone. Your horse was running around loose . . . Evelyn told them where to go, but . . . it's a lot of beach, and they couldn't find you . . . but David saw you and dragged you out—"

"But . . . no. No, it wasn't David—"

"And thank God he knew artificial respiration, because no one else was close enough to get to you in time. He looked after you until the rangers got there." Carol stopped and took a jagged breath, tried to smile, her hands trembling around Wim's.

"But it wasn't . . . it wasn't." Restlessness overwhelmed her and she sat up uneasily.

Sam appeared in the doorway. "Well, look at you!" he exclaimed joyfully. Behind him Wim caught a movement, and Carol frowned. "Sam, this isn't—" But she was interrupted by Tangi bursting into the room.

"You're looking *bonzo!* Wow! Hey. *Ki'ora!*" the girl cried happily. But once the words were out she seemed suddenly at a loss for what to say next and stood smiling with uncertainty at Wim.

"Well, come in, Tangi. Now that you're here," said Carol, testy. She got up and took the tray. "Wim, I'm going to bring you more food. And you have to eat it. And Tangi—you can stay ten minutes. That's all."

Sam left with her, blowing a kiss to Wim. Tangi said, "Wow. Wish my mum looked after me like that. Breakfast in bed and all. Maybe I would've stayed home more, eh. Lucky you—" She came closer to the bed but stopped when she saw the painting. "Oh," she said, pleased. "Didn't know if she'd put it up for you or not. She wouldn't let anyone up here, you know." She gave Wim a shy glance. "It's yours. If you'd like it. Uncle David wanted you to have it."

Tangi's words were tumbling around her like the waves; she couldn't get her bearings. She fought the impulse to lie down and turn toward the wall again. "David," she said at last. "David. My mother said he saved me—" She watched Tangi's eyes go dark and unreadable. "But . . . but it wasn't him, was it?"

The girl shook her head. "No," she answered in a low voice. "He told me he found you on the beach and made sure you were breathing. But the others were farther away, and they thought it was him way out in the water bringing you in, and Uncle David said it was better to let them think so."

"Yes," said Wim, and she remembered why they had all been there.

They averted their eyes from each other at the same time. *Oh Aunt Kia,* Wim thought, and anguish welled up in her. *Oh Aunt Kia, I'm sorry. I'm sorry I let you go—*

Carol returned with sandwiches. "I made some for you, too, Tangi," she offered.

"Ta. But I have to go," the girl muttered, and edged out of the room.

Carol gave a frowning little laugh. "Strange girl," she commented. She pushed the plate of sandwiches toward Wim. "Eat." After a moment she said anxiously, "I thought, if you were feeling better, I might work half a shift . . . but I could call them—"

"I'm fine," Wim said. She ate mechanically, tasting nothing. Carol waited until she was done before getting up to leave. She took the plate and went toward the door.

The panic slammed Wim without warning. "Mom—" she whispered. Her mother turned swiftly back. *Mom. I let her go.*

I didn't stop her. Was I wrong? "Mom?" *Tell me! Tell me! Did I make a terrible mistake?* Her voice stuck. The words got tangled. "Was I a mistake?"

Her mother stared at her. Wim clutched the sheets. "I mean . . . I mean—did you really think I was a miracle? Not a mistake?"

Carol said softly, "I still think you're a miracle. Every single day."

Later, Wim wandered downstairs. The house was quiet. No one was home; David's car was not by the cottage. She went into Kia's room. Her father had already begun to return the space to its original use as his study. The desk had been moved, boxes brought from the cottage, the bed dismantled, the mattress propped against a wall. There was not a sign of Kia left. Wim stood in the middle of the room and tried to feel something. She could not cry. A slow terror crept over her; she knew without doubt that she could not survive the same emptiness she'd felt after Jilly died. She sank to her knees. "Rereahu!" she called in a low voice. "Rereahu! Please . . . please." But she did not know what she was asking.

The blinds had been drawn and the room was a dim, dimensionless space around her. Nothing stirred except the fear whispering at the edges of herself, like a dry, unhealthy wind. She willed herself to cry, fiercely twisted her face, clenched her fists. But no tears came. After a moment she gave up and gazed around hopelessly.

She had seen the boxes when she first came in, but nothing had registered. Now, suddenly, she stumbled to her feet, searched among them frantically. It did not take long to find the journal; it was at the top of a box of papers, waiting for her. Carefully she lifted it out.

She turned the yellowed pages one by one, running her hand lightly over Emmanuel Dart's coded words. Gradually she became aware of a strange comfort, as if the journal was a dream she'd woken from and understood completely. She stepped closer to the window, meaning to raise the shade so she could look more closely at the indecipherable writing. A sliver of filtered light fell over the open page and she caught briefly the reflection of her movement in the glass that covered the genealogy chart hanging on the wall. She glanced at herself, at the page superimposed over her image in the glass, and gasped softly. She held the page closer. *She could read it in the glass.* Emmanuel Dart's code was backwards writing.

She jerked open the shade and went to the mirror over the dresser. She held the journal up, read briefly, turned the pages until she came almost to the end. Her breath caught in her throat, she peered close and ran her finger slowly along a line of text.

June 1835. Two weeks out from the Horn of Africa. Capt'n Thorpe put in at Cape Town for supplies, but many too sick to go ashore. Much doctoring work. Bad storms. Teeanniwa seasick. Her Condition makes it worse.

The blood rushed to her face. She turned the page, hardly breathing.

June 20, 1835. Willie follows me around, bewildered. He knows nothing of women, and has never understood that he is a Married man these last two months. He wishes only to play with Teeanniwa as a child plays with its mother. The Captain has ordered me to look after Teeanniwa, teach her such English as I can, and tend to her needs. Dr Kendall tells me the Captain fears for the life of his coming grandchild.

Capt'n Thorpe bids us call the poor girl Annie. She is Christian now, he says, and his Son's wife. O but I can hardly look this man in the face! It is my conscience that bids me record all I know on these pages, for I am bound by the foulest Blackmail to reveal nothing to any living soul. Capt'n Thorpe has committed an outrage against God that is beyond Comprehension. He bought this poor girl from her Heathen captors for the price of ten guns and has taken her away from all she knows. We had barely cleared the harbor at Kororareka when he used his Authority as master of a vessel to marry her to his son, in order that he might claim the child he knew she would bear as his grandson and heir. But the child she carries is his own! For he uses Teeanniwa secretly as a concubine. His lust has taken command of his Senses and he has forced her into this marriage to hide his Sin.

This, then, was Emmanuel Dart's terrible secret: Thomas Alexander Thorpe—Kia's Grampy—was not poor simple Willie's son after all, but the illegitimate child of Captain Thorpe himself and the woman he bought from slavery. Wim put the journal down thoughtfully and frowned, gazing at the genealogy chart. All those sorrows, all those secrets—they had taken place so long ago. More than a hundred and sixty years had buried Captain Thorpe's sins. And now, what could it really matter? Was it only a question of a single generation, more or less? She gazed at herself in the mirror and thought, *I am the youngest descendant of Captain Charles Williamson Thorpe.* But it meant no more to her now than it ever had. Emmanuel Dart's journal only emphasized the questions it wasn't answering.

Who was Rereahu? Why had a man with a tattooed face come seeking Kia's Grampy when he was a young man, claiming him as a brother and demanding a necklace of green stone?

There were only two pages remaining in Emmanuel Dart's journal. Once again, Wim turned the book toward the mirror.

December 2, 1835. Annie's son is born today. He is small and sickly and Dr Kendall does not believe he will live. He has recorded in the Log that the babe was born too early. He tells me in Private he worries for the Captain's sanity. Damn the Captain! I cannot think of any but the terrible Sorrows the mother bears all alone in her heart. The Captain has named the child Thomas Alexander Thorpe and makes great show of congratulating Willie. False man! He even caused his crew to be given an extra dram of whiskey in celebration.

Poor Willie, through all, looks happy and bewildered by turns, and claps his hands with the Delight of a child who knows only that his elders are pleased with him. The birth of the child seems a portent, of what I cannot tell. Thank God we have sighted land today for the first time in more than a month. If God forgives us all, we will be Home before Christmas and Annie's child will live . . ."

The water-swollen pages had degraded badly toward the end and Wim struggled to make out the words in the mirror. One whole passage was obliterated by a dark stain. At times, Emmanuel Dart's handwriting appeared shaky and hurried, and she imagined him hiding the journal under his blankets at night and writing almost blind.

Teeanniwa sings and speaks to him secretly in her Native tongue, which the Captain has directed me to forbid her from using. But the Heathen words are wonderfully soft and soothing to the babe, esp. when he wakes. Kia orra, she sings to him, kia orra. I take pains to warn her when the Captain is near. Teeanniwa calls her son Tamatoa when they are alone, and she places around his tiny neck her own necklace, a pendant of green carved stone on a cord . . .

The words disintegrated under another stain. Wim wiped the mirror in frustration and leaned closer, angling the journal to catch the light.

. . . teaching her English, and she is quick to learn. I vow before God I will watch over her as best I can when we return home, and continue to help her in what little way I am able. She will live as Willie's wife in the Captain's house in Provincetown, and no doubt will be taught to attend the Captain's sickly wife, and will serve as secret concubine for the Captain himself. O poor creature! O sad and terrible story! I do not understand why God would allow such Misery as Teeanniwa is forced to bear. I have indeed learned the dark and unimaginable sorrows of the Human heart, of which Dr Kendall spoke at the beginning of this Journey . . .

She had come to the end of the page. There were no more. Along the inner binding of the leather cover she could see the torn edges of what might have been more pages, but it was difficult to tell for sure. She closed the journal and cradled it against her, looked around the room. A hundred and sixty years before, a Maori woman had lived out her unhappy story in this house. Te Aniwa. She counted the generations on her fingers.

Her great-great-great-great grandmother. Unfathomable. As distant from her world as the diaphanous horizon of the sea curving away under the sky.

She sighed and with an inexplicable sense of discomfiture, placed the journal back in the box and closed the top. It didn't seem to fit as well as it had before and she fiddled with it, uneasily feeling she had to hide any sign that she'd touched it. She glanced quickly around her.

David stood in the doorway.

They both froze, each as startled as the other. David spoke first, gesturing awkwardly with some papers he held. "I didn't see you," he said. "I just came in to put these back . . . the rest of your father's papers—"

They might have been seeing each other again for the first time, at once total strangers and utterly known to each other. He moved into the room and she stepped back, and the sudden astonishment and hurt in his dark eyes threw her into confusion. He said, in his formal way, "I'm happy to see you looking so well."

She said, "Thank you," hating the stiffness in her voice, wondering if she was meant to thank him, too, for saving her life. Then, flustered, she remembered he hadn't and was grateful when David turned away to put the papers on her father's desk.

"It's a good thing I checked. I packed these with my own material," he said. "I might have taken them by mistake when I leave tomorrow."

"You're leaving tomorrow?" she asked blankly.

He nodded in silence.

"*Tomorrow?*" she gasped. He turned swiftly and caught

her to him. She whispered against his heartbeat, "I don't understand!"

"Oh, *hine*—"

"But when . . . how long have I been—"

He took her face between his hands and looked into her eyes. "You've been up in your room for a week, *hine*," he said. He tried to smile. "Your mum set up guard by the door. She wouldn't let anyone in. Your friends Tammy and Evelyn stopped by a few times, and Tangi pestered your mother every day." He was keeping his voice light, but she wasn't sure if she was trembling or if David was.

"She didn't let you come see me?" she mumbled.

He said fervently, "It didn't matter. I never left you, *hine*. Not for a moment. I don't need to see you to be with you." His breath brushed her cheek and she lifted her face, touched his lips with her own, and this time he did not pull away. She closed her eyes and breathed in his breath and felt his body around her as she'd felt the ocean holding her.

"Who are you?" she cried in a low voice. "Are you Rereahu? Who are *we?*"

He kissed her fiercely, on her mouth and eyes, in her hair, on her mouth again. "Let's go out somewhere," he said finally. "I want to show you something."

She sat awkwardly in the car, arms and legs like jelly, stomach churning. She was uncertain where to look, how to sit. The August traffic forced David to drive at a walking pace down Bradford Street, and the afternoon sun burned them uncomfortably through the windshield. He turned the car abruptly down Shank Painter Road, giving her a quick, subdued smile.

"Let's get ice cream," he said. He stopped at the Dairy Queen and she followed him to a table. Even among the noise and dust and running children, the crowds of tourists and dogs and bicycles, a strange stillness surrounded them. He got two cones and handed her one. "Bloody awful stuff, soft ice cream," he said, grinning. He inspected his cone before lopping off the top with one bite. "It's catching on in New Zealand, though. Everything American is."

He gazed around at the crowds and licked his ice cream slowly. Gradually Wim relaxed. He was giving her time to collect herself. When she thought he would not notice, she studied him. Under the tattered umbrella, his skin was very dark. His dense, cropped hair accentuated the broad bones of his face. She gazed at his mouth. It was wide, full lipped. Powerful. She was filled with sudden wonder. She had kissed that mouth.

He turned and met her gaze. His eyes let her in completely. Intent. Longing. Troubled. The eyes of the man with the tattooed face. "What am I going to do?" he asked softly.

"Don't go."

"I can't stay—"

She cried, "You live so far away!"

He laughed a little. "No place is unreachable," he said. "The world isn't as big as all that." He smiled at her. "You remember me telling you about my friend Ian? The one who works with endangered birds? He told me once that birds have no concept of distance. It doesn't matter if it's an albatross with a wingspan of two meters or a hummingbird the size of your little finger. They just fly till they get to where they want to be."

"Like the *kotuku*—" she murmured.

He looked at her sharply and was silent awhile. Finally he took a deep breath and said casually, "You know, Ian's always needing people who're willing to slog around in the bush and watch whatever he needs watched. It's hard to hire people who'll stay for long at a job like that. They have to spend a lot of time alone—"

"I like being alone," said Wim.

"They have to be observant, and not get bored."

"I never get bored watching things."

"And I don't think it pays very well . . ." David finished.

Wim shrugged. They smiled happily at each other. David hesitated again. "There's something I'd like to talk about—" he began.

The stillness enveloping them seemed to pulse almost visibly. Wim said quickly, "Not here."

She directed him to Herring Cove. "I love this beach," she said. "It's magical. It's one of the only places on the East Coast where you can watch the sun go down over the ocean."

They walked along the pebbled sand until the sky deepened into dusk. They had long ago left the late afternoon crowds and now passed only the occasional surf fisherman. The dying sun broke dramatically through the dark clouds at the edge of the horizon and plated the water with molten gold. Great streaks of light shot through the indigo sky. Wim stood still. "This is how Aunt Kia died," she murmured. "Bursting into death. It's the way she wished she'd lived."

They sat side by side on the beach, shoulders touching. The air had grown cool, but warmth lingered in the sand. "I just don't understand anything," she said at last, gazing out over the water. "Aunt Kia was old, but she was so alive. I don't understand why she died. I never understood why Jilly died, either. The reasons don't seem to explain anything. It just happened. I've never understood the man with the tattooed face. He just happened, too. And you . . . us. I don't understand *us*."

He laughed quietly. "I'm not sure I understand much, either," he said. "Certainly not *us*. It's a mystery." Wim shivered as a cool breeze riffled in off the water. David put his arms around her, pulled her close, and said thoughtfully, "But mysteries aren't puzzles. Their power is in being a mystery. I don't think we're meant to figure them out. We only need to answer their call. Especially *because* we don't understand." He looked seriously into her eyes. "And you have, you know. Answered. And that takes courage."

She didn't respond. He held her warmly, but she was tense and anxious waiting for him to talk. After a moment he shifted a little so he could see her. "Henry Cooper was my great-great-great grandfather," he began slowly.

"The one who left New Zealand and never returned?"

David nodded. Paused. "Henry Cooper was his *Pakeha* name. His Maori name was Rereahu."

She gazed at him, not moving, feeling only that she was waiting. David continued, "Henry Cooper was the name the missionaries gave him. They had raised him since he was a baby. But when he was a young man, and after he'd left the mission to get married, he rejected everything *Pakeha*. He became involved in a Maori movement whose visionary leader was a *tohunga* named Kotuku."

"Kotuku!" she cried softly. "The man who could become the white heron!"

David nodded. "'That's when Henry Cooper took back the name Rereahu and had his face tattooed with a traditional *moko*. Rereahu grew up in the 1840s and '50s—unsettled times in the Bay of Islands. He must have been deeply affected by the unrest between Maori and *Pakeha*. Kotuku encouraged his followers to reject *Pakeha* ways and to hold to the old traditions. We can reclaim our voice, he would tell them. We can reclaim our stories. We must speak from the earth and sea and sky of Aotearoa."

"That's really why you came here, isn't it?" Wim asked softly, searching his face. "To reclaim your story."

He looked startled a moment, then he smiled. "You do have the most penetrating eyes of anyone I've ever known," he murmured. He leaned down and kissed her, first on one eye and then the other.

She wanted to relax under his touch, but something troubled her and she pulled away. "Why couldn't you tell me any of this before?" she asked in a low voice. "Why did you—and Tangi, too—keep everything such a secret?"

David did not answer. The only sound Wim heard was the constant, quiet rattling of pebbles under the waves. She was afraid to look at him, afraid he would shut her out again. After several minutes, David reached into his pocket and took out a thickly folded paper. He held it with what seemed to Wim like reverence.

At last he said, "All my life I've wanted to learn and teach the true history of my people. Maori have had their stories taken by *Pakeha* for a long, long time. Do you have any idea how much Maori culture has been lost, or twisted into quaint curiosities, or dismissed as silly superstition?" He cupped both hands around the folded paper fiercely. "I didn't want that to happen with this story. It's my family, our family's ancestor . . . I was trying to protect the story until it had fully spoken."

"Protect it? Against me?" Wim said bitterly. Then, bewildered, she asked, "But isn't it my story, too?"

David's smile was reflective. "I've had to do a lot of thinking since I came here. You see? There's a lot I don't understand, either." His voice grew so soft she had to lean closer to hear. "Maybe stories *can't* be claimed," he said. "Maybe stories have lives of their own, and grow and change like people do. Maybe they just go wherever they're needed. Maybe stories are the only thing that can truly connect us all." He looked into her eyes now. "I'm learning how to live with what I don't understand. You're teaching me, cousin."

Carefully, David unfolded the paper he'd taken from his pocket and smoothed it out on his knee. It appeared luminous in the last light. He handed it to her. "I think you can still read it. It will explain everything. But you'll see— " He shrugged, chuckling. "It will still be a mystery."

The paper was thick, and old, as old as the pages in the journal. The handwriting was strangely familiar. She drew in her breath sharply. "Emmanuel Dart!" she exclaimed, and began to read.

Provincetown, Massachusetts, May 20, the yr. of Our Lord 1841. To the Reverend Mr Garret, at the Mission in Kororareka, Bay of Islands, New Zealand.

Kind Sir: I send this letter into your keeping for a Mowree boy of your Mission, given into your care as a babe some Six years past. His mother gave him the name of ReereAhu.

I am gravely ill, Sir, and perhaps near death of Tuberculosis, and for this Reason it is my Duty to write of the truth concerning this boy's Mother, for a terrible Sin was committed against her in the eyes of God. I beg of you, give this letter to ReereAhu when he is of appropriate age, so that he might journey here to find his mother and bring her home to her Native land. For these last six years I have watched in helpless sorrow as this woman grows ever weaker with Grief, and my own heart cannot bear any more. She is called here Anne Thorpe, altho' her rightful name be Teeanniwa. She was taken captive in a war betwixt two heathen tribes and was brought as a Slave by the victors to Kororareka. There she was sold to Captain Chas. Wm. Thorpe of Provincetown, Master of the trading sloop Agatha Anne, *for the price of ten guns. He married her off to his only son, William, who is afflicted with the mind and manners of a child, for the purpose of obtaining an heir.*

Kind Sir, forgive me for broaching such delicate matters. But is not Truth before God more important than our frail Human sensibilities? It is whispered among the gossipers in this town that the child Annie Thorpe bore is not her husband William's son, but rather is the son of William's own father, Capt'n Thorpe. It is my observation that the Captain believes this, too, for he cherishes the child as his own. But all of them are wrong. Sir, Anne Thorpe's son, called Thomas Alexander, is no Thorpe at all, but is the full-blooded son of his Mowree father, a warrior who was killed in the tribal war.

Teeanniwa revealed to me that she was already with child when she was taken into slavery, and I have lately forced this same confession from Dr Kendall, to whom I was apprenticed.

He examined her when she was first brought on board our ship,
and he confirms that what she says is true. In fear for her well-
being, Dr Kendall did not tell the Captain, who, in his anger,
might have abandoned the poor girl on one of the South Seas is-
lands where he put in to Trade on our Voyage home.

The wind from the sea was rushing through Wim, burning
her face with sand, racing in her blood so her heart pounded.
She clutched the letter with both hands and continued reading.

I abhor Slavery in any guise, Sir, as I believe any Christian
must. I do not need to hear the Abolitionists talk to know that it
is the Devil's wickedness to separate a child from his mother.
ReereAhu's mother lives here, far across the sea from her native
shores, as does his full brother, Thos. Alexander, who his mother
calls Tamatoa. He is now a boy of almost 6 years. Remember-
ing your many kindnesses to me many years back, I implore
you, kind Rev Garret, to give this letter to ReereAhu so he might
learn of his mother's cruel fate. Encourage him to find some
means to journey here when he is grown, to bring his mother
and his brother home. In the name of God, I beg you to help put
right this terrible wrong. I can do no more, but I can die more
easy knowing I have spoken.

With respect, yr. Obediant servant,
Emmanuel Dart.

The wind gusted around her, tore the letter from her hands.
It rose up, the paper fluttering like white wings against the
darkness. Wim cried out and stumbled after it, but David
caught her arm. "Let it go," he said quietly. "It has spoken its
story. Let it fly away."

He reached again into his pocket and put something smooth

and heavy into her hand. Her fingers closed around it; it was warm from his body. She held up her hand and opened her fingers so it lay on her palm, faintly glimmering green in the light of the first stars. "Oh!" she breathed. "Oh!" She looked in wonder at David.

"Te Aniwa had two pendants," he said. "This is the one she put around the neck of Rereahu, her eldest son, when he was taken from her and given to the missionaries. The other she put around the neck of her other son, Thomas Alexander. Tamatoa."

"Grampy." She cupped her hand around the carved stone, the cord slipping over her fingers. She could feel the shape of the pendant more clearly than see it. She held it against her cheek and closed her eyes. She whispered, "But how did you get this . . . and the letter? And what happened to Rereahu?"

"He left Aotearoa and disappeared forever," said David. "Reverend Garret apparently didn't give him the letter until he was eighteen, when he left the Mission to get married. He was still known as Henry Cooper then. Perhaps it was the letter that disillusioned him about the *Pakeha.* Or maybe he was just swept up in the violent unrest that was growing between Maori and *Pakeha* in the Bay of Islands. I don't know. But he left the Mission to become one of Kotuku's most active followers, and in 1853 he signed on with the crew of a whaling ship bound for Cape Cod. I found the crew list — it's the last official record with his name on it. The ship arrived in New Bedford in late October 1854. In November of 1854, records show that a Mr. T. A. Thorpe of Provincetown reported to the authorities that a 'grotesquely marked heathenish man' had been hanging around in the vicinity of his grandfather's house . . ."

"He's still hanging around," Wim whispered.

David gave her the same private, compelling smile Wim remembered from the day she'd found him in the kitchen with her father. He concluded, "Before he left New Zealand, Rereahu gave the letter and the greenstone pendant to his wife for their little son . . . and they have been kept in our family ever since."

They sat in silence a few moments. A quarter moon had risen, casting a pale, rippling shimmer over the sea. Far out in the darkness she thought she saw something white briefly catch the reflected light. A gull, perhaps, or a late sailboat. Or a piece of paper drifting on the wind. "He never found his mother," Wim said softly at last.

David tightened his arms around her. They were speaking in whispers now in the vast night. "No. Te Aniwa had died years earlier, not long after Emmanuel Dart wrote his letter, when her son Thomas Alexander was still a small child. Rereahu did not arrive until Thomas was a young man. Old Captain Thorpe had died by then, too, believing all his life that his secret was the truth . . . that Thomas, whom he called his grandson, was really his own son with Te Aniwa. I had no way of knowing whether Rereahu ever actually spoke to his brother . . ."

"Until you met Aunt Kia," Wim said excitedly. "But you didn't even know about her! You didn't know that she had just come to live with us."

David said, "No. *I* didn't. But the *story* knew. And the story needed to speak. It just needed to find the right voices."

Wim opened her hand again, and by the light of the moon she could see the carved green pendant more clearly. It lay in her palm, a weird, contorted figure with a huge head and great round eyes of iridescent shell set into the stone. "And now the story's ended," she said, almost to herself.

David looked at her seriously, stroked her hair, whispered, "But what about this? Us? Are you sure the story's ended?"

She flushed, lay the green stone against her cheek in confusion. David said, "As long as we are here, our story continues. I believe that. Maori know that our *tipuna*, our ancestors, live with us and guide us. Their spirit, their voice, give us our *turangawaewae*. They give us a place to stand to speak our stories."

She gave him a troubled look. "But my ancestors aren't even who I thought they were," she said. "I'm not a Thorpe at all. How can *I* speak, if where I stand was a lie?"

David laughed quietly and kissed her. "Beloved cousin," he said. "You've uncovered one mystery to discover another. You see? Stories don't end."

Wim had no idea of the time when they finally walked back along the beach toward the now deserted parking lot. They had not spoken for a long time. Wim dangled the green stone pendant, let it dance and whirl at the end of its cord so it flashed in the moonlight. When they came to the wooden walkway leading from the beach to the lot, she turned and went to the edge of the sea, waded into the dark water, felt the sand give way beneath her feet. "Aunt Kia!" she whispered. "I found it, Aunt Kia. You wanted me to have it—"

The stone glimmered at the end of the cord like a green star hanging above the waves. She stepped deeper in. Suddenly she raised her arm, whirled the necklace. Let go. The stone rose in an arc over her, a flickering green flame in the darkness. She reached out—

And caught it. And slipped the cord around her neck. The greenstone lay cool and smooth against her skin, and her heart was full. "I'm not afraid, Aunt Kia," she called. "I'm not afraid."

She walked out of the sea and onto solid ground.

Epilogue ෨෧

The wind blowing in from the ocean smelled fresh; more rain was coming. It rippled over the marsh grass in the estuary and turned it a pale, silvery gray. The tide was on the ebb, and flocks of shore birds had descended on the newly exposed mud. Wim crawled on her stomach over thick grass hummocks and cautiously lifted her head. She was wet; she was always wet now, it seemed, and she had come to expect the wind that, even in summer with the sun breaking frequently through the clouds, was always chilly. But she did not notice it in her excitement. A high-pitched piping was coming from the reeds that hung over the tidal creek just beyond where she lay.

She'd lost count of how many days of watching it had taken to find them this close. She hadn't even been completely sure, until now, that the small brown ducks she'd seen flying low over distant reaches of the estuary were the rare brown teal. But the piping sounds, broken occasionally by a low, distinctive bleat, were unmistakable. The estuary was a labyrinth of meandering brown creeks that cut through the marsh and down across low dunes above the beach. She had set her camp higher up, on the near headland where she could scan the whole area with binoculars, and earlier this morning she'd seen a skein of ducks skim along the water up the coast and settle inland on one of the main arteries of the creek. It had taken her three hours to work her way around stealthily from the beachside and crawl through the marsh to her present vantage point.

She rested a moment before carefully pulling the binoculars from the waterproof case around her neck, then she raised herself inch by inch onto her knees. She peered over the tops of the grasses. A broad smile broke across her face and she mouthed a silent "Yes!" of triumph. The group of eight brown teal ducks —one of the rarest species in the country—dabbled peacefully along the shallows near the creek bank. As she watched, one of the drakes tipped tail up to feed under the water, and she held her breath to keep the binoculars steady. There was no metallic band around the duck's leg. Another bird tipped down, tail waggling. No band. This was an unknown, uncounted group of ducks. A warm satisfaction spread through her.

The ducks fed slowly, keeping to a protected area of the creek, and Wim watched until the sun was high overhead. She paid no attention to time or personal comfort when she was out in the marshes. Here she experienced no boundaries between her inner solitude and the solitude of water, wind, and earth. Even the wild storms that thundered up the coast no longer frightened her. Only darkness kept her tentbound, and then she read, or worked on her field notes, or sent E-mails on her laptop until she fell into a contented sleep.

She didn't know what made her suddenly turn her head. The wind through the hummocks, the rattling cry of king-fishers diving from fenceposts, the quiet muttering of the ducks . . . there had been no other sound. But all at once she caught sight of a deep, still pool in the creek that she had not noticed before. She caught her breath.

"Rereahu?" she whispered. "Rereahu?"

But she could not be sure. Perhaps it was only, after all, a golden brown patch of weed in water painted on by the shadows of scudding clouds and lacy webs of marsh grass. Then a cloud blocked out the sun. At the same moment, she saw the reflection of something large and white sweep across the darkened surface of the pool.

The great white heron landed on the far bank and hopped a few steps, his huge wings half extended, before he folded them gracefully against his body. She knew the bird could see her, but still, with deliberate care, it waded step by slow step into the pool until it stood no more than six feet from where Wim lay. Her heart was pounding so hard she could hear it drumming against the earth. The heron surveyed the water, his beautiful neck curved and his beak poised to strike. He was motionless, a carving of polished marble. Shadows from the wind-shredded clouds slipped over his plumage. Wim was so close she could see drops of water beaded like diamonds on the broad wing feathers.

A fine, misting squall came in from across the ocean. She did not know if it was the mist or her own tears that obscured her vision of the white heron. *"Kotuku!"* she called in a low voice. *"Tena koe, kotuku! Tena koe, e rangatira!"*

She was not even sure she'd spoken aloud. But the great bird lifted its wings and rose into the wind, hovering almost motionless directly over her before sailing off on slow wingbeats farther down the creek. She watched until it had disappeared into the mist. For a long time she lay where she was, watching the piping ducks, gazing at the water, until she was roused by the far-off honking of a car horn.

The world came tumbling back over her. It was mid-afternoon, today was Thursday, and her weekly supplies were due to arrive. She scrambled as quickly as she could back across the marsh to the beach. From there, she could see the headland that rose on the far end, opposite her camp, and could just make out the dirt track that switchbacked down the steep slope from the road above. She waved and received a honk in reply.

It would take the Land Rover several minutes to traverse the winding track down to the paddock bordering the marsh. By the time she reached the gate, it would be bumping across the roughly grazed field toward her. She hoped they'd remembered her request for a new rain slicker to replace the one she'd torn three days ago.

She'd already shut the gate behind her and was walking across the paddock before she realized it wasn't Ian's assistant, Fiona, driving as usual, or taciturn Gavin who'd come the first week. She dragged her muddy arm across her face, trying to wipe the misting rain from her eyes. The Land Rover stopped. A moment later she, too, stopped. Amazed. Heart racing.

She gasped, "David! David!" and ran over the slick grass.

"Charlotte Williamson Thorpe, I presume?" David said as he hopped from the Land Rover. They stood grinning at each other. Wim was out of breath. David said, "I needed a holiday, eh. I can't bear to mark another exam. I'm sick of students. Ian told me where to look for you—I wanted to surprise you. That's why I didn't let you know I was coming—"

Speechless, she shook her head. She reached for his hand and with her other pointed toward the sea. Flying along the edge of the water, flying between storm and light, *kotuku* was coming home.

Thorpe Genealogical Chart

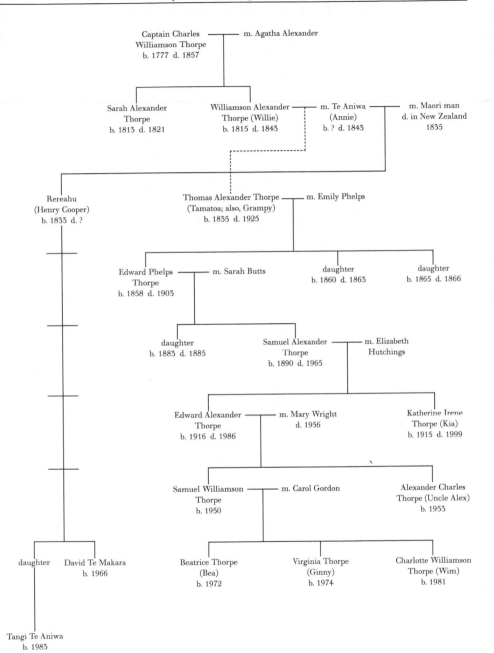

Captain Charles Williamson Thorpe
b. 1777 d. 1857
— m. Agatha Alexander

Sarah Alexander Thorpe
b. 1813 d. 1821

Williamson Alexander Thorpe (Willie)
b. 1815 d. 1843
— m. Te Aniwa (Annie)
b. ? d. 1843
— m. Maori man
d. in New Zealand 1835

Rereahu (Henry Cooper)
b. 1833 d. ?

Thomas Alexander Thorpe (Tamatoa; also, Grampy)
b. 1835 d. 1925
— m. Emily Phelps

Edward Phelps Thorpe
b. 1858 d. 1903
— m. Sarah Butts

daughter
b. 1860 d. 1863

daughter
b. 1865 d. 1866

daughter
b. 1883 d. 1885

Samuel Alexander Thorpe
b. 1890 d. 1965
— m. Elizabeth Hutchings

Edward Alexander Thorpe
b. 1916 d. 1986
— m. Mary Wright
d. 1956

Katherine Irene Thorpe (Kia)
b. 1915 d. 1999

Samuel Williamson Thorpe
b. 1950
— m. Carol Gordon

Alexander Charles Thorpe (Uncle Alex)
b. 1953

daughter

David Te Makara
b. 1966

Beatrice Thorpe (Bea)
b. 1972

Virginia Thorpe (Ginny)
b. 1974

Charlotte Williamson Thorpe (Wim)
b. 1981

Tangi Te Aniwa
b. 1983

aroha—love

aroha nui—with love

e noho ra—stay well (to a person staying)

haere ra—farewell (to a person departing)

haere rangimarie—farewell, go in peace

haeremai—greeting of welcome: come, welcome

He aha te mate?—What is wrong?

hine—term of endearment; "honey"

Ka ao, ka ao, ka awatea—It is dawn, it's light, the daylight breaks

ka aroha pai—well done

ka kite ano—we'll meet again

ka nui tenei—that's enough

ka pai; ka pai ra—good, well

kai—food

kai moana—food from the sea

kaitiaki—guardian, keeper, a guardian spirit

kakapo—endangered New Zealand bird

kia kaha—stay strong, be strong

kia kaha tonu—keep going strongly

kia ora (ki'ora)—greeting (less formal)

kia ora koe—thank you

kia tau te rangimarie—let peace be with all

kokako—endangered New Zealand bird

Kokiri te manu—The bird awakens

kotuku—white heron; rare visitor

kui (e kui)—form of address to a respected older woman

kuia—an older woman, an elder

Ma te Atua koe e tiaki—May God take care of you

mana—prestige, status (loose translation)

Maoritanga—anything that relates directly to the values and concepts of the Maori people

matakite—seer, prophet

Me mahi tahi tatou—We must work together

moko—tattoo; refers to the traditional Maori facial tattoo

mokopuna—grandchild

Pakeha—means "ghost-like"; commonly used to refer to white New Zealanders of European descent

porangi—crazy

rangatira—chiefly or noble person, or one possessing these qualities; a respected leader

takahi—endangered New Zealand bird

Takiri ko te ata—Dawn breaks

tama—young boy

te kotuku rerenga tuarangi—honored, rare visitor

tena koe; tena ra koe; tena ra koutou—various forms of greeting to one or more persons; also, "thank you"

tipuna—ancestors

tohunga—teacher of sacred customs; an expert in, and keeper of, traditional Maori knowledge

tuakana—older sister

turangawaewae—standing place; place of belonging

whakatata mai—come closer

Glossary of New Zealand terms

bonzo—great, fantastic

choice—wonderful, the best

crook—sick, unwell

grotty—dirty

petrol—gasoline

primers—elementary school

tip—dump or landfill

ute—pickup truck

warrant of fitness—car inspection sticker

Books used as language and historical references

The Collins Maori Phrase Book, by Patricia Tauroa. William Collins Publishers, Auckland, NZ; 1990.

Concise Maori Dictionary, compiled by A.W. Reed, revised by K. S. Karetu. Heinemann Reed, Auckland, NZ; 1984.

A Most Noble Anchorage: A Story of Russell and the Bay of Islands, by Marie King. Northland Historical Publications Society, Kerikeri, NZ; 1992.

The Oxford Illustrated History of New Zealand, ed. Keith Sinclair. Oxford University Press, Auckland, NZ; 1990.

Te Marae: A Guide to Customs & Protocol, by Hiwi and Pat Tauroa. Heinemann Reed, Auckland, NZ; 1986.

Tikanga Whakaaro: Key Concepts in Maori Culture, by Cleve Barlow. Oxford University Press, Auckland, NZ; 1991.

Author's note on historical content

In 1981 I moved to New Zealand and, although I lived there for only a few years, the experience had a profound impact on my life and writing. In particular, I was powerfully influenced and affected by the historical/cultural/social relationship between Maori and Pakeha, and found these themes recurring in my work. Over the next decade I returned many times to New Zealand for extended visits, and my first three novels were set there. During those years I was torn between a love for my New England home and birthplace in Massachusetts and the strange, compelling connection I felt toward New Zealand, which I had grown to consider my spiritual home. *Kotuku* is an attempt to bridge these two worlds.

Kotuku was inspired by two experiences that happened to me eight years apart. In 1973, right after my high school graduation, I got on a bus and moved to Provincetown on the tip of Cape Cod, Massachusetts. I was seventeen, I was going to be a writer and an artist, and I couldn't wait to begin. In Provincetown I found part-time jobs and places to live, and I stayed there for over a year, returning many times in the years after. I spent whole days, winter and summer, crossing the sand dunes, wandering alone along the gray Atlantic Ocean and gazing off toward the horizon. Provincetown, nestled on that tiny curled spit of sand in the vast ocean, first landing place of my ancestors, was my own jumping-off place into the world.

Eight years later, in 1981, recently married and living in New Zealand, I was wandering on the pebble beach at Russell, in the Bay of Islands, in the north of the North Island of New Zealand. Homesick and far from home, I was idly examining several mysterious objects I had found here and there in the tangle of seaweed along the high tide line. They looked to me like broken sections of small bones, but on closer inspection I realized they were denser and harder than bone—more like white clay. Later that day, curious, I took the objects to the museum in the town. The curator led me to a glass-covered case and there I saw more of the intriguing objects. But some of them were more complete than the bits I had found: They were white clay pipes with slender stems. The curator told me that they were pipes commonly smoked by sailors on New England whaling ships who put in at the port of Russell, known then as Kororareka, all during the 1800s. When the ships left port to begin their long, dangerous journey home, the sailors threw their pipes overboard for good luck . . . and bits of those pipes, made of white Massachusetts clay, have been rolling around on the floor of that Pacific Ocean harbor for almost two hundred years. What I held in my hand on that beach a world away from everything I knew was a little bit of earth from my own homeland.

Kotuku is not meant to be a historical novel, but although I have taken artistic license with the personal circumstances of my fictional characters, I have tried to be historically accurate in depicting the general situation of the period. Specific references to Kororareka and events concerning Maori and Pakeha in the Bay of Islands during the 1830s through the 1850s are based on material researched in two books, *The Oxford Illustrated History of New Zealand* and *A Most Noble Anchorage*.

I researched about the New England traders and whaling ships, specifically those voyaging to the islands of the southern Pacific, in libraries and museums in Provincetown and on Martha's Vineyard. The history of Maori unrest in the Bay of Islands during the volatile mid-nineteenth century is well documented, and in fact is fairly common knowledge in New Zealand. Kororareka *was* often referred to as the hell-hole of the Pacific during the busy years when American and British whaling and trading ships called into that port to trade with the local Maori and replenish supplies for the return voyage. Catering to sailors who had been at sea under appalling conditions for years, Kororareka was a town of taverns and bars and all the accompanying problems: drunkenness, prostitution, theft, and violence. As Emmanuel Dart noted in his journal, the missionaries in the area had their work cut out for them.

It was inevitable that with so much contact between the Maori and the primarily British and American visitors, tensions and conflicts would arise. Pakeha interests in New Zealand began to expand alarmingly after the 1830s. The initial, fairly straightforward trade relations between the two peoples began to give way to more complex issues of political sovereignty and land acquisition. Maori acquired guns from the visitors, and the intertribal warfare that had traditionally been part of Maori culture intensified . . . a situation the Pakeha quickly learned to exploit. Christian missionaries gained powerful and more influential footholds throughout the island. Pakeha diseases such as smallpox and influenza decimated the Maori population. Maori response to this invasion and occupation took many forms, among them the rise in the mid-1800s of so-called prophet leaders whose teachings were often a mixture of traditional beliefs and Christianity. Some of these teacher-prophets advocated peace and some called for violent rebellion, but all of them addressed the primary concern: the Pakeha was there to stay.

Contemporary New Zealand is a fascinating place to experience the formation of a bicultural society. Since the 1970s especially, the Maori voice—heard through activists, writers, artists, politicians, musicians, teachers, filmmakers—has evolved into an eloquent, powerful force influencing not only New Zealand but, more and more, other countries struggling to overcome histories of cultural and racial oppression.